The Hour of Witches Book 3

# WITCH CONTAINED

## KRISTA WALSH

Raven's Quill Press

Ottawa, ON

Raven's Quill Press

www.kristawalshauthor.com

Publisher's Note: This is a work of fiction. Names, characters, places, and incidents are a product of the author's imagination. Locales and public names are sometimes used for atmospheric purposes. Any resemblance to actual people, living or dead, or to businesses, companies, events, institutions, or locales is completely coincidental.

Cover Design: Deranged Doctor Design/2025

Witch Contained / WALSH -- 1st ed.

Paperback ISBN: 978-1-998398-21-8

For my family, bio & found - thank you for
having my back

# Chapter 1
*Alyssa*

I PULLED UP the hood of my sweater, then pulled it down. A minute later, I pulled it up again.

One of my least favourite parts of anxiety was my sudden inability to regulate my body temperature. That and the nausea. And the shakes. And the thoughts that refused to settle. And the… GI issues.

All of it. All of it was awful.

I did my best to focus on my breathing as I puttered around my kitchen. On every pass, I peered out the window at the midmorning sunshine brightening the clear blue sky. It was spring, the weather was getting warmer, the leaves were making their debut on the empty branches. With hands that stubbornly clung to a slight tremble, I poured peppermint tea from the teapot into two mismatched mugs, then carried them onto the enclosed balcony of my second-floor apartment. Years of running and working tables at Mooney's Pub meant I didn't spill a drop on my commute, but I made sure to set the second mug on the narrow table next to the occupied chair instead of handing it directly to the man who occupied it. The last thing Trace Wyatt needed right now was second-degree burns by tea.

Goddess knew, he deserved a break more than extra damage.

He'd endured so much over the past few months. We both had, sure, but I was recovering from most of my nightmares while Trace was still in the middle of his.

I watched him as I settled into my chair beside him. His eyes, such a unique blue they usually appeared violet, were glazed as he stared into the abyss. Literally into it. After all, the souls causing him so much stress were trapped inside him. From what he'd described, they were constantly fighting to escape the magical bindings he'd placed around them. More than once, they'd taken him over, turned his violet eyes yellow, and carried out gruesome and horrific carnage. It was an ongoing battle, and I wished I could do something to help him.

Until I came up with a solution, the best I could offer was my support and encouragement. Not nearly enough. Especially not when the shadows of his dark past had also risen to taunt him.

"Nickel for your thoughts?" I said softly.

His gaze cleared and a faint smile played on his perfect lips. "I don't know if my thoughts are worth so much."

"Inflation's a bitch. Besides, the penny's no longer in circulation." I nudged his leg with my foot. "Stop dodging the question. Not that you need to answer, of course, but I want to make sure you know the door is open to talk. If you wanted to."

I blew on my tea to give my mouth something to do other than blabber. The man didn't need my issues heaped on top of his. He'd been staying with me for the past two weeks, having given up his rental apartment—and because I'd insisted he should stay close to someone who could keep an eye on him and his unstable resident souls—but that didn't mean I had to assault him with my concerns for him.

As though he read my thoughts, his eyes softened, and he held out his hand. I shifted my mug to my other hand and slid my warmed fingers through his.

"I'm wondering what to do about Hazel," he said.

Of course he was. We hadn't talked about much else since her text message had come in last week. Hazel Blackwood was the spirit witch who'd trained Trace in the illegal arts—among other things—when he was only eighteen. When the heat had come down on her, she'd thrown the young Andrew Wyatt to the wolves, leaving him to go on the run for the better part of three years until he'd made a deal with Supernatural, Magical and Occult Affairs Canada to trap her and send her to Moongrave, Canada's supernatural prison up north. There she'd been for the past nine years. Only we'd recently learned she'd escaped the government's hold. SMOAC had kept her disappearance under wraps to avoid panic, but my friend, Task Force Captain Jet Dawson, had been charged with going after her, and so far Hazel had proved elusive.

"Any progress on coming up with a plan?" I asked.

He grimaced. "A few. None you'll like."

I tightened my grip on him. "You're not going to meet with her. Not without backup. Or a bomb to throw."

We'd been through this many times as well, but I would repeat it until I was sure Trace would listen.

"This woman arranged for Gramps to be kidnapped," I reminded him. "She ordered that you be *tortured*. She gathered the most powerful, nastiest witches Ontario could hold."

None of it needed to be said. It wasn't like Trace would have forgotten what David, the ghoulish elemental witch, had put him through in his attempts to force the souls out of him, or the battles we'd fought to take David and the rest of the coven down. If we'd known Hazel had been behind everything, we would have planned our approach differently. Or not. I'd gathered a good chunk of the Mooney clan to raid the house in Rockland, and we'd still only gotten out by the skin of our teeth.

So yeah, no, there was no way in hell I would let Trace approach her by himself.

He set his mug on the table and shifted in his seat so he could hold my hand in both of his. "Breathe, princess. I'm not marching into battle right now. And no, I don't plan to meet her without a plan and someone with me."

His calm, gentle voice broke through my spinning thoughts, and I forced my breathing to slow.

"Sorry," I said once my heart rate settled. "I've been living on the edge of anxiety for so many weeks I never know what will push me over. Although clearly the thought of you in danger is a trigger. Good to know."

Trace leaned forward, rested his hand on my shoulder, and pressed a kiss against my forehead. His thumb swept over the pulse in my throat, and warmth trailed after his touch. I grabbed hold of his arm to keep him in place, grounding myself in his presence.

"As long as I'm around, I'll do my best to catch you before you fall," he murmured. "It's the least I can do after all you've done for me."

I breathed him in, savouring the warmth of his skin against mine. I wanted so much more, but although he'd been staying with me—sharing my apartment, my bed—we hadn't taken the risk of moving things forward. Not when I worried about what might happen if Trace pushed himself too hard.

But our closeness helped clear my head, and soon enough I was able to pull away and take another sip of my tea. Trace lingered near me for another moment until he was sure I was all right, then he sat back in his seat and reclaimed his mug.

"Has Chip been able to narrow down where the bitch—sorry, I mean witch—is hiding?"

Chip—the horrible, punny nickname for Trace's computer whiz bestie—had been working overtime to track the source of Hazel's text. It amazed me he hadn't been able to crack the firestick-wall-thing she'd hidden behind, but I had no doubt he would. The guy was a miracle worker. An asshole, sure, but some kind of computer angel.

Or demon, to be more precise, although I didn't know what type exactly. Not a very well balanced one, anyway. How could he be when he rarely stepped outside?

"He knows she's in Ottawa, but he hasn't pinpointed a location."

"I'm shocked. Stunned, even. Has Chip finally found something he can't do? Someone smarter than him?" I leaned forward to set my hand on Trace's arm, widening my eyes in feigned horror. "Is he losing his power?"

Trace huffed a laugh. "Careful, princess. If he bugged your apartment, you might wake up tomorrow with no electricity."

I looked around the enclosed balcony. "He wouldn't have." Uncertainty tugged at me. "Would he?"

Trace looked at me. I looked back. Then to the ceiling I said, "Sorry, Chip. You're amazing and infallible. If you haven't found Hazel, it's because you don't want to."

Trace nodded. "Wise."

Under my voice I added, "Between you and me, can I still be surprised that the Great and Powerful Wizard hasn't found her yet?"

"Hey, now. He's no charlatan."

I shrugged and took another sip of tea. "He does love living behind that curtain."

Trace followed the groove in the armrest of his chair with the pads of his fingers. "Yeah, but he's not hiding anything. He just hates people."

I sniffed and closed my eyes. "Something I'm understanding more by the day."

A low laugh reached my ears, but it sounded bitter, strained. I opened one eye to watch as Trace stared out the window, his gaze once more unfocused. "Don't say that, Alyssa. I need you to love people. I need you to remind me the world's not a horrible, dark, greedy place. It gives me something to find my way back for."

I was sitting up and facing him before I knew I was moving. Tea sloshed over the lip of my mug onto my hands, and I set it down on the table without considering the pain. "Don't even joke about that, Trace Wyatt. You better keep fighting. If I have to stand here waving around a flashlight to convince you there's still light in this world, I'll do it."

My heart thrashed in my chest, growing even more unruly when he smiled his first full smile of the day. He took my hands and swung himself around so our legs were intertwined. His closeness pressed in on me, his scent of bergamot, musk, and fresh coffee tickling my senses and making my lips hunger for a taste of him. As though he caught every unspoken thought in my head, his pupils dilated, and his breath caught. "No flashlights necessary, princess. You're a light enough by yourself. The beacon guiding me home. Please believe that."

My heart clenched, my throat tightened, and I reached for him. I needed him closer, needed every last gap between us gone. This man had sacrificed so much for me, and I'd taken so many risks to keep him safe. I didn't feel grounded unless he was nearby, and I needed him to know it. More than anything, I needed him to keep resisting the souls trying to consume his.

I didn't know what I'd do if I lost him.

Trace skated the tip of his nose along my jawline, and I ran my fingers through his thick strawberry-blond hair, today left loose and framing his face. His breath fanned across my cheek, and I angled my face towards his, seeking, desiring.

The buzz of a phone made me jump and sent my already erratic heartbeat into overdrive. I pressed my hand to my chest as Trace leaned over and grabbed his phone from where he'd left it on the table.

"Speak of the devil," he said. "Or of the computer demon, anyway."

My eyes widened. "Do you think it's because of what I said?"

Trace chuckled and answered the call. "What have you learned?"

"Fucking nothing," Chip said. "The fucking witch has buried herself under so many different—Anyway, not important. I stopped trying to find her because she was pissing me off, so instead I focused on her people. They're scattered across the city, but a bunch of them are spending a lot of time in South Keys. Maybe it's a coincidence and there's a bakery in the neighbourhood they all happen to love, but it's setting off my spidey senses. I'll send you the address."

I held my breath, waiting for him to call me out on my lack of faith in him, but the line clicked as he hung up.

"You ever get exhausted knowing him?" I asked.

"Constantly." Trace rubbed his hand over his face, then held it out to me as he stood up. "But hey, at least we have somewhere to go."

# Chapter 2
*Trace*

I PLUGGED THE address Chip had given me into the GPS and headed from Centretown towards South Keys.

It felt good to be doing something other than sitting in the apartment waiting. I didn't deal well with waiting at the best of times, but with Hazel on the loose and my own future up in the air, these past few weeks had been torture. The only saving grace had been Alyssa, but even being near her was an agony of a different kind. Both sweeter and more painful than the war my resident souls were engaged in.

Every day, she moved around the apartment with mindless ease, making space for me, allowing me to help her clean and cook and *live* in her home. She would go to work at the pub, and I would sleep or work with Chip over the phone, or sometimes attempt to read one of the books from her shelf. Every night, I slept beside her, her body pressed against mine, her sweet aloe vera scent filling my senses.

It was the deepest relationship I'd ever been in. Hell, it was the only relationship I'd been in since Hazel when I was eighteen—if I could call that messed up, manipulative, abusive situation a relationship.

Despite everything, I was happy. And I wanted more.

I wanted to take Alyssa out to dinner and not have to worry about some witch smashing through the windows and trying to kill me. I wanted to spend evenings with her on the couch watching her favourite TV shows without the weight of the world pressing down on us. And, goddess, I wanted to make love to her. The ache for her was almost a worse distraction than the battling souls, and from the way her eyes darkened whenever we stood too close or kissed too long or touched too much, she wanted it too.

But we both knew how temperamental my guests could be, especially when my emotions were heightened, and that was not how I wanted our first time to be. Or any of the times after that.

When this was over, though, we wouldn't leave her bedroom until she was fully sated.

Until then, we had this lead.

"Is it bad that Chip's comment made me hope there is an

amazing bakery around here?" Alyssa asked as she looked up and down the street.

I grinned at her as I grabbed an elastic from the cup holder and pulled my hair into its usual half ponytail. "We'll swing by somewhere on our way home, how's that? Grab you a chocolate cupcake or something."

She rolled her eyes skywards in an expression of bliss, then shot me a nose-wrinkled grimace. "And something Not Chocolate for you, you freak."

My genuine laugh was cut short when my eye fell on a familiar face walking up the street towards where we'd parked. Emile. "You've gotta be fucking kidding me."

Alyssa followed my gaze and her mouth fell open. "You've gotta be fucking kidding me."

Weeks ago, he'd been the one to lead us to the people who'd abducted Gramps. I'd nearly killed him and Kurt in a fight outside the Museum of Nature and hadn't been able to stop the souls from killing Nathalie. No, not just killing her. My guests had taken over and roasted the woman until her remains couldn't even be identified as human.

Alyssa shook her head. "I told him to get out of town. I hope he listens to his superiors better than he listened to me."

"Let's have a word with him, see if we can get him to pay attention this time."

I waited until Emile came in line with the car, then gestured for Alyssa to open her door to cut him off as I got out and rounded the back to close him in.

"Hey—What the fuck, man, didn't you see me—" Emile stopped short at the sight of me, and his eyes flew wide. "Fuck."

He turned and bolted, but Alyssa stood in his way and I sensed the familiar weave of her magic stretching out across the sidewalk, creating an invisible barrier. When Emile tried to push her to the side and run past her, he slammed into it and bounced back, catching himself before he could land on his ass.

I grabbed his arm and shoved him against the side of my car, keeping a smile on my face so anyone looking out their window would think we were old buddies catching up. "Didn't think you'd still be in town. Last time we got together, I understood you'd be leaving soon."

"I—I—"

"Didn't. Yeah, I got that. So what have you been up to? Big plans keeping you around?"

"Well, I—"

"Where's Hazel, Emile?"

I didn't think it was possible for his eyes to open any wider and worried they'd roll right out of his head. "She—I don't—"

My patience strained, and the souls woke up and drifted to the surface, warming my skin and making my fingertips tingle. "Let's quit with the games, yeah? You're here because you're ordered to be here. Why? What does Hazel have you doing?"

Emile trembled against the SUV, his balding head beading with sweat. The last time we'd seen him, he'd been bundled up in his winter gear, but now, in the comfort of early May, he couldn't hide that the years hadn't been kind to him. His gut sat low and heavy on his waistband, and his skin was sallow—someone who didn't get a lot of exercise, good food, or sunlight. I suspected if we'd followed him to see where he was headed, we would have tracked him to yet another LCBO to top up on his afternoon snack.

For all his weaknesses, however, I knew he was no slouch when it came to magic, so I didn't know if this show of fear was to distract me from a sneaky attack or if he was terrified because he'd been caught.

Alyssa's magic slid around me, reminding me—and the souls—that we weren't alone on this very public street in the middle of the day, and I stepped back to give Emile a little space.

"You should probably tell us," she said, moving up to stand beside me. Her expression was one of open understanding with a hint of sympathy, and I took another step back to let her take over. "We're here, and we know more than you probably want us to. We know Hazel's leading this coven. We know she's harvesting souls for some reason. Do you know what that reason is?"

Emile turned to Alyssa and some of the immediate terror drained out of him, as though given the choice to deal with her or me, she was the less scary option. An underestimation, of course—I knew what my atmospheric witch could do—but he thought he was safe to summon his magic. It prickled over my skin as he wrapped it around himself, and Alyssa crossed her arms, no doubt seeing it clear as day. She didn't summon her own magic in return, not wanting to escalate the situation, but she did watch him closely, ready to throw up a ward if she needed to.

Emile shot me a quick glance before he unleashed his spell, and he must have noticed the glint of power in my eyes, because he blanched. I tilted my head and allowed that power to swell, reminding him what I was capable of. What had happened to Nathalie.

His shoulders drooped, the sensation of his magic withered, and he slumped back against my car, looking like he'd aged ten years in the past ten seconds.

"I can't tell you," he said. "You know I can't tell you. She'll kill me. You know I'm harvesting souls for her. I bring them to one of her people, they let me keep some and take the rest. That's all I can say."

Distaste curled Alyssa's nose for a microsecond before her smile was back in place. "People like Hazel don't reward their helpers, Emile. They use you for everything they can get, then they take the rest. Chances are she'll kill you anyway."

He dropped his gaze, and I suspected he'd already realized that for himself.

"Go home," Alyssa said. "I'm sure you have some kind of life waiting for you in Alberta. Something a little less awful?"

Emile licked his lips and gave me a pleading look over her shoulder. "I have my cat. I miss her a lot. I'd really like to go home to her."

I narrowed my eyes at him, letting him know he might get the chance if he played nicely.

Alyssa nodded. "A cat's a good reason to stay alive, don't you think? Talk to me, tell me what you know, and then you can get on a plane and actually leave this time. Believe me, Hazel will be too busy to notice you're gone."

"I—" Emile started and stopped yet again, but this time we waited.

Well, Alyssa waited, and I was more than happy to let her lead. The woman was magic. After we'd dealt with our problems and I finally got back to my regular life of tracking down and dragging in Canada's worst supernatural offenders, I wondered if I might convince her to join me once in a while.

"I don't know what she wants the souls for," he said in the end. "But she's gathering more people, and she's definitely after something." More sweat trickled down the side of his face. "I don't know anything else. But I'm leaving." He pulled out his phone, and I caught a glimpse of the airline website as he pulled it up on his browser. "I'm buying my ticket right now for the first fucking flight out of here because my heart can't handle this bullshit. It was fun at the start, you know? Challenging, pushing boundaries, hanging out with old friends. But Nathalie's dead"—he shot me a nasty look—"and Kurt's also dead"—this time he glowered at Alyssa, even though neither of us had known the witch had fallen—"no thanks to your family. So I'm out. My cat is all I have left, and I want to go home and give her a cuddle before Hazel's people track me down and end me. So there. Ticket's bought. I'm gone. Thanks for nothing, assholes."

He shouldered me out of the way and started down the street, but I grabbed him by the arm, and he went so still I worried he might shatter. "One last thing before you go."

His throat bobbed with a swallow, which I took to mean he was all ears.

"Where is Hazel staying?"

Emile looked from me to Alyssa and back to me. "I don't know."

But even as he spoke, his gaze darted down the street, and I looked over my shoulder to a grey two-storey.

"Good enough." I let him go and waited until he'd taken a few steps before I called him back. "And Emile? If I catch you hanging out with crowds like this again, you'll be joining Kurt and Nathalie."

He blanched, nodded, and picked up his pace.

Alyssa stared after him, seemingly lost in thought, then shook herself and turned to face the grey house. "What do you think? Call in the reinforcements?"

It was an option. We could raid the house and try to stop things here… but I didn't see it. Hazel wasn't stupid. If this was where she was staying, she'd have defences we wouldn't get past without every mundane on this street playing witness.

But those mundanes might also be a help. They meant if we got Hazel out in the open, she wouldn't be able to wield her magic against us either. We could confront her safely in a way we might never have another chance to do.

I looped my fingers through Alyssa's. "You know what? It's a beautiful day, the streets are busy, the risk is low. I say we go knock on the door."

# Chapter 3
## *Alyssa*

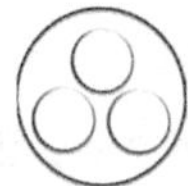

I WALKED AT Trace's side as we made our way towards the house Emile had pointed out.

"What do you think the odds are that we're walking into a trap on this?" I asked.

"Decent," he admitted. "I don't think Emile was prepared to run into us on the street, but I wouldn't put it past Hazel to assume I'd track her down."

"So what's the plan? We invite her out onto the driveway for a chat? Ask what her plans are, politely request that she leave off whatever she's up to?"

"Something like that." Trace squeezed my hand and gave me a smile. "Nothing's going to get fixed today, so don't worry about having a showdown in the middle of the street. We're here to get information straight from the source. Try to piss her off enough that she lets something slip that she doesn't mean to. We know she's involved, so she's lost the element of surprise, and she knows we're hunting her, so we don't have that advantage either. If we can at least play with all our cards on the table, we have a chance of being strategic rather than fumbling around in the dark."

It made sense, but my stomach still sloshed with unease as we walked up the pathway towards the front door. Before we reached the stoop, I spotted the green-and-yellow magic smeared over the door and grabbed Trace's arm to pull him to a stop. "We have traps."

He puffed out a breath. "Of course we do. What can you see?"

I scanned the front of the house and spotted more traps on the front window next to the door that looked into what I thought might be the kitchen. "If we had knocked or decided to play Peeping Tom, we probably would have found our faces melted."

"Not playing nice, then. All right, good to know." He frowned and stared at the house as though it were a challenger in a duel. "What about the garage?"

I released his hand to return to the driveaway and spotted another trap along the access panel. "More yellow. Very subtly woven, too. I bet if we'd tried to magic our way through the code, the spell would have backfired and, again, face-melt. Not that I can really tell the type of spell based on the signature, but I definitely get a Not Friendly vibe."

"Let's bring the car up, and we'll sit and wait, see if there's any movement inside, try to catch someone coming or going." He shot me a grin. "Unless you had better things to do with your day than sit in a car for long hours of boredom without even snacks to keep us going?"

"You mean I have to spend more time with you? The horror."

His gaze softened, and he held out his hand for me to take it again. I happily looped my fingers through his, relishing the contact.

We went back to the SUV and pulled it up the block so it was parked across from the house. While we waited, I pulled out my phone to check for any messages from Simon. My chaos demon bestie and business partner was watching the pub today, as he'd done more days than usual over the past few weeks, but I didn't want him feeling like he was managing everything by himself.

I did a few of the inventory checks I was able to do from my phone, placed a few online orders for supplies I knew we were short on, then messaged Simon to give him the update.

**Me: Tracked down Hazel's place. Playing babysitter on her front door for a while to see if we can pin her down.**

**When I get home tonight, I'll take a pass over the books you sent me. How goes?**

I didn't expect him to answer right away. We would be right in the middle of the lunch rush, and he was probably worked off his feet keeping up. Becca and Darrel, our daytime servers, would be there to help him out, but Simon likely wouldn't get a chance to reply for another hour or two.

While Trace watched the door, I split my attention between watching and scrolling on my phone, but I was very aware when he stiffened and sat up, even before he said "What do we have here?"

I looked around him to see what he'd noticed, and my stomach dropped out when I spotted the blue SUV with the subtle Ontario Witches' Council logo, a woven OWC, on the side. They'd parked across Hazel's driveway in the wrong direction, preventing anyone from backing out.

"What are they doing here?" I whispered, as though they could hear me from across the street.

"I guess we aren't the only ones getting leads. But hey, if they want to do the honours of saying hello, I'm happy to let them take point."

So was I. The witches' council wasn't always the most engaged body of government. They tended to let the local coven leaders—e.g., my family—deal with any issues that arose, only stepping in when there was credit to be stolen or wider political consequences to avoid. So yes, if they wanted to get their hands dirty for a change, I would welcome their involvement. Keep my friends and family safe, let Trace enjoy his closure from a distance.

As we watched, two people got out of the SUV. The man was shorter, almost squat, with short, dark hair, and a wide, muscular torso that made me think of a concrete planter box. The woman was almost his opposite: Tall, blond hair looped up in a bun, and somewhat stick-like in figure.

The guy split off to walk the perimeter of the house while the woman went up to the front door. I held my breath, waiting to see if she knocked, but she stopped before rapping her knuckles against the fibreglass. With her back to us, I couldn't see her expression, but her shoulders tightened and she stepped backwards down the stoop and tilted her head to look up at the second-storey windows.

The guy returned, shaking his head, and the woman said something, gesturing to the spells. The guy pulled a gadget out of his pocket—something that wouldn't have fit into her pocket because women pockets—and tossed it at the door. The magic woven across the surface flashed in a burst of light that left me blinking, and a moment later, both of them marched up the step and the woman knocked.

Minutes passed with more knocking and no answering.

"I guess no one's home," I said.

I'd barely added my commentary when the guy raised his hands, pulling deep purple atmospheric magic between his palms, and launched it at the door. The lock burst, the door flew in, and the two council witches disappeared inside.

"Huh," I said. "I'll admit, I didn't expect that."

Trace glanced at me. "You didn't know the council could be so ruthless?"

"I would have said effective. Think they'll find anything?"

"If they do, we'll never hear about it. There's no point sticking around. Either they'll grab Hazel or whatever evidence she has in there, or there's nothing to find. We'll have Chip watch the house just in case, but it looks like we're back to waiting for him to find her for us."

His phone buzzed in the cup holder between us, and he reached for it. When he glanced at the screen, his brow furrowed and his jaw tightened, and I had no doubt about who'd messaged him. Hazel's timing was flawless.

I looked around to see if I could spot her. She had to know we were here, right? Otherwise, her messaging now was a major fucking coincidence.

"What does she want?" I asked.

"She sent details about where she wants to meet. The old museum in Almonte."

"The mill?"

He nodded, and I pictured the place. I'd gone there often

enough with my family when I was a kid. Forests, fields, and, if you timed your visit well, walking trails with no one to break the silence. There was also the old cloister. It was often used for weddings, but I'd always believed it might be a stepping stone into another realm.

Fitting place for an evil bitch looking to corner someone— or kill them.

"When?" I asked.

He scrubbed a hand over his brow, tossed the phone back into the cup holder, and sagged in his seat. "Three days from now."

I swallowed my worries and reached for his hand. We'd come so close to catching up with her, but now here she was, still ahead of us, still calling the shots. "Hey, at least we have a timeline. We won't be walking into this unprepared."

He met my eye. "I don't want you walking into this at all. Coming here today, she couldn't have started anything out in the open. But if we're going into a fight? This woman is dangerous, princess. And if she knows how much you mean to me, she'll target you." A yellow gleam swept across his violet eyes. "I won't let her do that, I can't—*argh!*"

He squeezed his eyes shut and pressed the heel of his palm to his temple, but I'd caught the bright flash of the souls within him pushing to get out. His fear for me had lowered his hold on them. A balance he worked for every minute of the day.

His nostrils pinched and flared and his shoulders heaved as he fought to steady his breathing. A few minutes passed before he dropped his hand, though he kept his eyes closed.

Doing my best to keep my voice soft so he wouldn't hear the tremor in my words, I said, "If you go in there by yourself, you won't be able to keep control and she'll have you. Whatever the danger, Trace, I won't let that happen. So let's work together on this, okay? Let's show her how unstoppable we are as a team."

He blinked his eyes open, and I was relieved to find only streaks of his own silver magic running through the violet, though I appreciated how superficial that relief was.

"All right," he said, his voice rough. "But if I tell you to run, you run and don't look back. Agreed?"

I swallowed hard. "Agreed." It killed me to say it, but he knew this woman much better than I did. "Let's hope it doesn't come to that. We have a place and a new message. Let's see if the Great and Powerful Chip is ready to work another miracle."

# Chapter 4
## *Alyssa*

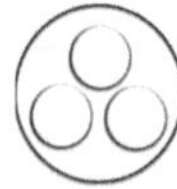

TRACE DROPPED ME off at home before driving to Stitts-ville, wanting to bring his phone to Chip so the computer mastermind could work his magic. I fully intended on staying home to get a few chores done and hit the accounting spread-sheets early, but after fifteen minutes of staring blankly into my computer screen, I gave up.

Hazel had known we were there earlier. She was coming for Trace, and Trace didn't have the ability to defend himself safely. We needed to get his souls under control, and I needed to get out of this house before my fears pushed me into a tail-spin. Not wanting to subject the pub to my frazzled thoughts, I grabbed my keys and drove forty-five minutes to my parents' place in Ashton.

At this time of day, my dad wouldn't be home. He worked a nine-to-five at the local bank, and his schedule was as predictable as the calendar. Mom was a healer at the Peaview Supernatural Hospital in downtown Ottawa, which meant I stood a good chance of her being around. She generally tended to work four days on, three days off, with the occasional night shift thrown in. I tried to stay on top of her schedule so I would know where to find her, but lately time had flown out the window. Days, hours, minutes—they'd blended together in the face of the threat Hazel posed.

I knocked twice to give everyone the heads up I was here, then stepped inside.

"It's Aly!" I called.

"Pip? What are you doing here?" Gramps shouted from his downstairs apartment.

His voice was a soul snuggle. He'd always been the anchor of the Mooney clan, not only the patriarch of the family but the head of our coven as well. We'd come so close to losing him a few weeks ago, and it was only because of Trace that he was still here.

He came up the stairs, his white beard unruly, not yet tamed by his daily routine. I looked at the clock as it ticked towards midafternoon. "Isn't it a bit late for you to still be loafing around?"

Gramps's gaze followed mine, and he shrugged. "I've been

marathoning that regency drama. *Bridgerton*. That's a damn good show."

I raised an eyebrow. "Bit spicy, don't you think?"

"Probably best for both our sakes not to deep-dive into what your nana and I got up to back in the day."

I tried not to think about it as he slung his arm over my shoulders and led me into the kitchen.

"But you didn't come here to talk about kissing shows with the old man, I'm sure. What's going on?"

My shoulders slumped, and I sagged against him. "Hazel reached out to Trace again. She wants to meet him in three days. The meeting is stressful enough, but I don't know how functional he'll *be* in three days."

"The bounty hunter's getting worse?"

"Barely hanging on. I was hoping Mom might have some ideas about how to help."

"Help with what?" the mom in question asked as she came into the room. Her hair was damp and she was dressed for work, so my timing was perfect.

"A binding spell of some kind? Something I can do to help Trace keep hold of those souls. If Hazel wants to meet with him, it's because she has another plan to lure his guests out, and he might not have enough strength left to stop her."

Mom frowned. "I can't think of anything off the top of my head, but I'll look into it. You'd be looking for a gentle containment spell more than a binding spell. Something too strong would latch the souls to him for good."

I shuddered. "Yeah, no, we don't want that. The opposite, really. Finding a way to get them safely out of him would be the preferred option."

Unfortunately, getting them out wasn't as easy as a magical purge. We needed to find somewhere for the souls to go—somewhere someone like Hazel wouldn't be able to swoop in and absorb them herself. And after being stuffed in an amulet for two hundred years, I doubted the souls would be interested in hopping into another piece of jewellery as a temporary measure.

Mom pulled my head down to kiss my forehead. "Don't worry, Aly, we'll figure this out."

Gramps nodded. "This is the Mooneys' problem to solve. Trace has been carrying the burden of our mistake for too long as it is. We'll fix this."

I believed them. I really did. I just hoped they found the answer before I lost everything that was left of the man I'd fallen for.

Fallen for. Great. That was the first time I'd admitted to myself how deeply my feelings for him had burrowed, and it was in the same context as his possible death. Why did it feel like the universe had it out for me?

I rubbed my palms on my denim-clad thighs.

"Breathe, Pip." Gramps squeezed me tighter. "Don't let that brain of yours get the better of you. What have I always said?"

"I'm worthy of getting the best-case scenario."

"That's right. Your brain will always try to make you believe the worst outcome is the only option, but you're just as entitled to a positive twist as anyone else."

I leaned into the old words, drawing strength from them.

"All right. You're right. Okay." I exhaled slowly, then drew myself away to stand on my own.

Mom took my hand and gave it a squeeze. "I'd stick around and brainstorm with you, but I have to go extract a tentacle from a… never mind."

"Don't worry about it. Tentacle-removal should be your priority." I rubbed my arms, a comforting self-hug as another wave of unease gripped my stomach. "We'll find time to talk."

I walked out with Mom and stopped by her car as she opened the door, but she turned to me before getting in and wrapped her arms around me in a tighter, better hug than I ever could have given myself.

"He's lucky to have you, Aly. Whatever he's going through, he has you to stand by him and support him. That will help him stay strong until we find what we need to help him."

Tears pricked my eyes, and I hugged her back.

Mom tensed and pulled back, and her eyes were bright with

revelation. "I just had a thought. Somewhere we might want to start. It would be an intense solution, and neither of you might be comfortable with it, but at least it's something. My books are in my office at work, so let me read into it, and I'll get back to you, all right?"

The desire to push her for more information was there, but I knew my mother. She was as stubborn as a rock when she wanted to be—and when it came to the safety of her children, that rock was mountain sized.

"Thanks, Mom."

She got into her car and drove away. I shuffled towards my Nissan, but before I could unlock it, Gramps was behind me.

"What are your plans now?"

I shrugged and kicked some mud off my tire. "We're in that annoying waiting stage. With all of it. So I guess I'll head home? Lie on my bed, stare at the ceiling, and play out a million scenarios for how we're going to take down this witch?"

"Be careful, Pip, all right?"

I raised an eyebrow. "With what? My ceiling? I'll probably be okay."

"I mean with this witch coming after your boyfriend."

A flush warmed my cheeks at the term. I was twenty-eight years old, for the goddess's sake. Yet hearing Trace referred to as my boyfriend made me feel like I was in high school again.

"We will. As best we can, anyway."

"What approach are you taking?" There was my mercenary grandfather. I'd been wondering when I'd see him again.

"He's going to meet with her. Find out what she wants. Before we figure out the meeting, we want to see if we can arrange things with Chip and maybe Jet to snare her and send her back to Moongrave."

At least, I thought that was the plan. Unless Trace wanted to get rid of her for good. If so, I wouldn't blame him, but I also wouldn't let him face that challenge alone.

"If you need us, call," Gramps said. "The Mooneys have your back, just as we always have."

I gave him a tight hug. "Thanks, Gramps. I know I can count on you if it comes to it."

My phone buzzed, and I pulled it out of my pocket to find a reply from Simon waiting for me.

**Simon: Something's come up. Cover my shift.**

That was it. No explanation, no greeting, no cute, smiling emoji.

With those words, my blood ran colder than it had all day.

"Everything all right, Pip? You look like you're about to pass out."

I turned my phone to show him the message. Gramps had known Simon as long as I had. The three of us had gone out to celebrate when we'd added Simon to the business licence four years ago. So I understood when his expression morphed to reflect my worry.

"Something's been going on with him for the past few weeks, but this..."

"Come on, Pip. Let's get to the pub and see what's going on."

# Chapter 5
*Trace*

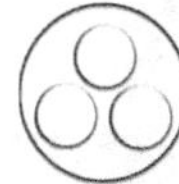

I STOOD IN the living room of my best friend's well-defended house and stared at his computer screen over his left shoulder. I knew better than to get too close to his professional setup. Chip wasn't known for his understanding or patience if anyone moved a single dust particle from the curved desk that housed his computer, his three monitors, and all his other technological bits and bobs.

"You're breathing on my neck," he griped as I leaned in to read the words scrolling across the page he'd loaded.

"The font can't be more than six point. How do you expect me to read it if I don't get closer?"

"I don't expect you to read it. That's what you have me for. In fact, I don't even know why you're here. Go home and be with your pub owner."

"Believe me, there's nowhere else I'd rather be, but until I have a better idea what Hazel's plans are, Alyssa doesn't deserve having to put up with me."

"And I do? Should I be flattered?"

I clapped him on the shoulder, and he stiffened under my touch, then shrugged me off. "Of course you should be," I said. "Who else do I trust with my worst?"

Chip snorted. "Lucky me."

Despite his arguments, I caught the faint spark in his eyes and knew we were good. This man had been at my side for almost a decade. After the three years I'd spent on the run from SMOAC, I'd taken steps to become a bona fide bounty hunter, and one of my first moves had been to scout for a computer guy to help me pin down my marks.

Chip hadn't come highly recommended by anyone. In fact, he hadn't been mentioned at all because no one knew who he was or that he even existed.

He'd found me.

I'd just experienced my third failure in catching my quarry after a reputed tech witch had failed to get the information I'd needed. I'd crashed on the oversoft mattress in a dingy hotel room here in Ottawa when my phone had rung. Private number, of course. And there had been Chip on the other end of the line telling me he was bored of watching me flounder.

He'd gone by Shadow Demon back in those days, and once we'd brought in our bounty together, that had been the first thing we'd fixed.

Now, so many years later, there was no one I trusted more to help me navigate my current problem. Hazel was out there somewhere, planning her attack against me and, no doubt, trying to stake her claim among Canada's covens again. The bitch had always been ambitious, and her success in escaping SMOAC's bindings would have gone to her head. If anyone could take advantage of her arrogance and use it against her, it was Chip.

"All right, well, since you're here, let's try to make this a short visit, shall we?" Chip said, drawing my attention back to the screen filled with tiny writing. "She's still hiding behind these texts. I suspect she's pulling the same trick as those guys you… took care of in the park the other week. Buying phones, using them once, and trashing them. I can get you a generic idea of where she sent the text from, and like I already did—which you failed to make use of—I can follow her people, but if she's being this careful, she's likely not sending her messages close to where she's staying."

"I didn't fail to do anything. We followed your lead."

"Mmhmm, and did you catch Hazel?"

I frowned at the back of his head. "Touché."

"I can feel you flipping me off back there. Don't hate me

for pointing out the truth."

"What about the witch with the demonic magic? Any word from her? Or has SMOAC gotten anything out of Corpsy?"

The demonic witch had been the fiercest enemy we'd faced in the Rockland fight. The woman had somehow absorbed a demon's magic, and it had made her a true powerhouse. Barely anything had touched her, and her ability to summon hellfire had nearly ended us. Because of it, we'd had to evacuate the house and leave her behind, giving her ample room to escape.

As for Corpsy—or David, as he'd introduced himself before he'd tortured me—he'd been brought in by the feds and no one had heard about him since.

"Corpsy's dead," Chip said.

"Excuse me?"

"He suffered a fatal 'accident' eating his peas with a plastic fork while in lockup. The Smokers aren't bashing down doors trying to figure out what happened."

The news didn't sit well with me. We knew Hazel's reach had to extend into the department for her to have escaped their custody, but if that reach was still active, it created a whole other layer of threat.

"As for the demonic witch—Doreen, turns out her name is—she's still AWOL. I caught sight of her once on some traffic cam footage, driving west, but I lost her. She's probably bunking down with Hazel, but not a peep from her since."

I slammed my fist down on the desk, then raised my hands in surrender and stepped away at Chip's warning glower. "Sorry—wasn't thinking."

"Mmhmm." He wiped down the surface where my fist had landed as though checking for stains or cracks. I was lucky he hadn't grabbed me by the back of my coat and thrown me outside. No one messed with this computer station.

"Was she always this clever?" I asked as I paced the length of his living room. "I don't remember her being this thorough about anything."

Chip swung his chair around and crossed his arms over his dark blue pullover. "No? I seem to recall a little detail about her chucking you into SMOAC's waiting arms to give herself a chance to escape. You don't think she made all kinds of contingency plans to disappear?"

And she had. For three years. The only reason I'd caught her was because…

"Her daughter." I stopped my pacing and strode back to Chip. "Do we know where Ameline is these days?"

"Still in Edmonton." I'd known Chip had kept an eye on the people closest to Hazel for my sake, but the speed with which he answered made me think he'd been keeping especially close tabs on her. "And as far as I've been able to see, Hazel hasn't been in touch with her."

"Probably not a lack of trying on her end."

Ameline was the only person Hazel cared about on this earth, or so it had always seemed. Even then, I'd long suspected that her daughter had been a means to an end. Proof of her power rather than an individual entity. Still, it had been because of Ameline that we'd been able to catch Hazel last time. Hazel had taken risks to go see her, and the agent I'd worked with had made use of the relationship.

Ameline might be out of province, but maybe we could use her to our advantage.

"Do you think you could reach out to her and see if she's heard from her mother?" I asked.

Chip snorted. "Yeah, because that'll go over really well. What should I do? Impersonate a fed?" An eyebrow shot up. "I could impersonate a fed."

Normally I wasn't one to straight up encourage law breaking—I was far more of a skirt-the-edges-of-legality type—but when it came to Chip, I took whatever help I could get and trusted him to cover his tracks.

"Okay," he said, rolling his neck. "If I'm going to do this, I need time to prepare. So you get out, get back to your girlfriend, and leave me alone until I contact you."

My heartbeat, which had only just started to slow, ramped up again. "Why do I need to leave?"

I didn't want to leave. Chip's house was covered in so many defences that I was sure no one would find me here. I also trusted him to deal with me if the souls overwhelmed me. Alyssa would try to help and possibly get hurt in the process. Chip would go full demon and kill me, but at least he'd make it quick.

As though he heard my every thought, he pushed himself out of his chair and did the rare thing of closing the distance between us. Although he didn't make contact, he stood close enough that I was well inside his personal space bubble.

"Trace, man, I get that you're going through some scary shit. I see the glint in your eyes when you're not wholly yourself. I'm not a fan. You need to sort this the fuck out and get back to yourself, and there's only one person who can help you do that. I'll give you a hint—it's not me."

I met his stony brown stare, so lacking in worry or pity, and focused on slowing my breaths.

"You're right."

He clapped me on the shoulder, then shoved me towards the door. "Good man. I'll be in touch."

I walked out, and the door slammed behind me, the locks triggering with their deafening ker-thunks. On heavy legs, I trudged back to my SUV and dropped into the driver's seat. Before starting the car, I pulled out my phone and checked my messages. A series of emotions gripped my chest when I read one from Alyssa.

**Princess: On my way to the pub. Something's up with**

**Simon. Meet you at home?**

My concern for her and what she might find at work battled with the warmth I felt at her reference to home. Not *my place*, just *home*. As though it were as much mine as hers.

I let out one last heavy breath and let my head fall back against the headrest.

So many years ago, I'd promised myself I would never again let my heart get in the way of my life. I'd fallen hard for Hazel, and her betrayal had made me believe I would never trust anyone again. But Alyssa… she'd changed my world. She'd burrowed her way into my chest, set up camp, and planted her flag, and all without effort. In such a short time, she'd come to mean more to me than anything else I'd fought for over the past nine years.

And if something was up with her best friend, then there was no way I'd let her face it alone.

With a new focus—and a nice distraction from my own problems—I threw the SUV into drive and started towards downtown.

# Chapter 6
*Alyssa*

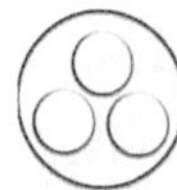

THE DRIVE FROM Ashton took longer than I wanted, with accidents and construction holding us up minute by agonizing minute. By the time we reached Centretown, I was a sweating mass of nerves.

Simon hadn't replied to any of the five texts I'd had Gramps send on my behalf. The last one hadn't even been delivered.

"Okay, try Reverie," I said.

The half-fae, half-succubus would know where my business partner was and probably what was going on with him. Those two had been tight since they'd met in the middle of the battle against Clyde Corrick's army. Before the fight in Rockland, Reverie's concern for my friend suggested she also wasn't comfortable with the recent changes in Simon's personality.

With the way my usually supportive, level-headed, compassionate friend had become impatient, surly, and possessive. Despite a few hesitations and concerns about their relationship, I trusted her to have Simon's back if he was in trouble.

"I can't find any Reverie in your contacts," Gramps said.

"What? Oh. Yeah. She's under BFF Thief." When Gramps raised his eyebrow, I shrugged. "I'm still working through some things there."

"Do you want me to call her, or…"

"Ew. No. Text is fine, thanks."

"You young people and your loathing of telephones. I don't understand it." He shook his head but brought up her number. "All right, sent. I'll let you know what she says."

Finally, I pulled into the parking lot behind Mooney's Pub and turned off the car.

For a while, I didn't get out. Everything about the pub felt wrong. My heart was racing, my palms were clammy, and I had a sneaking suspicion I was going to need to run to the bathroom in the next few seconds.

"It's all right, Pip." Gramps rested his hand on mine.

"The pub is closed."

Only after the words left me was I fully able to register the fact. We only closed for major emergencies. The last time had been after Trace and his recruited coven had smashed through the bar in their attempt to arrest me. And even then, Simon had been here organizing the cleanup and repairs. But he wasn't here. I hadn't gone in yet, but I knew he was nowhere close.

With a shaking hand, I opened the door and stepped into the parking lot. Gramps rounded the car and twined his fingers through mine in a show of support. I clung to him as we walked to the back door, and he used his key to unlock it. My wards were still in place—the only magic we allowed in the pub so we didn't set off Simon's chaotic power—which assured me no one was standing inside who shouldn't be, but that didn't comfort me much.

Because, although I'd been here yesterday, the pub felt empty. Abandoned. Had Simon opened at all today?

I walked to the counter and looked around. There were dishes in the sink that had yet to be cleaned, and the kitchen still smelled of food.

"What in the goddess's name…" I poked my head into the kitchen. Everything had been shut down, but it was obvious Jonathan and the rest of the kitchen staff hadn't been given time to clean up before they left. "Did Simon rush everyone out?"

He'd said to cover his shift, but he'd taken everyone with him in the middle of our busiest time of day.

"Here, Aly," Gramps called from the bar. "There's a note."

I felt as though I were floating. Everything seemed surreal—the blue walls swirling, the chairs brown blobs in my way. My phone was in my hand, clasped tight in my grip, as I crossed the floor to where Gramps held a piece of paper out to me. I took it in my free hand and read Simon's messy scrawl across the plain white surface.

*Something came up. Not sure when I'll be back. Love you.*

Just like his text, that was all there was. I checked the back of the paper to see if he'd written any postscripts, but there was nothing except for those few terse words.

I tossed the paper on the counter and turned my attention to my phone.

**Me: Seriously, where the fuck are you? I'm worried.**

Once I sent my text, I noticed a reply from Reverie.

**BFF Thief: Stuff is happening. As soon as I can, I'll be in touch. Try not to worry—I'm going to get him back.**

I stared at her message. And stared. And stared.

"Breathe, Aly." Gramps's warm hand was on mine as he pried my phone away. Then my other hand was in his and he was leading me to the nearest table.

"What is going on with my life right now?" I asked, not sure if I should laugh or cry. "My best friend is just… missing? Trace is getting eaten up from the inside. I barely have the energy to run my pub. A woman is making headway harvesting souls in my city. I don't know where to start putting all these pieces together."

"By breathing," Gramps repeated. "You won't get much of

anything done if you're passed out on the floor."

He made a good point, so I drew in a slow, deep breath, held it, and let it out.

"Good. Now that you're back, we can prioritize. I stole a look at your phone as I put it away. Whatever's going on with Simon, it seems like this Reverie person understands what it is and is working with him on it. Do you trust her?"

I thought of the sultry woman with the flawless tawny skin and the perfect curves and the deep, star-filled eyes that were so easy to fall into. I thought of the way she'd thrown herself into the fight against Corrick and had shown up with Simon in the fight against Hazel's witches. Trace had given me the rundown of her history, how Delvin—the demon who'd ended my healing career—had owned her because of a bad deal, and only with Trace and Simon's help had she freed herself and transformed the demon sex club into a classier, cleaner demon bar. Sure, she was the kind of half-demon who devoured the souls of her victims during nights of unbridled sexual pleasure, but from everything I'd seen and learned, she cared for Simon.

Hanging on to that thought like a lifeline, I pulled my shoulders back and took another deep breath. "I think I do." Something I never thought I'd say.

"Then let her handle it. Give it a day or two and check in again but have faith in our boy to know what he's doing and believe that he has the help he needs. You know he'd ask if there was anything you could do."

He was right. He had to be right. Because the alternative was that Simon was in over his head and too afraid to call me in and that something was seriously wrong and I'd never see my best friend again.

"Alyssa?"

Trace's voice at the back door brought me to my feet. I didn't have time to ask what he was doing here before he swept me into his arms and gave me a tight squeeze. "Is everything all right? Where is everyone?"

My throat closed again as I wrapped my arms around him. "We're not sure." I filled him in on Simon's messages, and Trace pulled back to look me in the eye. "Do you want me to start digging? We can make that a priority while Chip is working on the Hazel angle."

I blinked. This man must have broken all kinds of road laws to make it here from Stittsville since I'd texted him, and now he was willing to set aside his problems to help with mine. Again.

Without thinking, and with no regard for my grandfather standing right behind me, I rose on tiptoe and pressed my lips against Trace's. His grip around me tightened and he returned the kiss, a sweet but intense connection that hinted at everything he was holding back.

The door closed as Gramps went into the kitchen, and

although he'd meant it as a courtesy, it was the reminder I needed that we weren't alone. I pulled away, and Trace rested his forehead against mine.

"Seriously, princess, what do you need from me?"

"Exactly what you're doing. Just being here. Near me. The entire world could fall apart, and I feel like having you beside me would give me the strength to keep my balance."

The words were out before I could consider them, but as soon as they were, I appreciated how true they were. Little by little, Trace had dug out a corner of my soul and planted himself in it, and I had no qualms about telling him.

He brushed my hair behind my ear and kissed the top of my head, his other arm tight around my waist. "Right back at you, princess."

"What did Chip have to say? Any progress?"

"He's working on a lead. It might be the in we need to set a trap for Hazel before we meet with her."

"Good. Excellent. That's wonderful. About time."

Trace smiled, his violet eyes swimming with amusement and understanding. "I know you're worried, but we're doing this right. No running in and seeing what happens. You do remember this is what I did before I met you, right? Hunting people down, throwing magic, dragging them off to the authorities?"

A flush crept up my cheeks as I dropped my gaze. "Mr.

Badass Bounty Hunter. I know. You've got all the skills and experience and know-how. I'm the anxiety-ridden pub owner who enjoys spending her nights watching reruns of my favourite sitcoms and whose idea of a wild night is slipping some whiskey into my tea."

Trace pulled back, his eyes narrowed. "You don't."

"What can I say? I live life on the edge." I dragged my hands down his chest, gripping the collar of his shirt in my fists. "You might be all powerful, but I still worry about you. I think I've earned that right."

He dipped his head to kiss me again. "I love that you worry about me. But don't lose your stomach lining over it. I'm not worth that."

"Of course you are. Who needs a stomach lining anyway?"

"You kids done?" Gramps asked as he returned from the kitchen. "I can take another tour of the stoves if you're not. It's nice in there. You upgrade again?"

I shifted so I stood beside Trace, my arms around his middle. "One of the ovens… something, something, fuses. I don't know. You'll have to ask Jonathan. But he convinced me to replace one a month ago or risk a massive fire."

"Best to avoid those," Gramps agreed. "We seem to be putting out enough of them right now."

I swallowed a groan, but I needn't have bothered. They heard it anyway. At least that's how it seemed when Gramps slammed his hand on the cherrywood bartop, making me jump.

"All right, enough feeling sorry for ourselves. Let's figure out how we're going to make this witch burn."

# Chapter 7
*Alyssa*

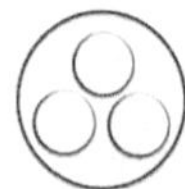

Before I knew what was happening, I was sitting at one of the artfully painted tables with a half-pint in front of me, Trace to my left, and Gramps across from me with a notebook between us.

"First things first, we're going to sort out the pub. As long as Simon's MIA, I'll take it over."

I sat up straight, my eyes wide. "What? No. Gramps, you're retired. You said you were done with this place."

"Bah." He waved his hand as though he hadn't filled my parents' house with rants for years about how he never wanted to hear the name of Mooney's Pub again before he finally handed the reins over to me. "I can suck it up for a few days or however long it takes to get everything back to the way it's supposed to be. No one knows this place better than I do, even with the newfangled ovens." He squinted over the bar. "And what is that?"

I looked over my shoulder to see what he'd noticed. "The Community Award? We won that last year for best city pub."

"Huh. How'd I miss that?"

"You were in Cuba."

"That would be how. Anyway, like I said, I know this place, so it'll be in good hands, and I'll ask Tory to step in and help on the floor. They were always a good hire over the summer, right?"

My cousin was a good choice. They knew the pub and how I ran things, and their wife was four months pregnant. I wouldn't want either of them near the fight against Hazel.

"I'll text them," I said.

"Good. That way you two don't need to stress about the business while you take on Hazel." He scowled. "And please tell me you're going to take her down. Her and that demonic witch. Those women have caused too much trouble in my family for me to tolerate their presence in my city."

Trace nodded. "I promise, Edwyn."

Again Gramps waved his hand. "Gramps, please. The only people who use my name are the kind who serve me papers, and I never get on well with them."

I noted the subtle flush in Trace's cheeks and squeezed his

hand under the table. Bit by bit, we were wedging him into my family, and he could either accept it or go running. There was no in between.

"How can the Mooneys help?" Gramps asked, urging us through any momentary awkwardness. "We have three days, closer to two now I guess, based on what Pip told me about that woman's text to you. That gives us time to round up the whole clan if you need it."

My heart swelled at his offer of our coven's resources, yet another indicator that he had already chosen to adopt Trace as one of his own.

"That would be…" Trace cleared his throat. "I might take you up on that. Right now, Chip is working on the daughter angle."

"Daughter?" I eyed him, and my silent questions must have poured off me, because he grinned, the faint dimple creasing his cheek.

"Not mine, I promise. Ameline was thirteen years old when Hazel and I… back when all those things happened. Now she's living on her own in Alberta, but we have reason to think Hazel might reach out to her."

"No love lost between them?" I asked.

"Doesn't seem to be. I got to know Ameline a little bit— she had a bit of a crush on me back then, I think. We haven't stayed in touch, but back then, even at thirteen years old, she didn't like what her mom got up to."

I could almost picture a younger Trace's ego puffing up under the attention. No doubt it had made him feel so much older and more powerful than he already was. All the easier for Hazel to manipulate him into boosting that power.

It did make me wonder if mother and daughter were as different as Trace seemed to think, and I made a note to mention it to Chip the next time I saw him. If there was nothing to it, I didn't want to be the one to strip Trace of a fond memory. Goddess knew he didn't have many of them.

"What about the location she mentioned?" I asked. "The museum. Do you think she's already laid some traps for us there, or do we have an opportunity to get in there first to lay some of our own?"

Gramps raised an eyebrow. "Museum?"

"The old mill in Almonte," I said. "That's where she wants to meet."

His eyes hardened. "There's old magic in that place. If she gets the upper hand there, she'll have an impressive amount of power on her side."

"Old magic?" I asked.

"One of the doorways to the mirror realm," Gramps explained. "It doesn't open anymore, but it wasn't properly sealed, so there's magic trickling through."

The mirror realm was the origin point for most supernatural

kind. It was the place the fae called home, a place the vampires avoided. Queen Meril, queen of the supernaturals, reigned over the territory of the realm that aligned most closely with the Canadian border. The unseen wall had gone up hundreds of years ago. In that time, the divide between supernatural and mundane worlds had grown wider, but we all knew the other side existed and the problems that could arise if Meril ever had cause to bring that wall down. Supernatural autonomy lost, wars with the mundanes. Chaos.

The thought of Hazel drawing on such pure magic raised goosebumps on my arms. "I don't suppose there's a way to convince her to change the meeting point? A coffee shop, maybe? We could sit down over tea and croissants and have a good chat."

Trace's mouth pressed into a thin line. "It's no coincidence she suggested somewhere near a doorway. She probably hoped I wouldn't find out that little detail until it was too late to protect myself from it." He rubbed his hand over his chest. "The influx of power might make the bindings around the souls even more unstable. That much easier for her to get at them."

I gritted my teeth and pounded back the rest of my drink. "I'm so fucking tired of people trying to take advantage of these poor spirits. They gave themselves up willingly for the good of their kind, and almost from the start, they've been manipulated and used against their will. I've had it, and I'm sure they're done with it too. We need to find a way to get them out of you. Ideally *before* you meet with Hazel."

Gramps rubbed his hands over his eyes. "Believe me, Pip, I wish it were that easy. But you know—"

It was my turn to wave him away. "I know. You and Nana tried for years to destroy the amulet and free the souls. I got it. It's a challenge. But your grandfather had to have a solution in mind when he created the amulet. Unless you think he was bullshitting the spirits from the get-go."

Gramps's shoulders slumped. "I don't want to think so, but who knows. It was so long ago, there's no way to say for sure."

"Unless we raised his backstabbing ass from the grave," I muttered. Then I perked up. "Can we? Yeah, yeah, necromancy bad, etcetera, etcetera, but would it be possible? Raise him up, ask dear old great-great-granddad how he intended to free the souls when their work was done, and then… do that?"

Trace and Gramps exchanged a glance, and while I might have thought they were judging my question, I noted the hint of calculation in both their gazes.

Finally, Gramps shrugged. "It's not impossible, I suppose. We know where Earl is buried. What we don't have is a necromancer trustworthy enough to do the job."

The wrong one could snatch him up and turn him into a battery, just like the ones he stole.

Trace scrubbed his finger across his upper lip, and I read

the silent debate in his eyes. His expression cleared as he made up his mind. "I do. One of the perks of my job is that I make connections from all walks of life. She's an odd one but good at what she does."

I didn't know why I was surprised by this. He'd made it clear from those early hours of our acquaintance that he was in with all kinds of people. To this day, I couldn't forget the slimy, glossy skin of the facestealer Trace called Shiny. They seemed to have some kind of history from Trace's old cases, and although I'd never dug deeper into it, it hadn't all been hostile.

Then there was Reverie. The day Trace and I had walked into Club Crescent-as-was, she'd laid eyes on Trace and greeted him like an old friend. At the time, I'd been too overwhelmed with the demon pheromones being pumped through the vents to be jealous, but more than once since then, I'd wondered what the nature of *their* relationship had been.

Then I reminded myself that whatever relationships Trace had been in before me didn't matter. I wasn't even sure Trace and I were *in* an official relationship. And even if we were, and even if he and Reverie did have a history, there was no way he'd compare me to a half-succubus. Because I could never compare to a half-succubus. They were literal sex demons. She would have blown his mind and ruined sex for him forever, and there was no way I would ever live up to it and—

"Pip?" Gramps cut into my spiral, and my cheeks flushed as though I'd just downed a shot of tequila and Tabasco.

"Yes?"

"What do you think? Should Trace reach out to this necromancer?"

I cleared my throat. "Yeah, I think it's not a bad idea. No one else living today seems to have an idea about what to do with these souls—no one we trust enough to ask, anyway—so maybe going back to the source is the best option."

At the moment, as far as Trace's souls were concerned, my ancestor was our *only* option. We either had to bind his guests more securely or find a safe way to eject them, and although I preferred the latter, I didn't care what the solution was as long as it kept Trace safe.

"All right," he said. "I'll message Sarah, and we'll see if we can meet up with her before the meeting with Hazel. Where is Earl buried?"

Gramps finished his drink and set the glass back down, matching it with the existing water ring. "There's an old cemetery up near Almonte. He's tucked in there."

I fought the rope of anxiety looping around my throat. "Almonte?"

Gramps raised his shoulder. "What can I say, Pip? We're living in a world of coincidences."

# Chapter 8
*Trace*

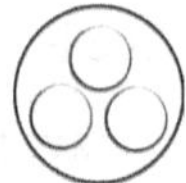

GRAMPS WAS RIGHT. The coincidences were piling up, and we needed to start breaking them down. Was I being paranoid to think they were all connected? That Hazel's decision to meet at the museum, the leaking gateway to the mirror realm, and the proximity of Alyssa's ancestor's grave were more than a simple twist of fate?

Because when I phrased it like that, it didn't sound like coincidence at all. It sounded as though Hazel had done more homework than I'd realized and was prepared to crush us under her heel. Not that I was sure how she might use Alyssa's family history against us. Though maybe that wasn't her intention. Maybe she was making a point about how much she knew about my allies.

My insides twisted at the thought of having to face her again. Before we'd found her at the house in Rockland, it had been close to a decade since we'd crossed paths, yet she'd haunted my life in so many ways I'd never been able to outrun her. I'd been an impressionable eighteen-year-old, and she had taken advantage of every facet of my naivety. Every decision I'd made since then had been with her in mind—what choice would she have made so I could do the opposite? What choice would set me on a better, smarter, kinder path?

I was far from perfect, and I didn't always make the best choices, but every step I took was an attempt to get away from *then*, with no clear idea of what I was moving towards.

Or at least, that had been true until Alyssa.

Now my pub-owning witch stood before me as something I wanted to strive to deserve. And just as I'd come to realize that, there was Hazel again.

Yet another fucking coincidence, or had her years in Moongrave Prison given her the skills to time the perfect destruction of my life?

Alyssa's hand on my arm made me jump, and I turned to where she stood beside me on the front patio of Mooney's Pub. Gramps had taken her car to go back home and ready himself for his shift, and she'd stayed with me, which was how I preferred it. Given all we'd learned in the last hour, I wasn't ready to let her out of my sight again so quickly.

"You all right?" I asked.

She bowed her head against my chest, and I wrapped my arms tightly around her. The scent of her aloe vera body wash tickled my nose, and I sank into the subtle sweetness that was so uniquely her.

"Wednesday both can't come soon enough and seems way too close," she said. "I can't shake the feeling that it's going to change a lot of things, one way or another."

She was right, of course. We just had to do everything we could to make sure it changed in our favour.

"Let's start by calling Sarah," I said, stepping away from Alyssa but taking her hand so she didn't stray too far. "If we can meet with her tonight, maybe we stand a chance of getting a good night's sleep."

She laughed, the note of it riddled with skepticism, and led me back into the pub. While she set to work checking her wards and doing a quick clean before locking up, I pulled out my phone and scrolled through my old contacts.

It had been a good five years since I'd last worked with the necromancer. Sarah Hickson had helped me out on a particularly nasty hunt involving a serial-killing groundhog shifter who had a taste for hitchhikers. The guy had remained so far under the radar that SMOAC had never figured out who was behind it. Only when I'd spoken with the soul of one of the victims had we figured out the whole groundhog piece. It was the first time anyone had ever heard of a groundhog shifter, but I'd been informed by my contacts within the government that from that day forward, no one ever discounted Canada's rodents.

"Trace?" Sarah said on greeting. "What in the cemetery brings you to me? It's been a decayed corpse since we last talked."

The woman enjoyed her deathly puns more than she enjoyed breathing, I was sure of it.

"Hey, Sar, how's it going?"

"Oh, you know, staying not dead. Be a shame to lose my livelihood by joining my clients, wouldn't you say?"

"Glad to hear you're still working. I have a job for you. More of a personal favour. Bit of a stretch, no guarantees he'll be up for a chat, but it would really help me out."

"A challenge? Consider me intrigued. It's been a while since I've spoken to someone more than a week gone. Tell me the deets."

I looked to Alyssa as she came back to stand beside me. No doubt she could hear Sarah's side of the conversation as well as mine—for someone who worked with the dead, the necromancer was full of life—but I held the phone up anyway, wanting to give Alyssa the reins if she wanted them. But she shook her head and let me continue.

"Two-hundred-year-old witch. Buried up near Almonte."

"Witch, huh? Hmm." I pictured her pursing her lips and wobbling her head as she considered the difficulties that came with bringing back supernatural spirits. "They tend to be feisty. Not much with the wanting to be chained."

Which would be ironic in this case considering the man's crimes of chaining hundreds of souls to an amulet with no way out.

"Sure, I'm up for giving it a shot. I won't even charge you if it doesn't work, how's that sound?"

"More than fair. I don't suppose you're free tonight?"

"Not on your life. I've got three grieving spouses looking to find out where the wills are buried. I know, I know, but I gotta do what keeps food on the table, am I right? How's Thursday sound?"

Alyssa winced, and I cupped the back of her neck, brushing my thumb across her racing pulse. "Could you swing tomorrow? We'll pay you whether you bring him back or not. Bit time sensitive, this one."

"Sure, I can throw some dirt around and make space for you. Text me the location of the cemetery, and I'll meet you there at eleven o'clock in the p.m."

I hung up, and Alyssa slouched her weight onto her hip. "I guess that's the best we can do for now. Any word from Chip?"

Although I'd just been on my phone, I looked again to see if I'd missed any messages from him. "Not yet. But it's early."

Despite my reassurances, I was surprised. Chip wasn't normally a sit-around-and-wait kind of person. He got things done, regardless of how inconvenient it was to anyone else.

"So what's next?" Alyssa looked around the pub. "I texted Tory while you were on the phone, and they're on their way, and Gramps will be here soon to help open up and get things running, which leaves us to do… whatever, I guess."

My gaze dropped to her lips, and my mind was filled with thoughts of all the *whatever* we could get up to. But the souls inside me had other ideas as they tried once again to claw their way out of my body. I doubled over to catch my breath, using the nearest chair to prop myself up. The pain tore through me, sending my muscles into spasm as I fought to stay in control. Then Alyssa's hands were on my back, and her beautiful magic seeped into me, relaxing muscles that wanted to bunch up, soothing the nausea churning in my insides.

I focused only on my breath and the surge of healing energy winding through me until the souls settled. Only then did I open my eyes to take in Alyssa's worried gaze and cup her cheek in my hand.

"I'll be okay."

She turned her face to kiss my palm. "I know you'll keep fighting. But don't push yourself too hard, all right? If we have to wait until Chip gets back to us, then let's go home. Grab something to eat. Maybe sleep?"

Neither of those things were top of the list of how I'd prefer to spend my time, but Alyssa was right.

"Sounds good, princess. Maybe we can throw on some episodes of *Parks and Rec*."

Her eyes lit up. We started towards the back door, but before we could step outside, my phone rang. I didn't know the number, and every muscle in my body tensed, the souls reacting to the strain.

"Trace?"

I looked up to find Alyssa standing on the threshold, worry once more shrouding her features on my behalf.

Taking a deep breath, I answered the call. "Hello?"

"Is this Andrew Wyatt?" The female voice was quiet, shaky. I didn't recognize it, but some of my tension eased. At least it wasn't Hazel.

"It is."

"This is Ameline Blackwood. I understand you're looking to murder my mother."

# Chapter 9
*Trace*

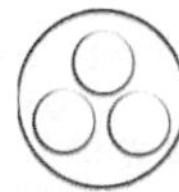

ISTAGGERED ON my feet and stared at my phone as though Ameline were about to crawl out of it and into the pub.

"Hello?"

"Yeah, hi, sorry. Ameline. Wow. I wasn't expecting to—Sorry about your mom."

It wasn't like I could deny my intentions. Hazel was coming after me. If I could send her back to Moongrave, I would, but if it came down to kill or be killed, I wouldn't hold back.

"Don't be. She's a bitch, and she deserves whatever's coming to her."

I raised my eyebrows at her response, but she didn't give me time to comment. "Anyway, I just wanted to let you know I've booked a flight out of here tonight, and I should be in

Ottawa by midnight. If you're making plans against her, I want to help."

It was nine years ago all over again.

"You don't have to, Am. I know how much it wrecked you last time."

"You know what wrecked me? Watching my mom try to steal a bunch of souls and tell me she was doing it to make my life better. You know what doesn't make a kid's life better? Hearing that your parent needs to kill other people to make it happen. We weren't at war, it wasn't self-defence. She was doing whatever she could to gain power and using me as her excuse. Or at least, telling me I was the excuse. It was all her. Everything is all about her. And clearly that hasn't changed. So yeah, I'm going to help you. If we don't need to kill her, fine, I guess I could be happy about that, but I definitely want her ass to be returned to prison where she's out of my life."

I blinked, still not quite sure what to make of this spitfire on the other end of the line. In so many ways, she sounded like Chip, and I wondered what he'd said to light this fire under her.

"You have my number," I said. "Let me know when your flight lands, and I'll make sure someone's there to get you."

"Your buddy already said he'll meet me. Chip, right? Who am I looking for, exactly? He hung up before I could ask, and he doesn't strike me as the kind of person who'll stand there with a big *Welcome* sign."

I stared at Alyssa, who looked back at me, having only picked up some of Ameline's side of the conversation. "Chip offered to pick you up?"

Now Alyssa's eyebrows shot upwards, and I was surprised her brain matter didn't follow.

"Yeah. I told him I'd take a rideshare or something, but he insisted, so whatever. At least someone will know where I'm supposed to go."

"I—um—" I had never known Chip to voluntarily leave his house for anyone. The man only stepped off his property in emergencies or to visit his parents in Kingston once a year. "He'll make sure you know it's him. I wouldn't worry about that. It might be more subtle than a *Welcome* sign, but you won't miss him."

A pause on the line, then, "Is he cute?"

My mouth fell open, and Alyssa grinned and nodded.

"I'm informed by some that, yes, he might be considered attractive."

"Cool. See you later."

She disconnected, and I was left staring at my phone, no more sure what to make of it now than I had been when I first answered.

"Well. That was a thing."

Alyssa cackled. "I wonder if Chip knows what he's gotten himself into."

The man had *offered* to pick Ameline up. "Oh, I think he's very aware."

As we drove back to Alyssa's place, we made a list of all the things we needed to do before our meeting with Hazel. The list wasn't long, but it was full of items that would depend entirely on whether we got to Almonte first and if everyone was able to come through for us.

"What does Ameline bring to the table?" Alyssa asked. "Is she a witch?"

"She is. A time witch."

Alyssa shifted in her seat to face me. "Excuse me?"

I nodded, understanding her shock. Time witches were incredibly rare. Even rarer than my telekinetic magic. It was a remnant of some ancient fae power, a result of mixed blood-lines and magics. Time magic allowed the witch to manipulate the world around them by mere seconds, slowing it down, stop-ping it, or even reversing it. I'd never heard of a time witch being able to affect more than two seconds at a go, but two seconds could save a life in battle.

"Her great-grandfather on her dad's side was a time witch, and the power skipped a few generations. She was decent with her power at thirteen, so I can only imagine how far she's progressed with it."

"Thank the goddess the power came from her dad's side and not Hazel," Alyssa said with a shudder. "I can't imagine trying to fight that woman with both kinds of power. We're up to our necks as it is."

I grabbed her hand where it rested on the centre console. "We're not skint in the power department ourselves. Don't underestimate yourself. I've seen your work."

Her smile was strained, lacking all the confidence she deserved to hold. "I've had reason enough to practise the last few months, something I'm not thrilled about. I really did plan on being a healer, you know. I never wanted to use my power to cause harm. Now I keep being thrown into situations that force me to do it, and I hate it."

Guilt threatened to twist me up, but I shoved it down. I may have been the catalyst that pushed her down that road, but luck—or fate—had governed it. Clyde Corrick had shoved Alyssa Mooney into the crosshairs, and I wished the man were still alive so I could kill him again. In fact, maybe he *was* alive. It was more than possible the fae had kept him breathing to draw out his suffering. Maybe I'd still get a chance to throw a few punches.

I squeezed her hand. "This won't last forever. Hazel is one of the most powerful spirit witches in the country. If—*when*—we take her down, it'll be a message to every other witch eying my guests that they should stay away from me. As soon as we deal with her, we can focus on releasing my souls, and then everything will go back to normal. You can keep working at the pub, I'll continue my bounty hunting ways, and we can see what life looks like without constant threats bombarding us and throwing us off track."

I looked forward to that. I wanted to know what life could be like with Alyssa at peace. I could almost see myself coming into the pub after a week away chasing a mark and her smiling at me in greeting as she poured me a pint at the bar before coming around to sink into my arms and kiss me hello.

My chest ached with longing, and I exhaled slowly. It was an incredible picture, but everything about it would need so many other things to happen first. We needed to get rid of Hazel, I needed to free the souls, Alyssa needed to decide if she wanted to keep me in her life after everything.

I believed she did—I *hoped* she did—but emotions ran rampant during a crisis, and I had no way of knowing if what she wanted now would be what she wanted after the storm passed and the waves calmed.

"I'd like that," she said, and it took me a moment to realize she wasn't answering my silent spin but the outward hopes.

When I glanced her way, I found her staring at me, her green eyes open down to her very soul, and my heart pattered against my ribs as though eager to burst out of me and get to her. I grinned, unable to hold it back, and was certain I looked as dopey as I felt, but I didn't care. How long had it been since I'd had reason to feel like this?

How long had it been since I'd believed it was possible I ever would again?

Never get my heart involved.

It had been my top rule of survival for so many years—after never touching spirit magic again. But here we were. Heart firmly on the line. And unlike last time, it didn't come with strings. It didn't come with uncertainty about whether I was making the right choice.

Instead, all it came with was a desire to protect the person who now possessed a huge chunk of who I was. Which meant Hazel had better be really fucking careful what lines she crossed, because I was armed with enough power to raze the city to the ground to protect what was mine.

# Chapter 10
*Alyssa*

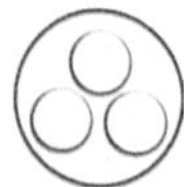

BY THE TIME we got home, I was exhausted. The roller-coaster of today's emotions had left me little more than a flaming pile of garbage, and all I wanted was to collapse on my big comfy couch, hide under a blanket and marathon some mindless television. Ideally while stuffing my face with cookies and ridiculous amounts of tea.

I didn't think Trace would judge me for any of that. In fact, I doubted it would take much to convince him to join me in everything except the cookies.

Unfortunately, we didn't have time for me to lose myself in hours of quiet recharge. We had less than three days to plan our attack against a powerful spirit witch. Too much of that unformed plan had to wait until we had more pieces put into place, but there were still details we could sort out.

"Is there any way we could make use of that leaking door-way?" I asked as I put the kettle on.

The days were finally warming up into comfortable spring weather, but that didn't mean the nights didn't call for plenty of hot beverages.

While the water heated, I grabbed a plate and my box of cookies. Then I put the plate away and brought the box to the couch. I might not be able to enjoy the TV-marathoning part of my recharge, but to hell if anyone would keep me away from the rest of it.

"I've been thinking about that," Trace said with his head in my fridge. He was rifling through it for something and stepped back a few seconds later with a bag of baby carrots.

"You are such a freak," I grumbled, and he flashed me a grin that warmed me straight through.

Ignoring my comment, he set to work organizing his own snack while I tore open the box of cookies and shoved a piece of chocolatey bliss into my mouth. I refused to be guilted into eating healthy right now. I'd bought the carrots, hadn't I? I ate them. I even enjoyed them. But this was a moment for junk food elixirs.

"I think we should take a drive up there tonight to get a lay of the land," Trace continued. "She picked the location, so we have to assume she's already been there and done some work, but if we're careful, we might be able to disarm whatever we find and rig them up for our own purposes."

It was a crafty idea that scared the bejeebus out of me, but what other choice did we have? We couldn't go in ignorant. That would guarantee we'd fail. Horribly. Probably very messily.

"Right. We'll get some sleep and take a drive after sundown. Maybe I should call in the family. Avery's wards might be helpful in case we set off something we shouldn't."

I ran through the rest of my coven. My brothers, Brody and Dylan, were better at offence than stealth, and my sister, Val, would grumble the whole time about how we were expending energy in attacking when we should be getting ready to run in case the worst should happen. Avery had been training with Mom to improve her healing magic, so that was another perk to bringing her, but every member of my family offered something. Gramps would be great to help us strategize, but he was managing Mooney's. Aunt Courtney would be a good second choice for that, but she and her wife, Jennifer, were in BC so it would take them time to get back. Like my brothers, my cousins Kyle and Grayson would be better suited for the fight to come, but I suspected Grayson would be happy to get in there early to lay a few traps of his own. From what I'd seen from him over the past few months—and what I'd learned about my family—he was following in Gramps's footsteps with regard to martial skills. Mallory was home, though, and her magic lined up well with mine. If she and Avery were free, we could make a solid team.

So many more cousins were mixed throughout the city, and I was certain they would come if called, but I would save them for the battle proper, when we'd need fresh, well-rested bodies on the field.

I texted Avery and Mal and went back to my cookies while I waited to hear from them.

"We shouldn't need warders," Trace said as he settled beside me, "but it won't hurt to have backup. I would have said I'd make sure Chip was keeping eyes on us, but with him *leaving his house* to get Ameline, we can't guarantee he'll be focused."

I chuckled, unable to hold back my shocked hilarity that Chip of all people was showing this much preference for someone he'd never met. As the thought occurred to me, I realized the truth. "He's been keeping an eye on her, hasn't he?"

"For my sake, he claimed, so we'd know where she was if we ever needed to get in touch with her, but now I'm wondering if there was more to it than that."

I raised an eyebrow. "Bit of an age gap, isn't there?"

Trace shrugged. "She's twenty-five."

A fair point. Until I considered Chip's demonic nature. "How old is Chip? Can't demons live an absurdly long time?"

"In the infernals, sure. On this plane, their lifespans are the same as ours. He's thirty. Same as me."

"Cradle robber," I teased.

Trace snapped a bite of carrot between his teeth as he waggled his eyebrows at me, and I couldn't help but laugh.

I didn't understand it. We were facing a showdown against a seriously powerful witch. A woman whose coven had nearly killed Trace two weeks ago, and me, and so many members of my family. Yet I felt lighter than I had in weeks. As though within these walls—or maybe close to this man—none of my problems could get to me. Life would stay solid and grounded because *he* was solid and grounded.

"Thank you," I said before I knew I was going to say it.

He paused mid-chew. "For what?"

I shrugged. "For being you. For being here. For not sneaking off to some crappy little rental on Metcalfe and disappearing on me again."

"I should be the one thanking you, princess. You're the one helping me face my past, something I've been running from for most of my life. I never would have found the courage to do it if you weren't with me."

I sagged into the couch and rested my head on his shoulder. In the kitchen, the kettle clicked off, but I didn't rush to get up and pour the water. The spell we were under right now, this lull in the chaos, was fleeting. I worried as soon as I stood up, it would end.

Then my phone buzzed, and the bubble popped anyway.

Trace kissed the top of my head and helped me sit up. I grabbed my phone and headed into the kitchen to pour the tea I now didn't want as I read the message waiting for me.

**Avery: We'll be wherever you need us to be.**

At least there was that. Tonight, we'd survey the battlefield. Tomorrow we'd check in with the enemy's daughter and a two-hundred-year-dead witch. On Wednesday, we'd ride into war.

# Chapter 11
*Alyssa*

TRACE PARKED DOWN the road from one of the museum parking lots, off a tucked-away side road, and we walked back to the mill in the darkness, guided only by the moonlight, which was thankfully close to full tonight.

Two figures lurked by the pay station at the front of the lot, and when we got close enough, Avery and Mallory stepped into view.

"Have you seen anyone else?" I whispered as I reached them and pulled first one cousin then the other into a tight hug.

Mallory shook her head. "It's been quiet. No cars, no dogs, no witches. Just us wondering what the heck we're doing out here."

"Searching for traps," Trace explained. "Keep your senses

open. If you detect anything, let me know and—"

Mallory grinned. "Don't worry, bounty hunter, we've got this. You think the Mooneys could grow up together and not learn how to make each other's lives miserable?"

I nodded, remembering the many pranks we used to play on each other growing up. And still did, admittedly. We were a bunch of children when we got together for a non-serious family event.

"Besides," I said, "do you forget what our real asset is here?" I tapped beside my eye, and Trace's shoulders sagged as he rolled his eyes skywards.

We Mooneys could see magic in a way many other witches couldn't. It was a genetic quirk of our clan to see the various types as weaves of colour, which meant out here in the dark there wouldn't be much chance of something bypassing us unless it was really well hidden.

"Should we split up?" Avery asked, peering around. "We looked at the map before we came out here. It looks like there are six or seven different walking paths. Do we know which one Hazel plans to use?"

"She'll be heading to the cloister," Trace said, "but there are a lot of ways to get there. I think splitting up makes sense, but let's keep communication open."

I pulled out my phone and loaded up Avery's number in case I needed to call her.

"Code word?" she asked, and I nodded to confirm. It was the standard phrase we used whenever one of us needed immediate help.

Then she and her sister slipped back into the shadows, taking the path to the left. Trace and I cut across the parking lot, keeping close to the gatehouse to stay out of sight, and took the path straight ahead.

We didn't speak as we walked, though at some point along the way, Trace held out his hand and I slipped mine into it. A soft breeze brushed through the trees, throwing leaves around my boots and shaking the mostly bare branches overhead. With the moonlight bathing the paths in dappled blue light, the smell of earth and tree and coming rain, the warmth of Trace's hand against mine, and the serenity that only comes when you're surrounded by so much nature, I could almost forget why we were here.

Yet despite the calming, soul-warming aspects of the scene, nothing was strong enough to squash the apprehension squeezing my insides. For all we knew, we'd already stepped into Hazel's trap. She had to know we'd scope this place out ahead of time, and she would have planned for it. What would we find when we stepped too far along this path? Suddenly, bringing only two reinforcements seemed short sighted.

But I breathed through my anxiety and focused on the practicalities. Hazel hadn't said tonight. She'd arranged for

Wednesday. That had to mean she was busy getting ready, and even if she'd prepared a few surprises for us eager beavers, that didn't mean they would take us out. It would simply put us on our guard and give us some insight into what else she might have prepared. Anything we learned tonight would be useful.

We rounded the curve and stepped deeper into the forested area. Trees closed us in on both sides, and the moon was blocked by the sheer number of branches overhead. The trails weren't lit, but that didn't matter. They were maintained well enough that all we had to do was follow the one we were on and we would wind up where we needed to be.

Avery and Mallory hadn't been lying about the silence, though. It seemed like everything was asleep. The usual foresty sounds I might have expected to hear—squirrels, birds, couples arguing about which way they should take when the path split—were gone, leaving only the sounds of me and Trace breathing and the leaves crunching under foot.

A glimmer of green caught the corner of my eye, and I turned my head to follow it, grabbing Trace's arm to pull him to a stop. I pointed in the direction of the magic and guided him to the edge of the trail, where we came across a small box. The green magic surrounded it, and only then did I notice the faint thread of power that led away from the box across the path to another box on the other side.

"Magical tripwire," Trace whispered. If we'd crossed it, we

would have released whatever enchantment was in those boxes.

I was impressed by the craftiness of Hazel's people. This was far beyond whatever we had come up with as kids. Not the tripwire part—that was classic—but the waiting enchantments? Very clever. I made a note to remember that on the next big Canada Day bash. With something less lethal in the boxes, probably.

Trace set to work disarming it, using his telekinetic power to wrap around the magic, containing it, suppressing it, and snuffing it out, and the green glow around the box faded. He tucked one into his pocket, and I collected the other.

"We'll take them home and see if we can dismantle the enchantment. Learn what kind of spells they'll be throwing at us," he said. "I doubt they'll be pretty."

Considering I'd seen Hazel's coven throw spells that decomposed a wall in a heartbeat, I had to agree with him.

"Good eye, Mooney," Trace said, nudging my shoulder. "You have the makings of a decent bounty hunter."

I stifled a laugh but held on to the warmth of pride filling my chest. I had a grand total of zero aspirations in that direction, but it was nice to know he thought I had what it took. Maybe I could find ways to put those skills to use making Mooney's run even more efficiently.

Especially if I had to learn how to run the place by myself.

No. I wouldn't think about that just yet. Simon had only

been gone a day. He would be back. Reverie had promised she'd bring him home. He could sort out his stuff, and when he returned, he'd be the best friend I'd known and loved for all these years. We could go back to normal, and no one would notice the pub had gone through some growing pains.

For now, I had to stay focused on whatever tonight might bring.

We found two more traps before we hit the cloister— another tripwire, and a buried enchantment that would have gone off if we'd stepped on it. My ability to see magic had saved us from the second tripwire, but Trace had noticed the vibrations in the air above the buried one. He'd pulled me to the side and thrown a rock at it, then covered my head when the dirt had blown in all directions with not even a sound to show for it. Only then had I watched the magic snap upwards, reaching like tentacles ready to grab us and… drag us under? Suffocate us? I didn't want to know.

Trace dealt with them, showing me how in the process, and we reached the cloister without any further surprises.

Once we got there, however, my alarms pinged.

The place was empty. There was no sense of magic, no visible or detectable traps marking the worn stone floor of the open-sided design. Either Hazel hadn't had a chance to set things up here yet, or we were missing something.

"We're sure she said the cloister?"

We strolled through, taking in the wooden pews that had been set up for visitors to have a sit. It had always been one of my favourite parts of the museum.

"She did," Trace said, his voice grim, "but I don't sense that magic Gramps talked about." He shook his head and looked around. "Be a good place for an ambush. Get us backed up against that wall with lots of space for her people to close in on us."

"Not tonight, though," I said, looking around and seeing nothing.

"No, not tonight. And if she expects us to come out here early, then probably not Wednesday night either." He threaded his fingers through his hair and spun in a circle, his expression twisted with frustration. "What am I missing?"

I didn't blame him for feeling confused. I couldn't help but feel that Hazel was ten steps ahead of us, not only making plans, but anticipating every decision we made. Which in itself boggled my mind. I got that she'd been the one to teach Trace most of the fundamentals he knew about magic and women and everything, but it had been nine years since she'd seen him. Twelve since she'd sacrificed him to SMOAC. How did she still know so much about him?

A silly question, maybe. After all, it wasn't like Trace had disappeared. Hells, he hadn't even stayed under the radar. He'd become a bounty hunter because of her—and he'd become such a *good* bounty hunter that he'd appeared all over the mundane and supernatural news. I was certain that even in Moongrave Prison, Hazel would have had access to newspapers and television. At least enough to keep tabs on her old protégé.

And if she'd been paying that close attention, then we had to prepare for her to know every move Trace might make.

"Stop," I said, holding up my hand.

Trace did as I asked without hesitation. He stilled mid-step, pausing even before lowering his foot to the ground.

I surveyed the scene, my thoughts flicking through possibilities. Hazel had planned for us to come here ahead of schedule. She'd known Trace would poke around and try to figure out what her intentions were. She would have laid a trap specifically for him.

But she didn't know me.

I breathed out slowly and stepped out of the cloister to the grassy, rock-ringed amphitheatre where folding chairs would be set up for events. I viewed the log building now used as a storage shed a few metres ahead of me, and the pavilion to my left filled with picnic tables where a reception might be held. A more modern building was just beyond that, which I could only assume was a place for a bridal party to prepare before the ceremony. These weren't the only buildings across the conservation area. Hazel could have chosen any of the more out-of-the-way places. Instead, she'd chosen one of the main tourist sites.

Why?

"Okay," I breathed. "You need to stop thinking like a bounty hunter. Ignore your instincts, ignore your experience." At Trace's confused expression, I pushed myself to be clearer. "Stop thinking like *you* and start thinking like Hazel. So far she's led everything because she's pulling from what she knows about you." I looked around us, at all the shadows and landmarks she might have used to her advantage. "It's time to turn the tables on her overplanning ass."

# Chapter 12
*Trace*

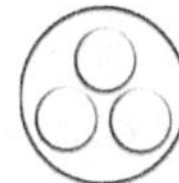

ALYSSA'S LOGIC MADE sense, so although it went against every voice in my head to walk away from the cloister, where I suspected the details of Hazel's plan were, we started across the grass. Although I hadn't detected the magic Gramps said was here, there was *something*. An energy, a vibration. Likely some other trap that some unsuspecting bastard might set off if they weren't careful.

Together we walked along the edge of the secondary parking lot towards the modern building to our left. Alyssa waved at me to stay put as she climbed the steps and peered through the window. Then she came back down, shook her head, and led me towards the pavilion.

I kept watch over my shoulder, feeling uncomfortable this

far out in the open. Why hadn't Hazel chosen somewhere more secluded? Yes, she planned to meet us at night, but this close to the parking lot, it was more than possible that someone might pull in and see us.

Then again, this close to the parking lot, maybe she didn't intend to fight me.

My thoughts stumbled on the idea, and I lurched to a halt. Alyssa glanced at me over her shoulder, making me realize I must have made a noise, and I rushed to catch up with her.

"She's not coming here for a fight," I said. "That's why there's nothing in the cloister. I'm right about the ambush, but her goal will be to restrain me. Maybe pull on the magic of the doorway to overpower me? Then drag me to the parking lot and take me somewhere else to get these souls out of me."

As I said it, her plan unrolled before me as though I'd shaken out a yoga mat.

Alyssa frowned. "Except she can't assume you'll come here on your own. Does she plan to overpower all of us? That's presumptuous of her."

That was Hazel.

"Her coven must be big. If she's feeling that confident, she—"

A scream cut me off, and Alyssa didn't think before she tore through the pavilion, down the wood-framed steps, towards the museum proper. I stayed close on her heels, and although

I wanted to warn her to slow down and watch where she was going, knowing how likely it was that we'd come across more of Hazel's nasty traps, I knew she wasn't likely to listen. Not when her cousins might be in danger.

We looped back towards the first parking lot, following a different trail. Alyssa skidded to a halt with a gasp, her wide eyes taking in something I couldn't see.

"What the fuck?"

Although the magic was invisible to me, I didn't need to get that much closer before I realized the full shock of what had stopped Alyssa. Mallory hung upside down in the air, dangling by her ankle. Avery stood beneath her, also trapped, her arm out in front of her as she tried to lurch away.

"We missed the trap," Mallory mumbled. She was doing her best to contort her body to reach her ankle, but gravity was working against her.

"Hang on, let me help," Alyssa said, taking a few tentative steps forward. "Trace, be ready to catch her."

Mallory was easily four feet in the air. If she dropped, she'd land right on her head, and I worried for her neck. So I stepped carefully, being mindful of the buzz of any other energy that suggested another trap might be hiding in the dirt road, and angled myself to catch the woman when she fell.

Alyssa raised her hands and moved her lips in a silent spell, and the hair on the back of my neck danced at the familiar signature of her magic. My own rose to play with hers, the two vibrations weaving in the sky so tightly I could almost make it out like tiny fireflies. Avery's eyes widened as she watched it, seeing the same thing as Alyssa could, and I envied her as well.

As soon as her surprise wore off, Avery battled again with whatever invisible bonds held her.

"I feel like such a fool," she said. "We knew there was something here but only caught it a second before it unleashed. There were two more—Trace, look out!" Her eyes widened again, this time directed over my shoulder, and I only just had time to whirl around and ready a spell as two dark figures hurtled out of the shadows.

Alyssa shifted one of her hands towards this new threat and joined her magic with mine to launch at them, keeping her other hand towards Mallory as she continued to unwind the spell holding her cousin.

The two witches bearing down on us splayed their hands at their sides, and I sensed the energy of their magic growing, spreading. I summoned a ward and pushed it out to stretch in front of Alyssa and me, Mallory and Avery safe behind us, and winced as the heavy spell slammed into it. My teeth shook, an uncomfortable buzz that crept along my jaw.

"Are you Hazel's?" I demanded.

They didn't answer before launching more spells. This time Alyssa turned her back on Mallory to throw two of her own.

They cut through my ward and struck the witch to our left, who wrapped his arms around his middle as he flew through the air, hit with one of her atmospheric pulses. The other, unscathed, sprinted closer. I summoned my telekinetic power and grabbed hold of a branch lying on the ground. It soared towards him and clobbered him over the head. Knocked off balance, he tripped on the uneven ground and rolled down a slight incline straight through the fence that guarded the path from the stream below.

The first witch was already back on his feet, more magic enveloping him. He threw a spell, and I didn't have time to block it, so I stepped aside. The spell hit the ground below Mallory, turning the dirt into a smoking paste, and Mallory let out a shriek as she dropped lower in whatever web had caught her. Alyssa rushed to hold her steady, but her attention was drawn to the witch readying another attack. I shifted beneath Mallory, avoiding the spell-touched mess, and widened my arms not seconds before the binding spell snapped and she tumbled into my hold. I set her down next to Avery and joined Alyssa in facing off with the witch.

He snarled and raised his hands. Alyssa bared her teeth in response. I split my attention between him and the witch I'd forced off the path.

Were these Hazel's people?

"Andrew Wyatt?" a calm voice called from behind me.

I stiffened but didn't turn around, not wanting to put my back to the person in front of us.

"My name is Al Nuñes. I'm here on behalf of the Ontario Witches' Council. It's come to our attention that you're in possession of a host of illegal souls, and I'm here to bring you in for questioning."

My heart stopped.

I kept my hands raised and straightened my back, not wanting to give away the terror coursing through me.

Beside me, Alyssa turned around to face Nuñes with horror written in every inch of her expression. "Excuse me?" she demanded. "Did I hear you correctly?"

"Alyssa Mooney?" he asked. "You're to come with me under charges of harbouring and collaborating with a spirit witch."

She barked out a laugh and her expression changed from horror to incredulity. "You have *got* to be fucking kidding me. How do we know you're not some of Hazel's lackeys trying to lure us in to kill us?"

I looked over my shoulder and watched Nuñes, a short, squat man with a short, squat mop of black hair, reach into his pocket and pull out his council ID. He didn't need to bother. I recognized him from outside the house in South Keys earlier today. His partner stood beside him, looking unimpressed by the situation she found herself in.

Alyssa's eyes narrowed as she took in the ID, then her attention shifted to the witches. "You're the ones who broke into Hazel's place. Which means you're after her too. Seems to me we're working for the same thing here. Why don't we work together on this?"

"I'm working for the safety and wellbeing of the witches of Ontario," he said, unswayed by her proposal. "You can come with us quietly, or we can subdue you, but either way you're coming."

Alyssa dropped her hands to her hips and nodded to the trap. "Were these you?"

"They were. We'll talk about how you were able to disarm them later. If you wouldn't mind?" He stepped to the side, an invitation for us to lead the way.

"Who told you we would be here tonight?" I asked, suspicion weighing in my chest.

Nuñes didn't answer, and neither did his partner, though she watched me closely.

I crossed my arms. "Look, if Hazel Blackwood is playing us, do you really want her leading you around? Can't we talk about this here? Without all the paperwork?"

Nuñes's wide shoulders tightened. "Does this mean you're choosing to be subdued?"

I gritted my teeth at his refusal to be reasonable. Hazel was obviously behind them being here, but why? To throw me off balance? To make it easier to get me?

We had options. We could fight our way free, figure out where these accusations had come from, and address them from a point of aggression. Or we could cooperate and try to get our answers on their terms.

I hated both options. Both took me too close to where I'd been twelve years ago.

Fucking Hazel.

What did she think I would do?

I appreciated what Alyssa had been trying to do, using her logic to get us off the path Hazel had created for us. It had been a solid idea, but she'd made one critical error. We might have moved away from my instincts, but we hadn't considered that Alyssa's might also be in play. That she might no longer be as *unknown* as she'd been a few weeks ago. Hazel had played us both.

"We'll go," Alyssa said before she and I could exchange a look. "Avery, Mallory, get Gramps. Tell him what happened and have him meet us at the council office."

Mallory worked to undo Avery from her bindings. "Will do."

Alyssa looked at me, and I nodded. She was making the right decision. I hated it, but it was the best choice. Yes, I'd broken the law—not to mention so many personal promises— when I'd stolen those souls away from Corrick, but we were the good guys here. We had to act like it.

So, without argument and with a dragging sense of dread, I fell into step beside Alyssa and headed off to the council's awaiting van.

# Chapter 13
*Alyssa*

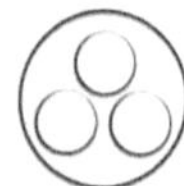

I SAT IN a mostly empty room, my hands bound in magic-nullifying cuffs where they were locked to a bar in the centre of the stainless-steel table.

The sensation of having my magic numbed was stifling, like I couldn't breathe properly. I squirmed in my seat, desperate to find some comfortable way of sitting, but with every passing minute, the odds of this chair morphing into a well-cushioned lounger grew increasingly less likely.

I'd been here for at least an hour and had been left alone so far. As soon as we'd arrived at the council's Kanata office, Trace and I had been split up, and I'd been escorted into this room with the promise that as soon as Gramps was here, they'd bring him to me.

I doubted it had taken this long for Gramps to get here. As soon as Mallory or Avery made the call, he would have been on his way, even if it meant he had to leave Tory to watch the pub as he came out to save me from yet another problem. If he hadn't been to see me yet, it had to mean he was somewhere else in the building, no doubt arguing with someone about holding us. Hopefully keeping his fists and his magic to himself.

A year ago, I would have believed it unlikely for my grandfather to get aggressive on my behalf unless he was clearly provoked, but I'd learned a lot about the old man in the past few weeks. Not only that he owed most of his success to the persuasive power the souls in the ex-amulet held, but also that he'd been some kind of magical vigilante in his youth. It put all my years of training into perspective, and I felt both reassured by his confidence and, I couldn't lie, a little terrified about what else he might have hidden from his family.

But, at the very least, I could be sure that Edwyn Mooney had my back. The Mooney family was a big deal in this province. A few Mooneys, Gramps included, were actually on the Ontario Witches' Council, and I was sure Gramps was seeing a little red at the fact that no one had given him a heads up about his granddaughter's arrest warrant.

He would get me out of here. Hopefully Trace, too. Also hopefully in time for both of us to get some sleep before we met with Trace's necromancer buddy tomorrow. And Hazel on

Wednesday.

Wow, I had a busy week scheduled. What a time for Simon to disappear on me.

I groaned and bowed my head against the table, grateful for the coolness on my forehead as my anxiety reared its ugly head and attempted to take the wheel on my whirlwind thoughts.

I breathed through the spin, refusing to get caught up in all the worst-case scenarios threatening to overwhelm me. I was worthy of good things. I would get this sorted and see own bed before the sun came up.

The door opened, and I sat up so quickly my spine cracked. I winced, and Gramps must have caught the change in my expression because he shot a murderous look at Nuñes, who came in behind him.

"You have her chained up in here?"

Nuñes wasn't fazed by my grandfather's ire. "Miss Mooney is here because she chose to work with a spirit witch. We can't take the risk that she's also dabbling."

"Stop fucking around, Al. Release her."

Nuñes still didn't react, but he did come around the table and unlock the cuffs. My magic flowed through me, as refreshing and delicious as a cool, crisp glass of water, and I sagged back in my chair as I rubbed feeling into my wrists.

"Now," Gramps said, sitting down beside me. "Finish what you started in the hall. Why is she here? Who told you about

Trace?"

Nuñes sat down, looking bored. He flipped open a blue file folder and spun it towards me. "You know these people?"

I glanced at the photo in the folder, and my stomach clenched. I recognized the faces of the three people staring up at me. Emile, Kurt, and Nathalie. Three members of Trace's old coven, a group he and Chip now referred to as the Bone Casters. Only one of them was breathing today, and he was on his way back to his cat in Alberta.

"I do. They're part of Hazel Blackwood's coven. Spirit witches, all three of them. They were practising here in Ottawa over the past couple months." I met his eye with a pointed stare. "Something the Ontario Witches' Council did nothing to stop, I might add."

"If you knew, you should have reported them."

Walked right into that one.

"I shouldn't have had to. I thought you people had your finger on everything that goes on in this city. We only learned about it because Trace was helping me search for Gramps, who'd been kidnapped by their coven."

Another finger in their direction.

I had a lot of reasons not to think well of the council as a whole. I appreciated why they existed, and I didn't do anything to get in their way, but they'd made it clear that they were happy to sit back and let other people solve Ontario's smaller problems, only getting involved when something happened that raised awareness on a provincial scale. Their non-action was what kept Gramps nice and busy on a day-to-day, essentially serving as the council representative for Ottawa's covens so things didn't need to escalate. And it was why I'd been so surprised to see them at Hazel's.

"So you acknowledge that Andrew Wyatt has connections to this coven."

"He prefers Trace," I corrected. "And you know he does. You know everything about his history because he worked with SMOAC nine years ago to take Hazel down. It's all on record."

Nuñes met my eye, unblinking, assessing, and I stared right back, unwilling to be intimidated. Trace hadn't done anything wrong. He had nothing to feel guilty about—and neither did I. If Nathalie hadn't walked out of our encounter with the Bone Casters, it had been because she'd attempted to use her harvested spirit magic to kill me and Trace had saved my life. That didn't deserve an arrest on his record. It deserved a medal.

"Do you deny that *Trace* Wyatt currently harbours illegally obtained souls?"

My mouth went dry. "I do."

Gramps looked at me, and I crossed my arms. I wished I knew what Trace was telling them, but I suspected he was being as honest as he could be. Or maybe less so in some twisted effort to protect me. I wasn't about to let him go down by himself, though. "I won't deny that he's currently harbouring *souls*, but I will argue that they were illegally obtained. Those souls were harvested willingly." At the time. "Trace transferred them into himself to save them. They chose to be contained by him."

All true. He'd sacrificed so much by taking them in.

"So you admit he practised illegal spirit magic."

I gritted my teeth at this man's unwillingness to see beyond the black and white. "I admit he worked against the laws of our kind in a heroic act of rescuing not only the souls but also my life and the lives of others. We've been working together to figure out how to safely release them, but we haven't found a solution yet."

"Oh, we have the solution."

The way Nuñes said it, without a fidget, without any intonation, raised goosebumps along my arms. "What do you mean? What have you done? Where's Trace?"

I was on my feet before I knew I was standing, marching towards the door. A band of dark purple atmospheric magic—just different enough from mine to tell he wasn't a member of my family—shoved me back into my chair.

"I don't suggest you try that again, Miss Mooney."

Gramps tensed. "You cast on her again, Nuñes, and I'll have you stripped of your position."

"You're here as a courtesy, Edwyn. Consider yourself lucky

you're not also up on charges if you knew about Wyatt's condition."

Gramps worked his jaw but wisely held his tongue. He couldn't say anything without damning the family, and we were too close to finding out what our ancestor's plan for those souls had been to risk it. Soon enough, that stupid amulet would be nothing more than a warning story for future Mooney generations. Trace would be free, I wouldn't have this guilt hanging over me, and we could move on with our lives.

"If you hurt Trace—or those souls—I'm going to go over Ontario's head to SMOAC," I said. "He has done nothing wrong. He—"

"Why were you at the museum tonight?" Nuñes interrupted.

I blinked. "What?"

"If we ignore everything else, you were trespassing on conservation land after hours. Why?"

"Because—" The question took me so off guard it took me a moment to remember. "Because Hazel is coming after Trace. She wants the souls. We wanted to get ahead of her so we can stop her. Since, you know, you and SMOAC lost her."

This time the lines around his eyes and mouth tightened, and I patted myself on the back for scoring a hit at last.

"Listen," I said, leaning forward. "I know we're skating some grey territory here, but believe me, we're doing you guys a favour. You know Hazel is back and that she's after power. You probably also know about the other witches that escaped SMOAC a few weeks ago hours after their arrest." Again Nuñes flinched. Interesting. I would have expected him to look smug that the feds had failed instead of the council. "They're working with her, and they're not to be fucked with. I've faced both of them. That witch with the demonic power? She can summon hellfire. Nasty piece of work. And the guy who looks like a walking corpse? Well, he's dead, which raises even more red flags about what's going on in the department. Hazel is bringing in some heavy hitters, and if she gets what she wants, she's going to cause so many problems in this province there's no way the Ontario council will have the power to fight back."

The look in Nuñes's eyes turned calculating. "All the more reason to keep Wyatt here until the souls are dealt with."

I didn't trust the council with those souls any more than I trusted Hazel with them. "You think Hazel won't find her way in here? The very fact you knew where we would be tonight, and about Trace, makes me think you're dealing with troubles enough in your council. I wouldn't be surprised if a quarter of your people are part of her coven."

The way he'd bashed open Hazel's door the other day made me think he wasn't one of them, but I watched closely for any sign of guilt. Instead, fire flickered in his dark eyes. I'd offended him. But he also wasn't arguing, which told me he had similar concerns.

"Let us go, let us deal with this, and you guys can take the credit. I don't even care. We want to solve the problem, not play politics."

I sat back in my chair and crossed one leg over the other. Gramps gave me a subtle nod of approval that raised my confidence. Look at me, being a badass dealing with authority. Before this, the extent of my experience with any government body involved taxes and permits. I was so far outside my element, and as proud of myself as I was, I was also about to throw up.

Nuñes tapped his fingers on the file folder. Then he flipped the page and I found myself staring at a photo of myself, one I recognized all too well. Because it wasn't me. It was a photo of the facestealer, Shiny, wearing my face outside the home of Viviane McCree, a murdered fae general.

I swallowed around the lump in my throat.

"Why does Dara Josef-Levesque have it out for you?" he asked.

He phrased the question in a way that told me he knew most, if not all, of the story, so I didn't bother explaining. "I have no idea. Corrick paid that facestealer to help him pin Vivi's murder on me, and Dara latched on to the idea that I was responsible."

It had taken nineteen hours and the near deaths of me, Trace, Simon, and Reverie to convince her otherwise. We'd piled up heaps of evidence at her feet to prove I hadn't been the one to kill her two generals, and she'd been determined not to believe it.

"Had you met the fae duchess prior to these events?"

"Never. I knew Vivi from the pub, but that's it. The first time I met the duchess was when"—I held back from mentioning Trace's name—"I was dragged in front of her. She was ready to kill me. Fortunately, she didn't get the chance."

Because Trace had put himself on the line to save me. Goddess, that man and his glorious risk-taking. Not to mention his endless faith in me.

Nuñes's mouth twisted in a thoughtful grimace, and suspicion snared me.

"Why?" I asked. "Do *you* know why she believed I did it?"

He tapped his fingers on the file folder again, a gesture I'd come to realize meant he was trying to decide something. His gaze flicked between me and Gramps, and after a moment, his shoulders sagged. "We have reason to believe it has something to do with spirit magic. With the souls now contained within Mr. Wyatt. What we don't know is if that connection poses a threat to provincial security."

I stared at Gramps, who met my eye and shook his head. "This is the first I'm hearing about any of this," he said.

I lifted the hair off the back of my neck and stared up at the ceiling as I breathed through this latest revelation. Dara had also been after me because of the amulet. Had everyone known it existed before I did?

"Look, I only found out about my family history a few months ago. I don't know why the fae might have it out for me, just like I didn't know what Corrick was after. The only reason Trace is involved is because he wanted to stop Corrick. You say you know more. How about you fill us in on the rest of it, and we can take that information and do something with it."

It was a bit of a long shot, but I needed to get out of here. I needed air. My lungs felt as though a giant hand had reached through my chest to give them a solid squeeze, and if I didn't see the sky at some point in the next few minutes, I was going to become a hyperventilating mess.

"Unfortunately, I'm not able to disclose any further information until we have a better understanding of—"

"Not acceptable," Gramps said. "Not only is this in reference to my family, but I am an elder on this council. You will spit out everything you know, or I will go over your head. You can throw whatever threats at me you want, but remember your place."

His magic flowed over his fingers in a show of strength—not a threat, but a reminder of his position in this city. Nuñes was strong, but he was nowhere on the hierarchy compared to Gramps.

Those fingers tapped again, and Nuñes's brow furrowed.

"Very well. All we know is that Dara has been asking around about the Mooney family. Something in relation to the unseen wall. Rumours have been coming from the mirror realm about unrest on the other side, something to do with the fae and the vampires, and she seems to believe it has something to do with Mooney's Pub. Word reached us a few days ago that the souls in question were absorbed by Mr. Wyatt. You understand why we can't allow him to walk free as he is."

I curled my hands into fists. "You damn well can. No one else would be able to hold them. Those souls deserve to be free—*properly* free. Not used by anyone else, including the council. Trace is the best bet to ensure they get the justice they're owed."

"Perhaps that's true, but it's not protocol. If he chose to use those souls, he would be unstoppable."

"But he won't."

"If Hazel Blackwood is coming after him, you don't believe he'll use whatever power is at his disposal to stop her?"

I pinched my lips together, my breaths coming hard and quick. But just as Nuñes grew smug—the faintest shift of expression on his stoic face—I shook my head. "If the souls choose to wield their power out of self-preservation, you can hardly fault them for it, but I've never met a man with more integrity than Trace Wyatt. His history is exactly why he's the best person—maybe the only person—to be trusted with them.

I have faith in him."

"As do I," said Gramps.

Nuñes looked between the two of us. "Excuse me."

He rose and walked out of the room, leaving us alone together.

I bowed my head into my hands. "Gramps, what the hell is going on here?"

He rubbed my back. "Don't stress, Pip. The council is doing what the council does. Putting on a show. But they won't want the responsibility of those souls either. Not when they would be forced to treat them properly for the sake of optics. If they'd gotten their hands on the amulet, it would be another story, but taking them out of Trace? Too much of a paper trail. They're going through the motions, but it'll turn out there's a purpose to this theatre."

"Which is?"

"They think whatever's happening in the mirror realm will spill over here. Dara's interest in our family worries them because of the potential magical crisis it could lead to. They're giving us the heads up so we fix it before it becomes an issue."

I scoffed and raised my head. "You've gotta be shitting me. So instead of inviting us over for tea and talking to us about this, they let Hazel lead them by the nose and arrest us?"

Gramps shrugged. "I guess this is more fun? Or they have reasons for wanting Hazel to think they're pliable."

The door opened, and Nuñes returned, this time with Trace behind him looking exhausted and more than a little irritated.

"You're free to go," the council witch said.

I rose and moved towards Trace, but Nuñes cut between us. "I highly recommend you find your solutions quickly, Miss Mooney. If the council does have to step in, it won't end well. For any of you."

# Chapter 14
*Trace*

B Y THE TIME we walked out of the council office, dawn was breaking. The soft blue-grey light bathed the public parking lot, highlighting the single car parked sideways across four spots.

"Come on," Gramps grumbled. "We'll head back to Ashton, and I'll take you to pick up your car after you've had some sleep and a bite to eat."

Neither Alyssa nor I argued. I made to open the front passenger door for her, but she took my hand and pulled me with her into the back. Her head on my shoulder was a comfortable weight, and my eyes sagged shut as Gramps sped along the highway into the country and towards the comfort-able split-level sitting on its large, open property.

I'd been to the Mooney house once before in the past few weeks, and it felt strange to walk through the door on my own steam instead of being carried in. Not strange in a bad way, more in a sense of… coming home. Which didn't make sense, as I barely knew these people. But with Alyssa's hand in mine, it seemed like the most natural thing in the world.

Avery shrieked and ran towards us, throwing her arms around first Alyssa, then me, with Mallory following her by a close second.

"Thank the goddess. Are you all right? Are you free? Do you have one of those monitors on your ankle to stop you from leaving the area?"

They fussed over Alyssa, Mallory straight up using her foot to nudge the hem of Alyssa's jeans to check for the monitor.

Alyssa sank onto a stool at the kitchen island and rested her head on her hand. "No monitor, but if they could have, they would have. I don't know how to process anything that happened tonight."

Other than Alyssa filling me in on her conversation with Nuñes, we hadn't spoken much in the car, all too tired and dazed by the whirlwind that had been our night, but now, under the warm lights of the chandeliers, the smell of food warming in the oven, the presence of friends, some of the shock was wearing off.

Mary, Alyssa's mother, came around the island and wrapped

her arms around me in a hug so tight and warm, I couldn't help but sink into it. How long had it been since my own mother had shown such affection? Ever?

"I'm so glad you're all right. When Mal called us, we didn't know what to do. I'm glad they were willing to listen to reason."

Alyssa snorted. "I don't think reason had anything to do with it. They're playing us, Mom. Using us. Again. Nothing new. But as long as it benefits all of us, I'm not about to call them on it." She frowned and swung around so her back rested against the granite countertop. "What I don't understand is why Hazel would have sent them after us. Because she had to have been the one to tip them off, right? How else would they have known to prepare for us?"

I pulled out a chair from the dining table and sat down, too tired to keep my feet. Mary patted me on the shoulder and returned to the kitchen to start loading up a plate with delicious-smelling leftovers.

"I don't know," I said. "The only thing I can come up with is that she has people within the council, and she figured it would be easier to pin me down if I was locked up instead of free and able to fight for myself."

Alyssa nodded vaguely. "That's what I told Nuñes. He looked offended by it, but not nearly as much as I would have expected him to be if he didn't suspect as much himself."

Gramps snorted. "That's because he's a smart kid. He

might be hardline, but he's one of the best. I admire him, even if I want to kick his ass for the way he treated you tonight. If Hazel has moles in there, he's not one of them."

I raised an eyebrow. "Can we use him, then? Having some-one from within the council on our side wouldn't be the worst thing. Not if we need to weed out Hazel's people."

Gramps nodded. "Once tensions die down and once I can get him on his own, I'll raise the issue. The fact that he let us go the way he did tells me he knows what's up and has chosen his side. He might not be able to do much except keep the council off our backs, but that might be all we need."

I shoved my hand through my hair, tugged out the elastic holding it back, and wrapped it around my wrist. I needed a shower. I needed to clear my head and make sense of every-thing I'd learned tonight. Not only that my secret was out—which meant I'd have to expect SMOAC to come knocking on my door sooner rather than later as well—but that whatever Corrick had set into motion by coming after the amulet was big enough to cross into the mirror realm.

"If Dara is worried about the effect of these souls on Meril's territory, then Hazel's decision to meet me near that doorway has to be for more than her personal benefit," I said, thinking out loud. "What is her game?"

I pulled my phone out of my pocket hoping to find a message from Chip, but so far he'd been quiet. Too caught up with meeting Ameline to notice the radio silence on our end. I couldn't wait to catch him up on the fact that I'd been arrested and he'd missed it. He'd be so disappointed.

"You won't figure it out on an empty stomach," Mary said, setting a plate of noodles covered in beef and broccoli in front of me. She waved Alyssa to the table and set the other plate next to me. "Eat, then sleep. In the morning, we'll bring in the rest of the family."

"A full Mooney conclave?" I asked, surprised and humbled.

She nodded. "I don't know how many times we need to tell you, Trace, but while you're tied to Alyssa, you're family." She kissed the top of my head, and my throat grew thick. "Now eat. I'm going back to bed. Avery, Mal, you can take the guest room."

Mary didn't make any offers about the couch for me, so I had to assume she assumed I'd be sleeping with her daughter, and my cheeks flushed. I tried to hide my awkwardness by shovelling food into my mouth, but I caught Alyssa's sly smile, and her wink made my stomach bottom out.

Her fingers curled around mine under the table, and I held them tightly while I emptied my plate, the calories and flavours almost making up for the crap of our night.

Twenty minutes later, our dishes put away, my stomach full, my eyelids heavy, I stood in Alyssa's purple-tinted childhood bedroom. It wasn't the first time I'd been here either, but unlike the feeling I'd gotten walking into the house—the sense that I'd been here a million times—my nerves danced like I was back in high school.

Alyssa came in and closed the door behind her, holding a T-shirt and sweatpants. "At the rate you're going through my brothers' clothes, we should probably get you a few spares to keep here."

She spoke lightly, as though it was no big deal that some guy had taken up such residence in her family that he needed a drawer at her parents' house, but I couldn't see it as anything other than ground shaking.

I accepted the clothes and set them on the dresser, then took her hand and drew her towards me. "You're amazing."

Her cheeks flushed, and her green eyes glittered as she looked around the room, unable to meet my eye. Not acceptable. I brushed the tops of my knuckles under her chin and waited until she looked at me.

"I don't know how I got to be so lucky to have gotten you as a mark, but I owe Dara more than I can ever say."

Her eyes shone, but she pressed her lips together to hide her smile. "Yes, well, maybe you could consider it an even trade. I'm still picking splinters of wood out of the walls from when you trashed my bar."

I chuckled and bent my head. "When this is all over, I'll help you pick out the rest. I promise."

She rose on her tiptoes to kiss me, and I ran my fingers through her hair, curling the light brown strands around my hand to angle her head, giving me better, deeper access. My stomach clenched, my pants grew tight, and I held myself back from pressing up against her. It had been a long day, and it would be an early morning tomorrow.

But I couldn't help but keep the kiss going, craving more. The adrenaline rush of tonight, the uncertainty of what the council would do to me, made me appreciate the fact that I was here and free and whole. With the one person I wanted to be with.

When I did finally pull away, Alyssa's eyes were glazed, her lips kiss-swollen, and the desire I saw swimming in her expression was enough to make me groan and bow my forehead against hers. Her fingers curled in the front of my shirt, and she held on tight, as though to let me go would be to fall to the ground.

"Wow," she said.

I chuckled. "That's all you, princess."

I wrapped my arms around her waist, and for a moment we stood there, breathing, enjoying each other's closeness. Until she wavered on her feet, and I pulled back. "Bed?"

She looked down at herself—at the dirt we'd both picked up during our scuffle with the council witches. "Shower?"

The quiet invitation stole my breath, and I swayed towards

her, so ready to take her up on it. It took a few swallows and gritting of teeth, but I managed to kiss her forehead. "You go first."

Her brow furrowed, the faintest glimmer of hurt shining in those summer-greens, and I caught her lips with mine again. "Believe me, it's killing me. But you're exhausted. The next time I shower with you, the water's going to turn cold by the time we're through."

Her skin flushed a deep red as her lips parted, caught on a breath. Then she laughed and gently shoved me away. "I'm going to get back at you for that one."

I grinned at her and watched as she closed herself in the ensuite bathroom. As soon as the door shut, I sagged onto the end of the bed and buried my head in my hands.

I felt like the world was folding in around me, leaving me with less and less room to manoeuvre. It left me reeling, the same way I had when I'd been forced to go on the run—the same way I had when Dara had dropped her ultimatum and panic had pushed me to betray Alyssa's trust. Something I still hadn't forgiven myself for.

Yet unlike last time, I didn't feel the same sense of despair.

I didn't feel alone.

Yes, we were facing so many unknowns, it was like we were standing on the edge of a very wide, dark chasm, and I had no idea what step would plunge me into the abyss, but with

Alyssa by my side, the ever-present ray of sunshine, I believed we could find our way without plummeting.

And if we did, well, I would push her to safety to fall myself and feel good about having done it.

Somehow taking the leap didn't seem nearly as terrifying when I was jumping for her.

# Chapter 15
## *Alyssa*

I WASHED THE shampoo out of my hair, then stood under the spray, letting the water droplets drip over my face and down my back, taking the stress of the day with it.

Although I wished Trace had joined me, wanting his company as much as the distraction, I understood his hesitation. At least, I thought I did. I suspected there was more to it than what he'd let on, but whatever his reasons, I wasn't about to disrespect his request for space.

I also couldn't deny that the space was nice for me as well. We had gone out to Almonte last night expecting something, but neither of us had anticipated Hazel might bring the authorities in on her scheme. What was she trying to do? Add legitimacy to her power grab?

That didn't seem right to me, which told me there was something we weren't seeing. If she had people within the council doing her bidding, then it was possible she was further ahead with her plans than we wanted to believe. And if that was the case, it meant we were racing against a tighter deadline than we'd thought.

My stomach twisted at the idea of that woman having any more leverage than she already did. I still woke up from nightmares about what had happened in that Rockland house. About Doreen, the demonic witch with the green and red power who'd channelled hellfire from her hands and set the house aflame. Or Mr. Ghoul's terrifying teeth and the way we'd found Trace after they'd tortured him.

We'd barely made it out of either fight, and now this coven had enjoyed an extra two weeks to gather their resources and get everything into position while we were scrambling to recover and catch up.

They were dominating this battlefield, and we couldn't let them continue.

I straightened my shoulders and summoned my courage, letting myself sink into the confidence I felt whenever Trace was on my team. He and I had achieved so much together, especially when my family was involved, and no matter what Hazel threw at us, we would get through it.

I just prayed we would all live to see the other side.

I rinsed off the soap and turned off the water, torn between wanting to stay in the warmth and finding the warmth—and my thoughts—too stifling. I needed to sleep and come at the problem fresh. Working myself into a spin and tipping into a panic attack would not be helpful.

So I stayed focused on practicalities as I brushed my teeth and slipped into my boy shorts and oversized T-shirt and thought only of the present as I left the steamy bathroom for the dim light of the bedroom. Then I stared in abject awe at the sight of a shirtless Trace standing at the end of my bed.

His dirty shirt was in the hamper in the corner, and although he still wore his jeans, the belt was undone and his fly was loose over his boxers, revealing more of the defined vee that formed at the base of his stomach.

I cleared my throat. "I'm finished."

His gaze landed on my bare legs, and I had the satisfaction of watching his pupils black out the violet irises. At least I wasn't the only one affected by the view.

"Right. Thank you. I won't be long."

I glanced down at the growing tent beneath his pants, and my face flushed. "Take your time."

He followed my gaze, and a pink blush spread across his own cheeks before he laughed. He closed the distance between us and bent to kiss my cheek. "Making us wait is only one more crime on Hazel's list."

I nodded, in full agreement, and he disappeared into the bathroom while I crawled into bed. My body sang with heat and desire, and I slid my hands downwards, thinking of that look in his eyes and the shape of his perfect body. But before I could reach my destination, sleep grabbed hold of me. I woke up once when a warm figure slipped under the sheets beside me and pulled me close, but that was the last I remembered.

"First you're accused of murder, then you get Gramps kidnapped, now you're arrested by the witches' council?" my sister Valery asked over dinner more than a few hours later. "Seriously, Aly, at the rate you're going, you'll lose me my job. Who wants their kids looked after by the sister of a known recurring felon?"

I rolled my eyes, not taking her words to heart. "I plead innocent of all crimes, your honour. You're just jealous that I keep winding up the centre of everyone's attention."

Val snorted. "Believe me, the last thing I want is to be the focus of someone's *murder accusations*. Really, Aly, who do you think I am?"

We exchanged a glare, then I winked at her and shoved more food into my face. I'd woken up with a grumbling stomach, and I wasn't sure if hunger was the sole culprit or if I'd simply been left unsatisfied this morning and needed something to fill the void. The way Trace was heaping yet another serving of mashed potatoes onto his plate made me think he was having the same mental struggles as I was.

"Is this really the time for comedy?" Dad asked as he shoved his glasses up on his nose. "I know you're both trying to keep the tone light, but I worry you're not taking this as seriously as you should be. The council has its eye on you and Trace. While Gramps and the others might have some pull to keep you out of the worst trouble, we don't know when they might pull you in again." He looked to Trace. "It's not like they don't have a case against you, I'm afraid."

Trace grimaced and nodded. "I know. I honestly didn't think I was getting out of there last night. Whatever they want to use us for, it has to be something big if they're willing to overlook what I did."

The food in my stomach soured, and I pushed my plate away. "I'm sorry."

He reached across the table to take my hand. "Don't be. If I hadn't been there to help you with Corrick, *he* would have these souls at his beck and call and we'd all be in a worse place than we are right now. Working together gave us our best chance to find a good solution. That hasn't changed."

I appreciated his words of reassurance, but I couldn't shake the guilt. The only reason he'd been there that night was because of me. I could have found another way to keep those souls away from Corrick. Like listening to people who might have known better and not going to see him in the first place.

"None of that, Pip," Gramps said, throwing more vegetables onto my plate. "If we all focused on our regrets, none of us would be able to get out of bed in the morning. Our only option is to stay focused on what we can change. So let's finish dinner, wait for the rest of the family to show up, and then we can make our list of problems we need to tackle."

It wasn't much of a pep talk, but it served its purpose. I was at least able to take a few more bites of potato before my body called it quits. Trace cleaned his plate, then joined me as we headed to the couch in the living room.

Few by few, the Mooney family trickled in. Many Trace had already met during Gramps's abduction debacle. Avery and Mallory had gone to pick up their parents, my aunts Courtney and Jennifer, from the airport, and my siblings, Brody, Dylan and Val, had shown up as well. But there were a few new faces. Cousins from my grandmother's side of the family, who normally focused more on the local administrative needs of the coven, had decided this was a big enough issue that they wanted to get involved, so I introduced Trace to Sonya, her husband Hayden, and their daughter Kaitlyn.

My other aunt, Hilary, her husband Tony, and their sons Kyle and Grayson would join us later, but for now we were the core group making a plan on how to save Ottawa, and maybe Ontario, from the growing threat of Hazel and her coven.

"Chip finally got in touch with me last night after we went to sleep," Trace said, pulling his phone out of his pocket. "Ameline arrived on schedule, and she's settled in with him at his place in Stittsville. According to what Chip tells me, Am hasn't heard from her mother in years, but she's received an influx of private calls this week, so she assumes that's Hazel."

"Will Hazel be surprised that her daughter is in town if Ameline hasn't answered those calls?"

Trace shook his head slowly. "In case her coven finds her before we're ready, Chip and Ameline have worked out a story that she's here for a job interview. Chip set up a false trail to confirm it if Hazel's people poke around. So I think we're in the clear there. But we won't push the story too hard. All we really need Ameline for is to stand in Hazel's way long enough for us to get into position."

I frowned. "You want to use her as what? A wall? That seems…"

Heartless? Thoughtless? Cruel?

Trace grimaced. "I know. But like I told you, she's not defenceless. With her time magic, she'll be one of the more powerful players on our team. And I don't mean we leave her out there to hang by herself. She might be the distraction, but we'll be right there with her."

Avery blinked. "Time magic? I know we learned about that field growing up, but I always thought it was a myth. I mean… manipulating *time*? That's demigod-levels of power."

Trace nodded. "It's incredibly rare. She can only affect a small bubble, maybe a dozen square feet or so. Anyone out of range probably wouldn't notice a difference."

Dad sank back in his chair. "Fascinating." He blew on his coffee before taking a sip. "I've studied all sorts of magics and still learn something new all the time."

"And we're sure we can trust her?" Gramps asked.

"As sure as we can be. Chip would have vetted her thoroughly before convincing her to get on a plane. If he believes her, I do."

Gramps rubbed his brow. "All right, so Chip has this woman lined up and ready to go. Hazel figured we'd check out the museum ahead of time, and she had the council waiting for us. With what you know of her, will she still be there Wednesday night?"

Trace sagged back in his seat. "Once she gets word that the council didn't keep us? Absolutely. She won't miss the chance to come for me."

"Then we have a little over a day to come up with and test a plan," Aunt Courtney said. She'd opted not to sit, preferring to pace the length of the living room with her hands behind her back. As though she were leading a meeting at City Hall. Or maybe an Ontario Witches' Council gathering.

"We should figure out how many of us are going and where we'll be." Trace rubbed the back of his neck. "I don't think she'll bring her moles in the council out for this, but that might not stop them from trying to thin our numbers before Wednesday."

Gramps tapped his thumb against his lip. "We should reach out to people who aren't Mooneys. People they won't think to detain."

I reached for my phone. "I'll send Jet a message. Maybe she'll be willing to lend us some of her team for the night. Especially if I mention the chance of revealing some rogue council members."

Jet Dawson, task force captain of Supernatural, Magical and Occult Affairs Canada, tended to follow all the rules of her department, but she'd pushed those boundaries a bit in Rockland, and I hoped she might be willing to do the same here. Considering what was at stake if we failed, it was in the government's best interests to help.

"What about Nuñes?" Trace asked Gramps.

"I'll give him a call in an hour or so. Give him space to have his evening coffee before I try to get him onside."

Having Nuñes deal with the council would be one less direction we'd need to watch. Anything that took some of the pressure off would be worthwhile.

"What would be best is if we could help Trace release these souls before the meeting," Mom said, eying him closely.

"Any luck on that yet?" I asked. "You said you had an idea you were going to look into."

Trace's eyebrows shot up as he twisted in his seat to look at me, and I dropped my gaze as my cheeks flushed. "Right, yeah, I guess I forgot to mention that I talked to Mom about your situation. Sorry."

He squeezed my hand. "I appreciate it." The hope with which he turned to my mom broke my heart, especially when the corners of her mouth turned down in disappointment.

"Unfortunately, not yet. I don't want to go into detail in case it comes to nothing, but I'm still looking into it. The books I have only touch briefly on spirit magic, but they refer to other texts." She sat up straighter and looked at Gramps. "In fact, maybe you could ask Nuñes about them. They won't be easy to come by without council sanction. Not considering the subject matter."

"Give me the titles, I'll see what I can do."

Despite being a bit let down that Mom didn't have better news for us, I felt more hopeful than I had since Trace had dragged himself into Mooney's Pub that first night after the fight in The Scorpio Lounge. Which was why, when I caught the slump of Trace's shoulders, I allowed myself to stroke his back to get his attention.

"We have that meeting with Sarah tonight, too," I reminded him. "Maybe great-great-Gramps will have some suggestions for us."

"Excuse me?" Sonya asked, her perfectly manicured eyebrow shooting up. She tossed her glossy blond braid over her shoulder and leaned in. "What's this about talking to the dead?"

I considered my cousin. She was in her late forties but kept herself in such good condition she barely looked a day over thirty. Not exactly the type I would associate with an interest in necromancy. But her blue eyes were shining, and she looked ready to butt in between Trace and me on the couch to not miss a single word.

"We figured that since the only person who might have had an idea of what to do with the souls in the amulet was our ancestor, maybe it wasn't the worst idea to have a chat with him about it. If he could tell us what his plans were, maybe it's possible to replicate them. Just… to get them out of Trace instead of out of the amulet."

"I want to be there," she said without missing a beat. "Do you know how long I've wanted to lay eyes on a summoning from that long ago?"

Hayden rolled his eyes to the ceiling, and Kaitlyn buried her head in her hands. "Oh my goddess, Mom, you are such a dork."

Sonya waved her daughter away. "Oh hush. You don't need to be there, and none of your friends can know anyway. So don't say a thing. Summoning a two-hundred-year-dead witch? How many council rules are you even breaking?"

I hadn't considered that side of it. "Perhaps when you call Nuñes, you leave that part out," I suggested to Gramps, and he nodded.

"Illegal or not, I wish you luck," Dad said. "I think you have the right of it. Earl might have something useful to say. The sooner we deal with these souls, the sooner we destroy Hazel's plan before she gets close to what she wants."

Jennifer grinned. "After that, while she's stomping her feet at having her dreams dashed, we can close in and take her down."

I watched Trace as my family prepared for our success against Hazel and couldn't help the seed of worry that grew in my gut. He didn't look nearly as confident as he should have. Which told me he suspected something we didn't.

Something that could swing out to crush us before we had a chance for our victory cheer.

# Chapter 16
*Alyssa*

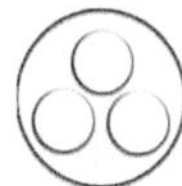

WE DECIDED THAT everyone in the room would come with us to the museum on Wednesday, along with Hilary, Tony, Kyle, and Grayson. Mom had already texted them before the meeting was over, and they'd agreed without discussion, saving themselves the trip out to Ashton today.

I never heard from Jet as the evening went on, and by the time the sun began to set, I was a little worried about what was going on with her. Since she wasn't replying, I sent a text to Madison Prince, the minister's chief of staff, in case she'd heard anything about Jet being unavailable. At this point, I was desperate for any kind of extra support. After Rockland, I didn't want to go in underprepared. It had been a miracle we'd walked out of that fight without losing any of my family.

While we waited to hear back from either Madi or Jet, I changed into a pair of black jeans and a warm, dark green sweater—trying to pull Cemetery Chic together on a whim—and met Trace outside by the car. Sonya was the only other person coming with us, and she'd opted to meet us at the cemetery.

"You sure you don't want to join us?" I asked Gramps where he stood in the doorway.

He shuddered. "You'd think I'd be more curious about this whole thing, but you know what? Turns out the thought of talking to the dead doesn't hit as hard as it might if I weren't so close to the grave myself."

Mom shoved his shoulder for saying any such thing, and I seconded the response. Gramps would probably outlive us all.

"Besides," he added, "I told Tory I'd be on call if they need anything tonight. I'd hate to have my phone ring in the middle of our chat with dear old grandad. Can't wait to hear what he says, though."

Trace and I got into the car he and Dad had retrieved earlier, and I gave him directions away from Ashton to the large cemetery off March Road. At this time of night, the place was quiet, which only made everything about a million times creepier. I wished I'd brought an extra sweater—something I could pull up around the back of my neck to cover the tiny hairs standing on end.

"Where are we meeting Sarah?" I asked as we got out of the SUV. "And do we have anything to worry about? And how weird and awkward is this going to be? And what do we do if it doesn't work? And—"

Trace set one hand on my shoulder and pressed the fingers of his other hand to my lips. "Hush. There's nothing to worry about. I have no idea what to expect, but we need to be prepared for this *not* to work. There's a lot fighting against us here. As for Sarah…"

"I'm here, I'm here."

A door slammed, and there stood a short woman with spiky red hair, a black vest over a purple shirt, a short denim mini-skirt over white-and-black-striped leggings and ankle-boots. She took a drag on a cigarette before tossing it onto the gravel parking lot and crushing it under her heel.

"Sorry. Gross habit. Going to put me in a coffin ten years early, but I needed to wind down. A few of my clients today were…" She shuddered and brushed off her arms as though clearing herself of something dusty. "I hate divorces, that's all I'm going to say. Anydoodle. Hi. Sarah."

"Alyssa," I replied. "Thank you for the last-minute help."

"You kidding? When Trace calls me in, I know it's going to be good. So give me the low-down. What are we dealing with here?"

Trace and I filled her in on the basics, leaving out a few of the more…controversial details, and Sarah clapped her hands together. "Awesome. Totally worth the drive out here. Let's go and see what Bones has to say shall we?" She snorted. "Not that his bones will do us much good anymore. Fortunately, we're not after his bones. We just need some dirt around his bones. After that, it's just a few words, some candles, and Bob's your uncle. Or, you know, Earl's your great-great-grandfather. Not nearly as pithy, but accuracy counts in things like this."

I blinked, unable to do anything else. The woman was a ball of energy contained in a very small human being, and I wasn't sure how she'd managed not to explode.

She blinked back at me, her heavily lined eyes looking owlish in the glow being cast off by the security lights in the parking lot. "Oh, sorry. Are we not ready to do this yet? I can get back in the car and have another smoke if you want to wrap your head around everything. Intentions have to be clear before we do the summoning, or we'll have all the ghosts in the place up and ready for a rave. Which, like, cool if that's your jam, but I've got two more summonings to do after this, so we should probably get started soon."

Trace chuckled and slid his hand down my back. "I'd say you get used to her," he said to me, "but you never really do. Best just to go along with it."

Sarah flashed him a wide smile. "This is why I like you, Wyatt. You never stress. We could use so many more like you around. We ready to go?"

"We're just waiting for my cousin," I said, and even as I spoke, Sonya's bright yellow VW Bug pulled into the parking lot. She stopped in the space beside Sarah's red beater, got out of the car, and immediately scurried towards the necromancer.

She might have looked out of place in her red slacks and white shirt with red polka dots if Sarah hadn't already proved you didn't need to wear black to commune with the dead. The excitement in her eyes dimmed slightly on taking Sarah in, but she kept her smile in place as she stepped forward. I understood—clichéd expectations were not exactly being met here.

"Sarah, this is my cousin Sonya. Sonya, this is Sarah. She'll be helping us speak to our ancestor today."

"It's so nice to meet you," Sonya said, extending her hand.

Sarah held her palms up. "Sorry, I don't shake. I'm usually too covered in graveyard dirt to be sanitary."

Instead of being offended, the light returned to Sonya's eyes. "That is so cool."

Sarah grinned, then turned to me. "Do you know where this guy is buried?"

I pulled the map out of my back pocket and handed it to her. I figured with her familiarity with cemeteries, she'd have an easier time interpreting the access roads. "I've circled the plot. And I brought what's left of the amulet with us in case you needed a focal point or something."

Sarah shrugged. "Helpful, not necessary. Might give you two something to talk about, though. Come on. It'll be easier to drive there. Should we all pile in my car or…"

I glanced between her beat-up red Toyota that didn't look like it'd make it over the next speed bump and Trace's sleek grey SUV.

"I'll do the honours," Trace said.

"Cool. Gas prices are fucking death right now. I keep wondering if this baby would run on corn fuel, but I haven't been brave enough to try it. Don't want to end up in a million pieces if the car explodes on the Queensway, you know? I've got plans for this corpse when my time is up, and it doesn't involve being spread across Ottawa's west end."

She laughed as though she were sharing some long-held joke, and I could only smile and nod. I couldn't say I would want to be scattered across Ottawa's busiest roadway either.

Sarah kept up a steady prattle about her day and the spirits she'd summoned this week as we drove across the cemetery, following her clear directions. We found the proper site, and while Sarah worked, Sonya filled the silence by asking her question after question about her setup (made up on the spot for focus), the symbolism of the colours (whatever had been on sale), and how she managed to learn so much Latin. The latter sparked a long, passionate conversation about the joys of learning multiple languages, until I worried the sun would rise before we got to the ritual itself.

Yet it was still the middle of the night when Sarah turned her attention to the grave, her eyes narrow and her shoulders tense.

"He's here all right," she muttered under her breath. Then she took her first real look at the grave marker. "Earl Finnegan." She raised an eyebrow. "Not a Mooney at all."

"The Mooney name comes from my grandmother's side," I explained, feeling the buzz of anticipation stirring in the pit of my stomach. I wasn't a medium and didn't sense the spirits around me like this woman could, but even I detected the shifting energy as I stood over my ancestor's burial site. "Every man who marries into the family is given the choice to change his name. Most of them do it because of the status it gives them."

Trace met my eye. "Is that so?"

I smirked. "Most of them also don't have an issue with taking the woman's last name. I know that's not the case for all men."

"My issue wouldn't be taking your name, princess. I've already given up one name, I don't have any ego about giving up the other. I'm more surprised the women are willing to share that status with the lowly spouses who woo them."

My smirk grew into a grin as my heart soared at his implication. Trace Wyatt the Untouchable making jokes about marriage? I was honoured. "I guess the Mooney men are particularly good at wooing."

"I have a lot to live up to, then."

The butterflies that had taken up residence in my stomach around the time Trace Wyatt had come into my life kicked up their familiar dance, fluttering their wings and strutting all their tiny legs, tickling me from within.

"I'm dying over here," Sarah said, though she didn't appear overly irritated or impatient, more like she was making a throw-away comment. Such an odd duck. But she'd achieved her goal of gaining our attention, so she turned to the faded headstone, closed her eyes, and threw her head back.

When she opened her mouth, a string of Latin flew from her practised lips. I only understood a handful of words—Earl's name, *spirit, join, communicate*. Clearly I needed to brush up on my ancient languages if I wanted to up my game in the witch community.

The wind around us blew, and goosebumps broke out along my arms and down my spine. Trace moved closer to stand with me, and Sonya hugged her arms around her middle as she looked around. I had no idea what to expect. Would the spectre of my ancestor appear to the bunch of us, or would he settle for speaking through Sarah? Or would he not bother to show up? After all, he hadn't exactly proved himself to be the most responsible or ethical of human beings, and I saw no reason why that might change now that he was dead.

All I could do was wait and stay focused on my breathing, not wanting to lose myself to the vibrations in the streams of black that spewed from Sarah in reaching tendrils, wrapping the entire grave site in their grasp. Their oily touch smeared across the back of my neck, and I cringed away from it, careful not to move too much or make so much noise that I pulled Sarah out of her spell. This entire experience reminded me that the nature of someone's magic was never what made something light or dark. Spirit magic was the closest that magic came to being dark, but even then, Trace had shown it could be used defensively in the right hands. Necromancy was no more evil than anything else. It all came down to how it was applied.

I ran those words through my head to avoid being completely repulsed by the feel and sickly hue of the power, but soon enough all thought of the moral ambiguity of raising the dead became moot as a shining figure hovered above the grave.

It was far from human shaped, more a green-and-yellow-hued ball. A fragment of my ancestor's magic, mixed with his soul and the souls he'd absorbed and used over the final years of his life.

"Earl Finnegan, your great-great-granddaughter has summoned you here to ask some questions. Are you willing to hear them?" Sarah asked.

I might have expected her to play up the exchange for show,

using some deep intonation or pretending to be in a chant, but she sounded just like her usual self, if a bit less wordy.

The glow from the orb pulsed, and Sarah turned to me. "You're up."

I cleared my throat and spoke to the orb, even if it felt a little like speaking to a light bulb. "You convinced hundreds of souls to enter an enchanted gem so you could gain their help in the completion of the Rideau Canal. You bound them on the promise that when the canal was complete, you would release them. When you made that promise, did you mean it?"

The orb pulsed again, and Sarah shrugged. "He says he did, but there's definitely some hesitation in the answer."

"Of course you were considering screwing them over." I rolled my eyes at the orb. "So nice of you."

The light around the orb dimmed, and I bit my tongue. I still had questions for him and didn't want to chase him away before I had the chance to ask them.

"How did you mean to release them? Your grandson tried to destroy the amulet and couldn't do it. How do we let them go?"

Sarah didn't bat an eyelash at the questions, and my respect for her rose. She must hear all kinds of wild things in her estate readings. Chances were a centuries-old magic crime was low on her list of interest. Yet after the orb pulsed again, her brow furrowed.

"You're not making a lot of sense, my friend. Can you try that again?"

She tilted her head as though listening. The orb pulsed once more, bright enough that I was blinded against the darkness of the cemetery, then vanished.

"Well shit," Sarah said. She pulled out her pack of cigarettes and lit one as she glowered at the gravestone.

"What did he say?" I asked.

She puffed a few times, then shrugged. "Means nothing to me, but maybe you'll have more luck interpreting it. He says the souls have to go back where they came from. He also gave a warning—'prepare for instability.' Something about the fabric of reality?"

"Oh," I said. "Is that all? Wonderful."

Because of course it couldn't be simple. Of course the problem that had fallen into my lap had the potential to tear the fucking world apart.

## Chapter 17
*Trace*

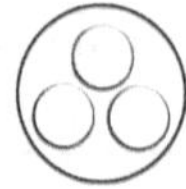

"Thanks, Sarah," I said as I handed over the cash I'd promised her.

She slipped it into her pocket and took another drag of her cigarette. "I'm not sure if I should give you a discount for that craptastic answer or demand a surcharge for the warning. What have you gotten yourself into now, Wyatt?"

I rubbed the back of my neck and wished I had a better answer for her than *a heap-tonne of shit.*

"All goes well, nothing you need to worry about," I told her. "I promise not to add to your workload."

She snorted. "Good. I've already got one foot in the grave. I'd like to give it a few more years at least before I slide the rest of me in to join it. Though at the rate I'm sucking back these fuckers, it might be sooner than I'd like." She looked around the cemetery. "We good to go? That was nice and quick, so I might have time to grab some nosh before my next client."

I looked to Alyssa, who was staring at the grave, her expression lost. As though she felt me watching her, she raised her head and nodded. "Yeah, let's go. We should probably update Gramps."

With her arms wrapped around her middle, she walked towards me, and I slid my arm around her shoulders, tugging her closer to my side as we followed the path back to the car.

"That was *so cool*," Sonya gushed to Sarah, struggling to make it over the grass in her high-heeled shoes. "Where did you learn to do that? Can anyone learn to do that? I've read some of the books but can't make my atmospheric energy work for me."

I took in the pair, the tall blond with the trendy clothes beside the short fire-head with the goth-punk drabs. Yet Sarah had no issue launching into some tips about how Sonya might get started, and I shook my head at the ease with which some people made connections. I usually had to threaten people to get them to talk to me.

Or toss them in the trunk of my car.

The memory of that fateful night drew my attention back to Alyssa. "Are you all right?"

"Yes? I mean, I'm no worse off than I was. I guess. Sure,

we just learned that if we don't do this carefully—or don't do it right—we could tear a rip in the fabric of reality, whatever the hell that means, but we're in a better place for knowing it now, right? Better than if we just swiped our hands and made an attempt without knowing what the consequences were. And if we fail, well, we can figure out the next problem, and the next. Eventually we'll land on a solution that fixes everything. It can't just keep getting *so much fucking worse*, can it? It's not possible. Wouldn't that go against quantum physics or something?"

I tugged on her ponytail to cut off her spin. "I don't know where it puts you on your anxiety scale when you start talking about quantum physics, but I'm guessing it's not a good place."

She snapped her mouth shut and gave me a rueful smile. "No, not exactly. Okay, so, I'm not okay. That's good to know, right?"

"It is. I like knowing where your brain is sitting. It gives me a chance to help you calm it down. We're going to figure out what he meant, all right? I know right now it seems like just another puzzle, but it's more information than we had before. If there's one thing I've learned after chasing people all over the world, it's that every piece of intel helps us reach our target. The how might not always be obvious, but it does. We just need to sit down and parse out what we learned."

Alyssa nodded. "Yes. Parsing. That sounds like a great idea. Maybe with cookies." Her expression perked up. "Maybe Dad baked while we were out. There could be fresh-baked cookies at home. Yeah, let's do that."

She picked up the pace, and we made it back to my car. Sonya and Sarah were already in the backseat, chatting as though they'd known each other all their lives. I wasn't especially thrilled that it sounded like Sarah was trying to recruit Alyssa's cousin into her business, but I also wasn't about to judge what piqued people's interests. If someone had told me I'd grow up to chase after bad guys and drag them to the authorities, I never would have believed it. Not young bookworm me or teenage rebel me. Yet, right now, there was nowhere else I'd rather be.

I dropped them both at their cars, then drove Alyssa and I back to the Mooney house in Ashton. Sonya followed us there. Her husband was home with their daughter, but she wanted to offer her input on what she'd heard tonight.

Gramps had the door open when we arrived, and I staggered on seeing him. He looked ashen, and his grip on the door was so tight his knuckles were white.

"Is everything all right?" Alyssa asked, rushing to his side.

He passed his free hand over his face and stepped back to let us in. "Nuñes is dead."

I stalled on the walkway, my entire body freezing as I processed the shock, then I reached the door and followed the other two into the living room. Henry sat in the armchair, his glasses in his hands, an open book splayed over the armrest beside him. His face was pale, his expression blank, and I guessed they'd only received the news moments before we'd arrived.

"What happened?" Alyssa asked, sitting with her grandfather on the couch. Wanting to give them space, I dropped onto the loveseat where I could see them both. Sonya settled on Gramps's other side.

"They found him slumped over his desk. No attack of any obvious kind, but I think we can assume."

The blood rushed out of my head. "They harvested him."

Gramps nodded. "I think so. And so does Pen. She was his partner. Still reeling a little bit, but the fury is strong in that woman. She's not going to take this sitting down."

I thought of Nuñes the two times we'd seen him in action. He'd had a solid head on his shoulders. Likely knew all the players in this game. Of course they would have had to take him out, though I didn't see that it would benefit them in the end. We were closing in. We had them penned. Didn't we?

A surge of unease rumbled through my gut and bile slid up the back of my throat. The sense that there was more to this than we knew kept growing. How was it possible that Hazel had organized so much from Moongrave Prison? That's where it had to have started, because there was no way she could have brought everyone together and set it into motion in the time since she'd gotten free.

"We need to figure out how Hazel escaped." When everyone turned to look at me, I pulled my shoulders back. "Whoever helped her has *been* helping her, which means they know what her plan is and what she's going to do next. If we figure out who and why, then we'll be in a better place to cut off her resources."

Alyssa pulled out her phone. "I'm still waiting to hear back from either Jet or Madison. I'm a little worried that they haven't been in touch." Her thumbs flew as she sent off another text. "I'll call them in the morning if we don't hear anything."

Gramps patted Alyssa's hand. "What about on your end? What did you learn from your seance?"

"That your grandfather was an asshole and we're better off without him," she said. Then she sighed and leaned into the couch. "He also said the souls have to go back where they came from. And that we need to be careful with instability."

Gramps frowned. "Back where they came from? The souls were from here."

"Were they?" I asked, leaning my elbows on my knees. "This was two hundred years ago, I'm sure the workers came from all over."

Sonya frowned. "I know I heard what you both heard, but somehow I don't think he was suggesting you hop on a plane and individually drop the souls off in their home territory. He mentioned the fabric of reality. To me that suggests something a little more… intense."

Gramps's eyes widened. "He said what?"

Alyssa nodded. "Sonya's right, and by the sounds of it, that whole fabric of reality part was connected to the warning of instability part. I'm telling you, Gramps, it was not the most optimistic of meetings."

He rose from the couch and paced the length of the room. Henry stared up at him. "What are you thinking?"

"The fabric of reality, sending them back where they came from, Hazel wanting to meet near that sealed doorway." He groaned. "What was my family thinking?"

Again my head spun, and I had to bury my face in my hand to try to wrestle my blood pressure back in place. "You think the souls came from the mirror realm?"

Alyssa paled. "You can't be serious. You said they were the souls of the workers."

"Some of them were fae workers, Pip," Gramps reminded her. "They were fighting to protect their people from war with the shifters. But the shifters are on this plane. The souls in the amulet are mixed. There must be souls from this plane and from beyond the wall."

"It'll be impossible to disconnect them," I said.

Alyssa swallowed. "And sending souls to the wrong places?"

I shook my head. "I wouldn't have thought it'd matter. But then, I've never heard of someone harvesting the souls of creatures from beyond the wall."

Sitting became too much for me, and I found myself on my feet pacing opposite Gramps. The room was too small, and I needed to get some air, but I also doubted I'd make it to the front door without my legs giving out. This was getting too big. Too much. Alyssa's spin in the graveyard suddenly seemed like an underreaction, and my thoughts threatened to follow her down the road towards quantum physics.

"All right," Alyssa said. "So. We need to figure that out, obviously. But somehow I doubt we'll have time to make connections in the mirror realm, take the trip over, purge the souls, and not start a huge diplomatic crisis before it's time to meet with Hazel."

"Unlikely, no," Henry said.

"Right. What's the backup plan? Trace, you stay the hell away from Hazel. That sounds like a good backup plan. Now that we know what kind of power you're carrying, we definitely can't let her take possession of your guests."

She was right. Hundreds of fae, witch, and shifter souls would have been bad enough, but supernaturals from beyond the wall were closer to the true source of magic. Their power was less diluted by mundane bloodlines, more potent. Which explained why I'd been having such a hard time keeping control over them. Not only because of how many there were but because of how much power they packed.

"I don't think staying away from her will be as easy as skipping out on our meeting, princess," I said, hating that I needed to disappoint her. "If I don't go, she'll find me another way."

Tears swam in Alyssa's green eyes. "Then what do we do? I'm trying not to be a Debbie Downer here, but by the goddess, Trace, this woman has us over a fucking barrel."

I couldn't argue with her. She'd infiltrated the council, created a coven, tapped into a connection to the mirror realm, and had us firmly trapped exactly where she needed us.

"I have an idea," Henry said, looking between the two of us. "But I don't think you're going to like it."

# Chapter 18
## *Alyssa*

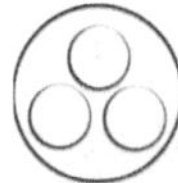

I ALREADY HATED Dad's plan and he hadn't told us what it was. Who started a plan like that? Worst. Proposal. Ever.

"You need to use the souls."

Yep, that was pretty much as bad as I'd feared it would be.

"Are you fu—are you kidding me?" I demanded.

Dad put on his glasses, closed his book, and set it on the side table. "I wish I were, Aly, but we're up against a coven of tremendous power, led by a woman who believes she holds all the cards because she knows Trace so well. We need him to act out of character." He looked to Trace. "Would she believe you'd use the souls?"

Trace shook his head, but he looked stricken by the suggestion. "With all due respect, I can't. I won't. I—You don't know—"

My heart broke for him. My dad hadn't been there the night the souls had taken Trace over and turned one of his old coven members into Fried Witch. She'd been little more than charcoal by the time he was through with her. And he would have unleashed the same punishment on the other two if I hadn't stepped in. He'd been devastated by what he'd done, but he was especially terrified that he'd scared me because of it.

And he had. Not because he'd defended himself—and me—but because there had been a moment, an oh-so-brief moment, where he'd had no idea who I was. I'd been just as much of a potential threat as anyone else in that park. The same thing had happened during the Rockland fight, and he'd struggled even harder to remember I wasn't the enemy then. I knew he was as concerned as I was that next time he would remember too late—if he remembered at all. I'd promised Nuñes that Trace had too much integrity to use them, and his reaction to my dad's suggestion was proof that I was right. But Nuñes was dead. That powerful council witch had gone down as easily as anyone against these bastards. I didn't want Trace to do anything he didn't want to do—but I also wanted him to survive.

As Trace paced closer, I grabbed his hand and pulled him onto the armrest beside me. He turned his haunted eyes on me, and I looped my hand through his. "If that's what it comes down to, you know I'll be right there with you."

He let out a husky breath. "That's what I'm afraid of."

"I know. But I keep getting through to you, right? The souls might not have recognized me, but you did. Even when they take you over, you're still in there, Trace, and you remember me. I'm not asking you to do this, and I'm not saying you'll need to. But if they don't give you a choice, all I'm asking is that you hang on to me, okay? Hang on to me, and I will do whatever it takes to bring you back."

His throat bobbed with a swallow, and he rested his head in his free hand. I stroked his hair and wished I had anything more to offer him than hopes and optimistic outcomes.

"First thing tomorrow, I'll try calling Madi," I said. "And then we need to round up the family and figure out where everyone is meeting us. We need as many powerhouses on this battlefield as we can get. If we're putting the onus on Trace, we can't let him stand alone."

"We won't," Gramps promised.

Sonya nodded. "I'll be there for sure. I don't really understand everything that's going on here, but it's clear enough that this is some serious shit. I won't have my daughter in danger if this woman gets her way." Rage filled her blue eyes when they met mine, and I understood all too well.

"I'll call Chip tonight," Trace said, his head still bowed. "Fill him in on what we learned and get a plan in place for tomorrow. We have to stop Hazel. If she gains access to the mirror realm, there'll be no stopping her."

I didn't know if it was the way he said it or the fact that, after all the chaos of the night, I finally had time to register what Hazel might want, but as Trace talked about the mirror realm, the answer struck me like a lightning bolt.

I sagged against him. "She wants to open the door."

Gramps stopped his pacing and turned to look at me. "What?"

"That's why she chose the museum. The door is closed, which means no one will be watching it on the other side. If she uses the strength of Trace's souls to smash the door open, she'll have access to the realm without anyone being able to stop her until it's too late."

And over there? If she brought her coven and continued harvesting?

Memories of *The Little Mermaid* spun through my head, of an animated Ursula growing bigger and bigger, creating whirlpools and storms, and attempting to destroy everything under the sea. Except I didn't think any of us were capable of driving a broken ship into her gut to take her down.

I was going to be sick. I was sure I was going to be sick.

Trace sat up beside me. "That won't happen," he said, and there was something so *off* about his voice that I raised my head to look at him. And found two glowing, yellow eyes staring back at me. "No one uses us without permission. Not again. We won't allow it. We will stand, we will fight, and we will destroy."

Trace's grip on my hand turned painful, my finger bones grinding together. I tried to pull away, but the more pressure I applied, the more agonizing it was, so I held still and waited as Trace squeezed his eyes shut. When he opened them again, only violet stared back at me. He immediately released me and shot off the couch.

"I can't do it. I can't control them. The more power they grab, the less influence I have. The cage around them is cracking, and I won't let it break."

I rose to my feet and wrapped my arms around his middle, bowing my forehead against his back.

"I know you're afraid, my boy," Gramps said, his voice tired and rough, "but if you don't take this risk, it's very possible no one else will be able to. I hate that it's all on you. It shouldn't be. To my dying day, I'll regret that it fell on your shoulders. But it is, and it has."

Trace's shuddering breaths vibrated beneath me, and he clutched at my hands around his waist. He was trembling all over, and I hugged him tighter, drawing in slow, deep breaths until he matched mine and gradually came down from the adrenaline spike. "All right. I'll do what I have to. But you have to promise me something."

He pinned Gramps with a stare, and my grandfather

nodded. "Anything."

"If it looks like I've lost control—If I can't hold back… I need you to get Alyssa away from me. And take me out before I can hurt anyone I shouldn't."

I let go of Trace and marched around to face him. "Excuse me, you will—"

"I promise," Gramps interrupted me.

I wheeled around on him. "No, you won't. What the hell is this? You can't both just dismiss me like that. I can take care of myself, and anyone who doesn't think so is fucking incorrect."

They'd pulled this exact trick at the MacLaren house, and the result had been me almost losing Trace. I was not a child to be coddled or taped in bubble wrap.

Trace grabbed my shoulders and fixed his gaze on me as though he heard every word I wasn't saying. "I have to know you'll be safe. I *have* to. Because if I'm afraid for you, then any tenuous hold I have on these souls will snap. I'll give in to them without hesitation. Do you understand? The only way that I stand a chance of coming back from this is knowing you'll be okay."

Tears stung the corners of my eyes, but I blinked them away, too angry and scared at the same time to let them fall. I hated that I'd become a bargaining chip for him, and that Gramps had agreed to it so readily, but if Trace was willing to take this risk on behalf of all of us, then the least I could do was promise to get out of his way. "All right. If it comes to that, I'll go without a fight."

His shoulders sagged, and he closed his eyes, a portrait of relief.

"All right, then," Sonya said as she stood up. "I'm going to go home and tell Hayden all about this meeting tonight, because hot damn, that was wicked, and then I'll see everyone in Almonte tomorrow. It's going to be fun. I'll be sure to wear my fighting pants."

She flounced out of the room, leaving the rest of us staring after her.

Gramps helped Dad out of his chair, and Dad wrapped his arms around me. "I'm sorry, Aly. That you're caught in the middle. But we'll do everything we can to make sure everyone comes out of this. You're not alone."

How often had my family said that to me over the years? So many I'd lost count. And they kept proving it. They never failed me. I wasn't alone, and we would get through this.

We had to. Because I wouldn't allow anything else.

# Chapter 19
*Trace*

ALYSSA AND I went upstairs to her room, and I closed the door behind us, locking us into the peaceful silence of the space that smelled and looked and felt exactly like her. Other than her apartment, this room was becoming my favourite place in the world.

"I hate feeling like this is our last night together," she said as she curled her arms around my middle.

I held her tight against me. "I wish I could say it's not. But I will say I hope it's not. I hope we have thousands of nights together."

She pulled back and looked up at me. "Do you?"

I frowned. "You don't believe me?"

She let me go and dropped onto the edge of her bed, sitting

cross-legged. "I know this is hardly the time to talk about this. You know, what with going to war tomorrow, and the fact that we're not really alone in this room, but… well… we got off to a bit of a rough start. The trashed pub, and the abduction, and you turning on me, and me driving you into a ditch. And the fact that you took in hundreds of souls to save my life and the results have been an endless series of horrible things that we're still not out of yet, but…" She gave an exaggerated shrug. "I… care about you. A lot."

The faintest of hesitations in her admission made me think she'd been about to say something else, and it didn't bother me that she hadn't. It meant more that she'd wanted to.

I considered sitting on the bed beside her but opted to drop to my knees in front of her. I wanted to make sure she looked me in the eye as I said, "I care about you a lot too. So much. More than I swore to myself I'd ever feel for anyone else again. Goddess, Alyssa." I shoved my hand through my hair and sat back on my heels. "After what Hazel put me through, I promised I would never let myself trust another woman. Not with my heart, not with my conscience. But you—after everything we faced on that first day. You tolerated so much. You have *forgiven* me for so much. And I'm so grateful that you have. That time and again, you put your trust in me, and I hope you know that being worthy of that trust has become my top priority in life." I took both her hands and kissed the backs of them. "You are strong, and beautiful, and resilient, and funny, and I am a better person knowing you than I could ever hope to become on my own. And no matter what happens tomorrow, I have not regretted a single decision I've made that's given you reason to care about me."

A single tear rolled down her cheek, and I brushed it away with my hand before cupping the back of her head and bringing her forehead to mine.

"Keep being my light, princess. Don't let whatever darkness Hazel wants to drag into this world put a damper on that. As long as you're shining, I'll find my way back."

"I promise."

I caught her whisper with my mouth, kissing her slow and deep. Her hands came up to caress my face, and the softness of her skin was such an incredible contrast to the roughness of my thoughts and the tumbling, surging souls.

My thoughts swirled back to the bar at Club Crescent and the way she'd looked at me as we'd breathed in the demonic pheromones. How badly I'd wanted to slide between her legs and take her right there on the bar—and how I'd known in that moment that if I'd tried, she would have let me. My memories left the club to the sidewalk outside. Our almost first kiss. When she'd healed my hand, and the feeling of her magic pumping through me had made me lose all sense of self.

I stood without stopping our kiss and pressed her backwards against her mattress, splaying my weight on top of her. Desire thrummed heavily in my blood, driving me onwards though I knew I should stop. Alyssa slid her hands under my shirt and clawed at my back, the faint pain shooting waves of pleasure through me that sent my blood south and pushed me to roll my hips against her.

Her tongue slid between my lips, and I stroked it with my own, inviting her in. I swallowed her moans, drawing out more as I glided my hand down her side, letting my thumb brush over her nipple.

I didn't understand what I'd done to earn her affection, regardless of whatever she wanted to name it, but to have her beneath me now, drawing me closer to her, winding her foot around the back of my knee to keep me in place, was a greater reward than any other achievement I laid claim to across my life or my career.

I trailed my kisses over her cheek, down her neck, tasting the flutter of her pulse. She released my waist to grip my hair, her fingernails scraping my scalp.

"I want you," I whispered against her skin.

"Then have me."

The vibration of her invitation where it rumbled in her throat nearly did me in, and I bowed my face in the crook of her neck, inhaling her aloe vera scent, savouring her warmth. I reached for her hand, slid my fingers through hers, and pressed them into the mattress beside her head. But I didn't stop her other hand from reaching down between us and undoing the button at the top of my jeans. The zipper came down next, and she teased my hardened length over my boxer briefs, cupping me, toying with me.

It felt incredible, and the base of my stomach tightened with need.

But along with the surge of desire came a different kind of intensity. An uncomfortable heat that spread through my blood and seared my veins, sinking into bone and sinew. The voices in my head grew loud, the souls more unstable, and I released her hand to grab her other one, holding her still while I tensed my entire body and struggled to regain control.

The internal war lasted minutes—hours—days. I had no idea how long the souls and I went back and forth before they finally steadied and returned to their dark depths in my centre.

Drenched in sweat and shaking, I huddled against Alyssa, and her arms came around me, holding me tightly, her fingers stroking my hair, the back of my neck, as she murmured soft words of reassurance.

"I'm sorry," I mumbled.

"Don't be," she said. "I'm glad they let us know now and not later that they have issue with that kind of inappropriate behaviour."

I groaned, both appreciating her attempt to lighten the

mood and hating that it was necessary. "But I enjoy that kind of inappropriate behaviour. And believe me, princess, I want to engage in it with you. Multiple times. A night."

Alyssa's hips rolled against mine again before she caught herself and chuckled roughly into my hair. "You better stop now, or I might not care that it's a ménage-a-centaines."

That earned a straight up laugh from me, and I kissed her neck before rolling off her and propping my head up on my hand so I could stare into her beautiful eyes. "You're incredible."

She smiled up at me and shrugged. "You're worth it." Her smile faded and her expression turned serious—downright lethal. "We are going to finish what we started, Trace Wyatt. This is the second time you've built me up only to leave me hanging. There will not be a third. We are going to kick Hazel's ass, we are going to sort out these souls, and then we are going to have wild, loud, uninhibited sex—preferably not in my parents' house."

I grinned and leaned down to kiss her. "If I needed more motivation to get control over myself, you have just provided it. Let anyone try to get in my way."

# Chapter 20
*Alyssa*

MY STOMACH WAS in knots the next morning. For the second night in a row, I hadn't slept well, too wound up with no way to vent the energy running through me. I was so angry with Hazel and even angrier at those souls for getting in the way of a perfectly viable and necessary outlet.

Necessary not only for my mental health but also, goddammit, because if things went wrong tonight, then I would never know how Trace Wyatt, famous bounty hunter, held up between the sheets. And if the foreplay was anything to go by, that would be a crime for which the universe could never atone.

I held on to that anger as we planned our evening.

Around nine o'clock, I finally got a call from Madison, but the moment I answered I knew I wouldn't be getting any help from that direction.

"Sorry I've been MIA," my friend said, sounding so tense I was amazed my phone didn't shatter. "We've got a few major events coming up that… yeah."

The last of my hopes that my friends would stand with me drained out of my boots. "I get it. I haven't heard from Jet either. Does this involve her?"

"It's all about her, actually. We got some new information about—anyway, sorry, I'm excited. This is really big. Her whole team has been busy making preparations. I haven't seen her all week."

My shoulders sagged. "That's intense. Good luck with everything."

"But hey, wait! What's going on? Is everything all right?" Madison's concern was a gentle hug, and I appreciated that even if I didn't live to experience a real one again, I could at least have this.

"Not really? Hazel's coming after Trace's souls, and we're meeting with her tonight to try to take her down."

"Well, crap. I'm sorry we can't be there to help."

"It's all right." I chewed on my bottom lip. "Actually, there's something else I might need you to do. Not tonight, obviously. And hopefully not at all, but… Ugh." I knew what her relationship was like with her family beyond the wall—tense, estranged, all that good stuff—so throwing this at her felt cruel, but not giving her the heads up would be crueler. "We think Hazel's playing some dangerous games with the unseen wall. We're planning to stop her, but if we fail, you might need to reach out to Meril's court and let them know to be on their guard."

The silence on the line was telling, and I pressed my lips together, giving Madi a chance to rally. Finally she said, "The mirror realm?"

"Yeah. Something about gateways and harvesting magic. And the witch's council might be corrupt? It's been a lot."

"Sounds like it." Her voice was stiff, lined with shock. Then she cleared her throat. "You have no idea how much I wish I could be there to help. Please, *please* be careful."

"I'll do my best."

I hung up and dropped my forehead down on the wall. When that felt good, I did it a second time. It was fine. We had my family and whoever Gramps managed to call in. We were a large, powerful group. Everything was going to be fine.

I returned to the living room to find Trace standing on his own staring out the window. I went up to him and wrapped my arms around his waist. "You ready?"

"No," he said. "But I don't think that matters. I just have to do it."

"We," I reminded him.

He looked down at me and kissed my forehead. "We."

Just as we'd done the other night, we arranged for everyone to park down the street from the museum parking lot, not wanting to make it easy for Hazel to ambush us before we'd ensured everyone was here.

The mass of Mooneys standing on the quiet highway warmed my heart. There were seventeen of us, with some of the strongest among our clan. Training and recent experience had made it a simple task to divide the rest of the family into groups of three, with a warder and two fighters on each team. Mom and Avery, our best healers in the family, would stick with the groups at the rear, making them easy to dispatch while also keeping them safest. I would be on the front line with Trace and Ameline, once she joined us, and while my healing was a bit out of practice, I would be a third point of contact should anyone go down.

Because we couldn't afford anyone staying down for long. Not against this coven with all its spirit and demonic magic. We would be stronger as a unit, which meant keeping everyone on their feet as long as possible.

Another car pulled up alongside the road, and Trace led me over to the black Hummer as the headlights went out. The door opened, and there was Chip, dressed all in black with his sharp eyes taking in my family. He kept his distance from everyone, but I noticed the way he walked around the front of the vehicle to open the passenger door—and the way he hovered so closely to the shoulder of the lithe young woman who stepped onto the side of the road.

Ameline was a pretty creature, with large eyes, delicate features, and a slim figure draped in loose, flowing clothes. I would have thought she was fae if I didn't catch the aura of orange magic swirling around her, ready to use.

"Am, it's good to see you." Trace took her hand and bent down to kiss her cheek. An image of what these two must have looked like twelve years ago superimposed itself over the present, and I was hit by a sense of pride that despite everything Hazel had done to him, Trace was still able to show kindness to the young girl he'd known.

Chip, on the other hand... I pressed my lips together to hold back a smile as he gritted his teeth, the muscles along his jaw flexing, and narrowed his eyes at Trace. Was that a flicker of demonic red mixed in with the deep brown? An interesting development that I never would have expected.

"Chip filled me in on your suspicions about what Mom is up to," Ameline said when Trace released her and returned to my side. "You really think she's trying to access the mirror realm?"

"It's the most likely scenario," Trace said grimly. "You

understand why we need to stop her."

She held up her hands. "You won't get any argument from me. I cheered the day they swept her off to Moongrave. Aunt Matilda was much better for me than Hazel ever was. Did you know you're not supposed to leave your kid home alone for weeks at a time? I know. Wild, right?"

She shook her head, and her gaze landed on me. "You must be Alyssa. That's some nice atmospheric magic you've got there. And wow, you're strong." Her attention strayed to the rest of my family. "A lot of you are. And you seem to like each other. Is this, like, a thing? Family as coven, actually getting along? I don't think I've ever been this jealous before."

Her genuine interest in my family pained me for her sake, but I'd gotten stuck on what she'd said at the beginning. "You can see my magic?"

She canted her head. "Yeah. Can't you?"

"As colours. You're orange."

Her eyes lit up. "Really? That's so cool! You're not a colour, but you're… pulsey. Drew's is more pushy, like his magic is trying to shove me off balance." Her eyes widened. "Sorry. Chip said you don't like Drew anymore. Trace, right?"

He nodded. "Fewer bad memories linked to Trace."

Her shoulders slumped. "Yeah, I know what you mean. Maybe I should have changed my name too, but I doubt it would have made a difference. I needed a whole life change after what happened." She brightened again. "But that's why we're here, right? We have a second chance to put things right. How can I help?"

"By staying in the car," Chip grumbled under his breath, but the words carried in the quiet night regardless.

"You know I can't do that," Ameline said, resting her hand on his arm. "But you'll be with me, right?"

He bared his teeth and stared skyward. "Probably better if I'm not. My skills and talents are best kept to my computers. In person, I get a little… uncontrolled."

Curiosity nudged me, but I knew better than to ask. Chip was at least part demon, according to Trace, and that's all he'd ever told me. But I knew demons. Daily Davis, Mooney's Pub's resident sloth demon, was born to do as little as possible, and I still wouldn't want to get on his bad side. Simon was one of the good ones, and even he'd gone off the rails. Unpredictability was in their nature. I was lucky that Simon's unpredictability was limited to his magic doing who knew what when interacting with someone else's power, or at least that had been true until recently. If Chip was worried about being present for the confrontation, I suspected he got a bit volatile.

Ameline paled a little, worry blossoming in her eyes, but Trace set his hand on her shoulder. "Chip will be in the car, not far at all, and I'll be right there. I won't let anything happen to you."

She shrugged. "Oh, I'm not worried about myself." I didn't believe her for a moment. "More for everyone else. But hey, let's get moving then, eh? The sooner we start, the sooner we're finished and I never need to hear Hazel's name again."

She pulled her shoulders back and left Chip's side without a backwards glance. He opened his mouth as though to call after her, then screwed his jaw shut, stomped back around to the driver's side, and jerked the door open.

"We'll keep her safe," I assured him.

He scowled, then nodded and locked himself in the Hummer. I doubted it was to keep Hazel's people out and more to keep himself in.

I followed Trace back to my family, who were making their introductions with Ameline, oohing and aahing over her orange-tinted power. She seemed to be right at home among them, and I hoped that while she was here she would find the connection she'd obviously been lacking.

As soon as everyone was in place, Gramps raised his hand and the bunch of us fell silent. "We've printed off maps of the various walking trails throughout this place. I don't think we need to worry about the forest over on this side, as it's farther from the door, which leaves three paths to cover. We'll send three teams down each path, and Trace, Alyssa, and Ameline, you'll head directly to the cloister where Hazel is due to meet us. Take down anyone you see. Aim to restrain, not to kill, but if they go for the throat, don't hold back. We don't know how many people might be here tonight, so stay on your toes, keep a lookout in every direction. No hesitations. With luck, we'll take down her lowest hitters before they have a chance to make a move. Combine your magic where you can, do not let anyone get between you. We are strongest when we're together."

I summoned my magic and nudged it towards Trace. He started in surprise, then reached out with his, and I wound mine through it. It was too bad he couldn't see it the way I could, the way his yellow-touched silver played with my purple. It was art. A magic in and of itself.

All around us, witches bound their magic to the others in their team, reinforcing their power, readying themselves to defend or attack. We weren't messing around here, and anyone who chose to mess with us would deal with the consequences.

I watched the teams split up and follow the paths to the various trails, while Trace, Ameline, and I remained together on the edge of the parking lot. We would go in along the main route, hopefully drawing most of the attention our way. Trace was the target, I would be expected, and Ameline would— hopefully—be the surprise we needed to throw everything off balance.

"This feels familiar," I said as we walked the same route we had the other night. "Think we can expect more council members to show up and arrest us?"

"Not tonight," Trace said, his voice grim. "If Hazel's hand in the council is as far reaching as we think it is, she'll keep them away from here. Officially, anyway."

Goosebumps rose on my arms. At first I thought it was the significance of what Trace was saying—that Hazel had so much power as to direct the movements of the entire province's witches' council—but it didn't take me long to realize the real source of my unease was the tingle of magic in the air.

I couldn't see anything, but it came in broad sweeps on the wind. Like the scent of smoke, or the prickle of electricity before a storm. It didn't get stronger as we walked towards the cloister. It never changed at all. When I looked at Trace, I noted the yellow glow creeping in around his eyes. Not so much that it overpowered the hints of his silver magic, but the souls were responding.

"Are you going to be okay?" I asked, keeping my voice low.

Trace nodded, but I caught the strain in his throat and jaw as he worked to maintain control over himself.

Ameline stared up at him. "Are you sure?"

"He'll be all right," I answered for him, squeezing his hand. "We just need to get through this."

Ameline shuffled closer to me. "I told myself I wouldn't be nervous about seeing her again. But now that I'm here…" She shuddered. "I really don't want to do this. I will, but goddess, I'm pissed that she's brought things to this point."

I wanted to give the other woman a hug. That she was being forced to stand off against her own mother wasn't fair. But Ameline had chosen her side, and I was relieved it was ours.

We reached the end of the first trail and cut across the wider lane to where the second parking lot lurked in the shadows. Up ahead was the cloister. So far we hadn't seen anyone else, but the magic was definitely growing stronger, the steady current in the air mixing with the more visible forces of witches summoning their power.

"Stay strong," I whispered. "Here we go."

We stepped onto the grass. The cloister was up ahead, nestled beside that grass amphitheatre with the rock ring creating naturally made benches. Everything appeared to be empty until we stood before the open-sided building.

A woman stepped out of the shadows, and even in the dim light, I recognized Hazel from our brief introduction in Rockland. Her long black hair, which I now noticed was streaked with hints of silver, blew loose around her shoulders. She wore a pair of flowing grey pants and a loose white shirt that made her black hair appear that much darker. Everything about her was beautiful, graceful, elegant. Her clear skin and the angle of her chin, her curvy figure and her poise. All her years in Moongrave Prison hadn't affected her self-confidence, obviously, and I made a mental note to write to my supernatural councillor questioning the conditions our worst criminals lived in. No one should look this good after being stuffed away in the cold confines of up north.

"Andrew," Hazel purred. "I knew you'd come. And you brought your little pet. That's precious. And who is—" Her eyes flew wide, and just as we'd hoped, the ever-planning Hazel Blackwood looked stunned. Unprepared. I suspected the members of her team who were supposed to be keeping an eye on her enemies were about to have a bad night. High-fives to Chip for keeping his guest out of view.

"Hello, mother," Ameline said. "Nice to see you here. You should have let me know you were coming south for a visit."

"Am? What…" She shook her head and smiled—the kind of smile I might have expected the big bad wolf to wear. "I should have known you'd show up. You always did have a flair for the dramatic."

Ameline snorted. "That's the accusation you want to throw my way? Really? Here. Have this mirror."

Hazel shrugged. "Like mother like daughter, if you want. Sure. But you should have known to stay far away from me this time. Tonight especially."

Ameline crossed her arms. "Why? Because you're going to absorb all our power and shove it into the doorway to open the gate to the mirror realm so you can continue your work on Meril's turf?"

Again Hazel appeared shaken, and I knew our theory was

correct. We knew her as well as she believed she knew us, and it was satisfying… even if the confirmation was terrifying. We could not let her win.

Trace's grip on my hand tightened, and I squeezed him back. We would get through this. It wasn't a matter of if. We *would* come out on top.

"Stand down, Hazel," I said. "We know your plan, and we prepared for it. You're not going to succeed. Even if you did, we have connections on the other side. Meril would destroy you before you harvested your first soul."

I hoped Madison was ready to send that message, because my confidence was flagging. The magic in the air was messing with my head. For so many reasons, I prayed she wouldn't have to. Not only because it would mean we were dead, but I also didn't want to put my friend in that situation when she'd worked so hard to distance herself from that side of her family.

But again Hazel surprised me. She threw back her head and laughed. "You poor, silly fools. You keep underestimating the power we can access. Every person you brought here today will die. All you've done is make my task that much easier."

Figures came out of the shadows all around us, at least a dozen of them if not more. Their own magic mixed with the yellow of the souls they'd consumed, filling their hands as they summoned their spells. There was no way the three of us would be able to stand against them alone. But we had to try.

louder and louder. Pressure built in my chest, hooking in deeper, pulling on my insides, shifting my magic.

Another scream tore from my lungs as I watched the yellow-purple light stretching from my middle. Tugging on my magic—my soul. She was harvesting me.

# Chapter 21
*Alyssa*

As soon as I realized what I stood to lose, I fought back as hard as I could, clinging to soul and magic in the most critical game of tug of war I would ever play.

Ameline kept throwing spells, orange swirls dancing around us, and with every new burst of her time magic, I reeled my power back in. But I was tiring fast, while Hazel was only gaining strength. Ameline could work her spells all day, and although she saved me a few seconds at a time, she would never be able to prevent Hazel from ending my life.

We needed something more powerful. Gramps was somewhere in this fight, no doubt working his way towards us, but it would be a miracle if he made it in time.

Trace.

I lurched towards him, desperate, hating that we needed him so badly. But Dad had been right. We needed those souls to work with us.

Hazel's laugh crept deeper into my head. *Stop fighting, little witch. You know I'm going to draw you out eventually. Aren't you tired? Don't you want to sleep?*

My muscles sagged with the thought, but I shoved her out again. She wouldn't wear me down with her mind games. Yes, I was exhausted. More tired than I'd ever been even after three uninterrupted shifts on busy days at Mooney's, but more than that, I was determined to save my family. The entire world. The entire *realm* from this woman.

And to do that, we needed Trace and the souls he wielded. But when I reached for him, he jerked away. "Don't touch me."

I raised my hands to defend myself against the vicious tone, and as Trace raised his head to look at me, I realized he wasn't angry but terrified. Only a glimmer of his silver magic remained in his eyes, and before the last of it disappeared, he gritted his teeth. "Go."

The yellow overpowered the rest, veins of it spilling out from around his eyes, down his cheeks, under his collar to reappear over his fingers. Just as it had done before he'd scorched Nathalie to cinders a few weeks ago.

Hazel lost interest in me, her focus wholly on Trace, greed and desire filling her expression. "Yes, that's it. There they are.

I knew you'd come out to play. You just needed better motivation."

She'd been using me. Toying with me to set Trace off. We'd known she would, yet we'd still fallen for it. Fuck me up a chimney.

I ran towards Ameline, and a witch nearly barrelled into me from the left, hit by a Mooney spell that had her face turning purple as she fought for air. She tripped over a stone half buried in the earth and sprawled to the ground, and I leapt over her and skirted another two witches caught in a brawl.

Ameline wasn't far from me, yet the entire battle had managed to surround her. Finally, I grabbed hold of her arm. "Keep doing what you're doing. Buy us whatever time you can. We need Gramps. We need—"

Pain sliced through me, and I dropped to my knees, bracing myself on the ground as I sucked in breath after breath. When I looked over my shoulder, I found Doreen back on her feet, her red magic swirling around her, spreading, growing more intense with whatever spell she was brewing. Fuck. I'd forgotten about her.

I summoned my magic into a ward around me, the purple shield widening to include Ameline as the younger witch threw out her time spells, binding Hazel so every move she made was halting. Hazel's expression twisted with frustration, and she threw her daughter a nasty look, but with Ameline safe behind my barrier there was nothing she could do. For now. Doreen was about to make a concerted effort to smooth the way again.

Sure enough, the spell that struck the ward was enough to make my magic fizzle out. This bitch was a monster. So much stronger than the last time I'd seen her. How many more demons had she harvested since she'd escaped SMOAC's clutches?

I twitched my fingers to draw more magic into my palms, and as I threw out another atmospheric pulse, it was joined by three others—my family stepping in to support my attack. The four spells bound together to create a blast so strong it threw the demonic witch into a wide trunk, and both woman and tree collapsed. The earth shook as the tree landed, and with the vibrations came a shift in the storm. The rest of our reinforcements spilled around the cloister, and I took in the status of the battle. Our side didn't boast as many as the number we'd arrived with, but we were still over a dozen strong, an even match with Hazel's coven.

Needing to have faith that we were enough, I threw myself into the fight with an aim to destroy.

Magic of all colours flew across the grassy expanse, bounced off the stone of the cloister, wrapped around witch and tree and picnic table. Wood splintered, stone crumbled, humans collapsed, and I was no closer to Hazel and Trace.

All around Trace, his wild spirit magic surged, branching

out in tendrils against anyone who stepped within the circle of his power. Three of Hazel's witches were steaming ash on the ground around him, yellow magic rising from their bodies and drifting towards the cloister, and I spotted Gramps jerking Brody by the arm to haul him away from a searching yellow spell. Trace had no control over who he attacked. He was as much at risk of taking down one of ours as one of Hazel's. I had to get to him. I'd promised him I would make sure he came back to us, and I wasn't about to let him down.

Hazel's stare was fixed on him, her lips moving over an unheard spell as she tried to gain control over the magic he'd unleashed. I fought my way around her, wanting to get out of her line of vision so I could creep up on her from behind, but her witches didn't make it easy. They pushed me back at every turn, and only by drawing on my magical reserve was I able to make progress.

Ameline hurled her spells towards me, and I looped mine through hers, creating an atmospheric time bomb that we tossed towards an elemental witch whose natural magic had been almost completely drowned out by the spirits they'd harvested. They must have noticed the attack hurtling towards them, because they blocked against it, but when the spell hit without a reaction, they grew smug and widened their arms as if to challenge us again. I smiled back as the bomb went off, sending the witch backwards into two others. The three went down in a heap, and I sprinted towards them, throwing a magical net over them and pulling it taut so they wouldn't be able to escape. Avery was there a moment later to add her net to mine, her stronger ward ensuring their submission.

Finally, I had a way to Hazel. I turned towards her and readied a spell, but before I could throw it, she swept one arm backwards, hurling a spell of her own. The yellow magic with its sickly hue flashed towards me, and I barely had time to dodge it. It struck the stone of the cloister wall, and the rock crumbled like dry dust.

*That wasn't very nice, little witch,* she taunted.

The bitch had been so quiet, I hadn't realized she was still in my head. There was no way I could sneak up on her while she could read my every thought.

*You've shown more mettle than I expected, and I'm impressed. But I'm also done with this game. Andrew is mine, his souls are mine. I'll give you a moment to say your goodbyes.*

She threw a tendril of magic around me that bound my power and pressed my arms to my sides. I thrashed against her hold, too tightly wrapped to budge. I needed help, but everyone else was fighting for their lives against Hazel's coven.

To my right, a glow crept up from the nook at the front of the cloister. A glow in the unmistakable shape of a doorway. Hazel had been feeding her spell while we fought, using the yellow magic I'd noticed rising from the corpses of her people.

Horror hit me as I realized she'd been channelling it, manipulating her people even after their deaths. They were nothing to her except more fuel for her power, exactly as I'd warned Emile. I hoped he was happy to be safe at home with his cat.

Hazel was so close to getting what she wanted. I looked to Trace, and his yellow eyes—his yellow *everything*—left me cold. He was gone. If he gave up the fight, Hazel would win.

She turned back to him, and a red haze crept towards me. Fucking Doreen was back again. How much would it take to make her stay down?

I looked for Ameline and panicked when I didn't see her, but then a hint of orange magic crept into my periphery, and I watched as it wriggled under Hazel's binding spell. As though I were watching it on fast-forward, the yellow magic shrivelled and wisped away, undone by Ameline's power. I looked over my shoulder and caught the witch's eye, awed by her skill. She winked at me, then turned back to two witches trying to sneak up behind her.

I whirled around, a spell already between my palms, and blocked a blast of red magic hurtling towards me.

It bounced off my atmospheric pulse and redirected to my left. I called out a warning as it bolted towards Dylan, but he didn't have time to ward himself. A scream tore from my lungs as my brother took the spell in the chest. Blood sprayed across the grass, and he crumpled to the ground.

Terror, grief, rage stormed through me, and I summoned more magic. I'd expended so much already, had no idea how much remained at hand, but I would direct every last drop of it into cutting this woman down. Brody charged with me, and I sensed Val's magical signature joining ours.

Doreen smiled over the hellfire swirling around her hands. Her eyes flashed red, a wicked, ominous glow, and then she sent the fire towards us. Val leapt out of the way, screaming as an ember leapt onto her leggings and caught. Brody unleashed his magic like an atmospheric scythe, slicing through the air and across the witch's body. The shriek that burst from her lungs as her arm tumbled to the ground, lopped off at the elbow, rattled my eardrums and stilled the fight for a breath, but it didn't stop her from coming at us again. Hands were a good focal point for a witch, but the magic was in our blood, not in our fingers, and now this witch had access to a hell of a lot of it.

She channelled her power into every droplet and sent it towards us. The spray misted across my face, burning my skin, burrowing deep, and I squeezed my eyes shut against the damage even as I kept moving, not wanting to give her the opportunity to take advantage of my vulnerability.

Another yank in my chest staggered me, and I looked down at Hazel's second attempt to tug the soul from my centre. I tugged back, wanting to pull her off balance, but she remained firm on her feet. I bared my teeth at her as I threw another spell towards Doreen. I didn't wonder how the demonic witch was still going. With that much power running through her, we'd need to strike a fatal blow to destroy her.

This fight had to fucking end. There was too much going on. I spotted Mom running from witch to witch. Avery taking on the other half of the injured while doing her best to throw out ward after ward to protect those of us still standing. Dad was wavering on his feet, and Hilary was by his side. Tears streamed down her face, rage shone in her eyes, and I didn't want to consider what might have triggered such an emotional reaction. Sonya bled from multiple places across her face, but her jaw was set and she wielded her magic with wild ferocity.

Although we were still going strong, we couldn't last much longer. Hazel's people had been halved, but as long as Doreen and Hazel were still breathing, we would always be outpowered.

*Come on, Trace.*

I hated that he had to do it, but we needed him to start fighting.

My magic pulsed and throbbed around me, growing sluggish after being put through its paces, and I pushed myself harder, warding myself even as I hurled spells around the barrier, doing everything I could to keep the demonic witch busy and drive her back, creating space for more of us to turn against her.

Doreen lashed out with a magical whip and grabbed me

around the ankle. I crashed onto my back and blinked the stars out of my eyes as she dragged me across stone, twig, and rough grass towards her.

"I'm so glad I get to be the one to do this," she said with a grin. Hellfire danced over the index finger of her remaining hand.

"Likewise," Gramps said over my head. I threw my power to him, and he grabbed it, mixed it with his, and launched it like a spear into the woman's heart.

Her mouth rounded as she staggered back. She dropped to her knees, then keeled over onto her side.

Gramps helped me to my feet, and I turned to Trace and Hazel. Hazel, who had taken on the same bright yellow glow as Trace and had bound herself to that slowly opening doorway. Triumph shone in her eyes.

I looked at Trace, desperate to help, and as I did, I watched him start to smile as well. A cold, heartless smile. Not his, but coming from the souls inside him.

Hazel frowned, uncertain, then her eyes flew wide and she mouthed a silent *no* as the current between them changed direction. The doorway dimmed faster than I would have imagined, and the glow around Hazel faded. She clenched her teeth, and I sensed her pulling harder, determined to get the upper hand, but Trace didn't falter, barely looked strained, as he stood against her.

"These souls are not for you," came his layered voice. "You mortals better realize that now."

"You… are souls," she rasped. "You exist… solely for my… purpose."

Trace's smile widened, and he pulled again. Hazel flew forward and crashed onto her hands and knees. The doorway slammed shut. Mooneys closed in on her, rounding up the four other surviving witches from her coven in the centre of us.

We'd done it. Trace had come through, and we'd caught her. We were ragged, out of breath, out of magic, but we'd done it.

Victory flowed through me, satisfaction, joy.

Until Trace's power seeped out of him and came for those of us still standing.

"No one will use us," he said. "*No one.*"

He looked at me as he spoke, and my blood chilled to the marrow.

I barely had time to summon my magic and form a weak ward before he threw his power my way. The family scattered, getting out of range of his blows, but his reach was wide. It kissed the ground, and the grass grew brown under its touch.

I quickly surveyed the scene around me. Mom beside Dylan, focused intently on sending her healing magic into him; Brody at his twin's other side, watching Trace to see if he needed to move them to a safer distance. The rest of my family was in the same place I was. Uncertain, afraid.

I didn't want to run. I knew what I'd promised—that I'd keep myself safe—but I couldn't leave him like this. I needed to try to bring him back. This wasn't Trace. This was the souls who resented being trapped yet again. Trapped by *our* family. I didn't know what to do. I didn't know how to reach him.

"Trace, please." I'd always been able to get through to him. I had to try. "It's me. It's Alyssa. The woman whose pub you destroyed. The woman who—"

A flash of yellow power slammed into me, strapping my magic down, and my knees hit the ground so hard my teeth rattled.

A flash of silver cut through the yellow, and the magical spread slowed, stopped. Trace squeezed his eyes shut, his body hunching in on itself, muscles twitching, joints cracking as he fought to contain himself.

My heart thrashed against my ribcage and my blood rushed in my ears, but I pushed through the terror. I needed him to hear me before someone else was forced to step in. Before they believed the only way to save me was to kill him. Or before he killed me himself.

"I'm here, Trace. I'm right here. I'm with you."

Still no reaction, and desperation tore at me. We'd known the risks, but I wasn't willing to accept the consequences. I couldn't lose him.

Yellow and silver writhed around him, like solar flares of power. One moment silver dominated; then yellow took over. I couldn't look away, couldn't breathe. This man was fighting so hard to come back to me, and all I could do was kneel here and wait to see if he succeeded.

I'd just unleashed massive amounts of magic, taken down a witch fuelled with demonic power, defended my family, yet I'd never felt more helpless.

Rays of yellow magic burst out from around Trace, and wards of all colours shot up around the surviving witches to protect us against the brunt of it.

Silver overpowered yellow again, drawing it in, encasing it. The spread of the magic shrank and returned to the source before both yellow and silver went out, as though someone had flipped a switch and shut Trace down.

I was vaguely aware that Hazel was gone, that her followers had likewise disappeared, but none of that mattered as Trace collapsed. I rushed towards him, and my breath, my heart, my thoughts stopped when I threw myself at his side only to find him lying unmoving, eyes open… but unseeing.

# Chapter 22
*Alyssa*

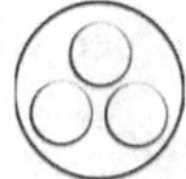

WITH MY HEART in my throat, I threw myself at Trace, pawing over his chest, not releasing my breath until I detected the pulse in this throat.

"He's alive," I rasped. "Thank the goddess, he's alive. Trace? Come on, wake up." I ran my hands over the stubble along his jaw, across his mouth, down his neck, but he didn't respond to my touch or my voice.

Tears blurred my vision as I rested my head against his chest, desperate to hear his heartbeat, to confirm with my other senses what that faint flutter in his throat was telling me.

"It's all right, Pip, we've got him," Gramps said, coming up beside me to pull me away. "Let Avery take a look."

I sat up and shifted to the side to let my cousin get closer.

I would have preferred my mom look at him, but she was busy with Dylan, her hands moving frantically across his body and into her satchel where she kept her ready supply of poultices, salves, and potions. I doubted anything she had in there would help Trace, but her experience would have been a comfort.

Avery hovered her hands over Trace's chest, and a furrow formed between her eyebrows. "I don't get it. I don't sense anything. Like, I do, but it's like it's all locked down, pushed so deep that I can't access it to see what's wrong. Physically, he's fine. The problem is his magic."

My gaze shot up to Trace's open, empty stare. With shaking fingers, I closed his eyelids. "You foolish man," I whispered.

He'd retained enough of himself to be aware that the souls had turned on me, and he'd pushed them so far down, he'd taken his own soul with them. His magic, his consciousness, was now trapped inside him, and I had no idea how to pull him out. Not without giving the souls another chance to take over.

Gramps clapped his hand on my shoulder, and I sensed the tremble like a mild vibration. "We need to get out of here. Hazel could very well come back with reinforcements."

I shot a look at the dead demonic witch and exhaled a large breath. "At least we took that woman down. Whatever else we lost here today, we achieved that much."

Ameline stared at the closed doorway. "I think we achieved more than you realize. That doorway. It was so close to open I swear I saw through to the other side. I hate to think of every-thing my mother might have claimed if she'd opened it." She turned her wide eyes on me. "We can't let her do it."

My words and heart were ice cold as I replied, "We won't."

I was done with fear around this woman's machinations. Right now, towards her, I held only anger, with all my fear reserved for the man on the ground in front of me.

"Let's get him up," Brody said as he came to my side and helped me lift Trace's body. We draped him over my brother's shoulder in a firefighter's hold, then I finally allowed myself to turn towards Dylan and Mom.

"Will he be all right?"

I was afraid to ask. Tears cut down my mother's cheeks as she poured another potion into the gaping wound across Dylan's chest, but she nodded. "He will be. My poor baby. Always believing himself so tough, but when it comes down to it, he's still so vulnerable." She brushed her bloody hand across his hair to clear it from his brow.

"We'll get him to the hospital, Mary," Gramps said as he tucked my hand under his arm. "He'll see dawn, no question about that."

I grimaced. "Do we trust the hospital?"

Gramps sighed. "On this, we have no choice. I'd say we'll call the council to bring in extra security, but…"

"I'll call Madison," I said. "I need to update her anyway, let her know she doesn't need to panic about Meril. Anyone she trusts to stand guard, I'll trust."

Mom nodded and stood aside as Kyle and Grayson, both of them looking rough and worn, picked Dylan up between them.

Hilary stood alone, with Mallory's arm around her shoulders, standing over Tony's body. A spell had taken him across the face and neck, leaving charred wounds through his throat. My stomach churned, and I reached for Hilary's hand. "I am so sorry."

She didn't notice my words or the gesture, and I let her go. Gramps left me to see to his daughter, and she collapsed against his chest as her first sobs broke through.

The anger Hazel had stirred in my heart burned brighter. Her bid for power had cut through my family. She'd scarred us, left us wounded, but she would not break us. I wouldn't allow it to happen. She had picked the wrong family to cross, and she would live to regret it.

Brody drove Trace's SUV, and Avery sat next to him in the passenger seat while I sat in the back with Trace. The drive to Ashton was quiet, taut with grief and rage. I texted Madison, letting her know she could stand down and asking for help with my brother, then I sent a message to Tory asking how the pub was going. It took a while for them to reply, which I took as a good sign, and their quick thumbs-up emoji was a weight off my chest.

No one spoke except for soft check-ins around and about the injured, and by the time we reached my parents' place, it was a relief to get out of the car.

Brody kept hold of Trace as we went into the house. He plodded up the stairs, bearing the weight on his shoulder without complaint, and laid him down gently on my bed. I stayed in my room long enough to remove Trace's shoes and make sure he was comfortable, kissed his forehead, then followed my brother back downstairs to where the rest of my family waited.

"Well," Gramps said as he dropped onto the edge of the loveseat. "That was a night."

I don't think he was aiming for a lighthearted quip, but more than one of us let out a rough laugh, as though the need for the break in tension was so strong we were desperate to grab at any small positive. At the sound, all of us seemed to take a deep breath, and with the extra oxygen flooding my brain, I was able to appreciate everything we'd achieved tonight.

The doorway was closed. Hazel's lieutenant was dead. Trace still had the souls.

It was a few incredibly large wins that were overshadowed by the heavy losses, but we stood to lose so much more if we allowed ourselves to be distracted by them. There would be time to mourn, but not yet. Not when Hazel was still out there. She'd failed, but she would try again. She wouldn't be satisfied with the single attempt.

"We need to know where the other doorways are." I rubbed my face, working the feeling back into my numb cheeks, my lips, my chin.

Gramps rumbled his agreement. "We'll track them down. At least that doorway's closed. By opening it as much as she did, then us sealing it, there's no way she's getting it open again."

"We're sure she won't try for a main door?" Dad asked as he served water and tumblers of brandy for anyone who wanted one or the other. I definitely fell into the "other" camp tonight, but I went for the water instead. I needed to get back up to Trace and keep an eye on him, and doing that sloshed wouldn't benefit either of us.

"She won't." Ameline's soft voice spoke up from the doorway, and I was shocked to find Chip standing behind her. They hadn't come fully into the living room, and the demon looked as uncomfortable here as I'd ever done in his home, but I was glad he'd come. It would mean a lot to Trace to know his friend had voluntarily stepped into someone else's house to check on him.

Or to stay by Ameline, but I suspected Trace would have been happy with that as well. It proved Chip had something of a heart for all his demonic nature.

"How do you know?" Avery asked. My cousin sounded exhausted. She sat slumped in the armchair next to Gramps, her head propped on her hand, her legs stretched out in front of her.

"Because my mother is a coward."

Ameline stepped forward, and orange magic swirled around her in a faint aura that looked so pretty under the soft glow of the table lamps. Or maybe I was just really tired.

"She'll never go for the hard route when the easy one is in front of her. If there are other half-sealed doorways, that's where she'll be. She won't want to start a war in the mirror realm. At least, not until she has enough power behind her that she thinks she'll win. The only reason she made her move today was because she had Doreen beside her. Now Doreen's dead." Her eyes narrowed. "Good riddance."

"You knew her?" I asked.

Ameline nodded, and I couldn't ignore the way she leaned into Chip. "That woman harvested more demons than I can count. She was a bitch on top of that. Even before the demon magic. It's no wonder she went that route. The world's a better place with her corpse rotting in the grass."

"To be fair, it won't be rotting in *that* grass," Brody said, and when Dad shot him a look, he shrugged. "It's true."

It was true. We had more Mooneys driving out to the

museum right now to clean up the scene and make sure there was no evidence of our fight by the time the place opened tomorrow. Normally we'd ask the council for help with that, to make things more official and not seem like we were covering anything up. Unfortunately, the council had proved itself to be in a questionable state right now. We were on our own.

But that didn't mean we were going rogue. The invoices and paperwork would be sent to the council as soon as the situation was resolved.

"All right, so we make our list," I said. "We track down the other doorways, and we…"

I trailed off, not knowing what we'd do after that. If there were only one or two possible locations, we could stake them out to ensure Hazel didn't act against them, but if there were a dozen? More? We were already stretched too thin, and after tonight's fight, there was no way we'd be able to stand against her, even with Doreen dead.

"We need to sleep." It was the only logical next step.

Gramps frowned. "We need a plan. If the Ontario council is out of the game, I'll touch base with the Quebec council. Angélique might have some people she can send our way. At the very least to help us monitor the gateways." He looked around the room at our flagging family members and shook his head. "No, you're right. We need to sleep." He looked to Ameline and Chip. "Do you two want…"

Chip held up a hand. "No thanks, Gramps. We're off." His sharp brown gaze landed on me. "Cheers, I want updates."

I nodded, not put off or offended by his curtness. That he was asking at all showed he cared, and that counted far more than a friendly manner.

He and Ameline left, and the rest of the Mooneys folded in on each other, leaning on one another for the support we so desperately needed. Brody looked bereft sitting by himself on the other couch. It was strange to see him without his twin by his side, the two poking at each other, goading the other into a reaction.

I held out my hand, and he tugged me down beside him. Val changed seats to the one next to him so we sat together, three of the four, an incomplete unit. Dad watched us, then blinked away the tears that welled in his eyes as he checked his phone again for any updates from Mom.

We sat there until the first hints of dawn spilled through the windows, and when I finally pulled away to go upstairs, just as afraid of what I'd find up there as I'd been when Trace first collapsed, I prayed to the goddess that whatever came next, we'd seen the worst.

And knowing how likely it was that the worst was yet to come.

I opened the door and stepped into the darkness of my bedroom. I thought of the last time I'd done this, after we'd pulled Trace out of the clutches of Hazel's coven. The damage they'd done to his body. His exhaustion, his pain. Although he was physically whole, I couldn't help but worry they'd done this time what they'd failed to do last time. I was terrified they'd broken him and I'd never get him back.

Tears pooled on the side of my nose as I slid into bed beside him and rested my head on his chest, finding what comfort I could in the steady beat of his heart.

Soon we'd need to get him to a hospital to make sure his body didn't give out while we figured out the rest, but I wasn't ready yet. I couldn't shake this nagging hope that he would open his eyes in another few minutes. He'd fainted, that was all. He was fighting to come back to me. He'd get there.

"Come on, Trace. I'm waiting for you."

# Chapter 23
*Trace*

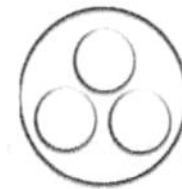

I'M HERE!

I shouted it as loud as I could, but without a working mouth, it was pure thought, and there was no one to hear me. I was trapped inside my own head. My soul was mixed with the screams of hundreds of others, and although they weren't trying to consume me, they were all around me, closing in, suffocating.

I wouldn't last here. I needed to find my way out. But if I pulled myself free, they would come with me, and they were still so strong. So incredibly strong. It had taken everything I had to compress them in the centre of my being, and my hold on them was secure. But one tweak, one unplanned stretch, and the binding would snap, they would be free, and Alyssa would be in danger.

I needed her to know I was still alive. Still me. But unless she found me hidden way inside here, I could only bide my time and hold on.

My thoughts of her held me steady, but with every passing moment, the details of her slipped away, my thoughts growing cloudy. Instead of her green eyes, I saw brown. Instead of her highlighted brown ponytail, there was long dark hair. A harsh laugh. A wicked smile.

*You should have stayed with me, Drew,* Hazel's voice filtered through my head, some of the last words she'd said to me before SMOAC had taken her away. *You could have become so much more than you are.*

Everything she'd wanted for me was happening. I was fading under the weight of these souls, just as I would have done if she'd gotten hold of me. Then she would have harvested everything—taken the power and run. Whatever happened now, I prayed she wouldn't get the chance. That... that someone— who were they? Why couldn't I remember their name?—would keep her away.

*Hold on. I just have to hold on.*

# Chapter 24
*Alyssa*

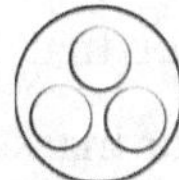

ESPITE EVERYTHING, I woke up feeling well rested. Sure, I woke up well after noon, but my body had obviously needed the complete shutdown. My dreams hadn't bothered me, the sounds of people moving downstairs or coming up to bed hadn't woken me.

And Trace hadn't moved. He remained just as he was, breathing, alive, but still unconscious.

For a long while, I lay beside him and stared at his handsome features. The longer-than-usual stubble that caught the afternoon sunlight and glittered with golds and reds. The thick, strawberry-blond hair a tangled mess and littered with leaves and dried grass. The defined nose with a bit of a twist at the bridge where a semi-decent healer must have mended a break.

The bruises under his eyes, no smaller than yesterday from not having gotten nearly the same level of rest as I had.

Because of course he hadn't. Although everything on the surface appeared calm and stable, he had to be waging a war inside, and it wasn't one I could help with except to keep encouraging him from out here.

I stroked the side of his face and brushed the leaves from his hair, then laid my hand on his chest to register his heartbeat under my palm. "Remember that time you jumped out of a window to catch one of your marks? I watched it on the news, how you managed to grab him, grab the railing, and haul both of you back up. I couldn't decide if you were a horrible show-off or the sexiest man in the world. Now I know you're both." I nudged him to let him know I was teasing. "You're a superhero, Trace. You can do all sorts of impossible things. Which means you can beat this."

When he didn't open his eyes and immediately prove me right, I got up to go to the bathroom. After taking care of my morning needs, I grabbed a bowl from under the sink, a towel, and a cloth, and came back to wash the dirt and blood off his face. I tucked the towel underneath him, then wrestled him out of his filthy shirt and scrubbed his chest and arms. After that, I rolled him onto his side and cleaned his back.

I detached from the man I'd fallen in love with and stepped into the training I'd taken on throughout high school when I'd dreamed of becoming one of Ottawa's great healers like my mother.

I removed Trace's dirty jeans and threw them in the laundry to join everything else and washed down his legs. I turned off all thought as I washed the rest of him, wanting him to be comfortable in his own skin while his mind protected itself.

He'd grabbed his overnight bag from his car, so once he was washed, I gave him clean boxers and his clean T-shirt, but went for the pair of sweats I'd grabbed from Brody instead of his jeans. No one liked sleeping in jeans.

That done, I found one of my dad's extra razors and turned my attention to Trace's face, carefully trimming back the day's beard growth until he was left with the amount of stubble I knew he preferred.

There he was. The man I'd grown so used to seeing in the mornings. The man who'd made himself such an important part of my life.

I kept myself busy throwing all our clothes in the laundry hamper, putting away the cloths and towels, opening the curtains to let the afternoon sunshine trickle in to give more light to the otherwise dreary room.

The front door opened and closed downstairs, and my heart caught in my throat. That had to be Mom coming home from the hospital. I didn't want to leave Trace, but I needed to find out how my brother was doing. And how long we could keep Trace here before we brought him to the room beside Dylan's. I bent over Trace and kissed his forehead.

"Keep fighting, you hear me? I'll be back soon."

Then I left him to sleep and made my way downstairs on shaking legs. My palms were clammy, and I rubbed them on my thighs repeatedly to dry them off as I reached the bottom of the steps and made my way into the kitchen where I heard people talking.

Takeout containers sat on the kitchen counter. I wasn't much in the headspace to eat, but I didn't let that stop me from dropping an eggroll and a spoonful of veggie fried rice on a plate.

Dad rubbed my back as I passed him, but he only had eyes for Mom.

When I sat down at the kitchen island, I followed his gaze, and everything in me lightened. Although she looked worn out and like she hadn't slept all night, she looked happier than she'd been when she'd left for the hospital. Happier than I ever thought to see her again.

"Dylan's all right?" I asked.

She gave me a shaky smile. "He will be. He was awake when I left this morning, thank the goddess. In pain, and they're going to keep him for a while to make sure there's no internal damage, but he was lucky. So fucking lucky."

She broke down in tears, and Dad rushed to throw his

arms around her and hold her while she cried. I covered my mouth and allowed my own tears to fall. My big brother was going to be okay. He was a headstrong, argumentative, aggressive bastard, but I was so happy he would live to be headstrong, argumentative, and aggressive another day.

"Kyle and Grayson are with him now," Mom continued, wiping her face with the back of her arm. "I didn't want to leave him alone there. Your friend sent people over to watch the door, but with everything going on…"

I knew what she meant. We had no idea who we could trust.

She came around the island and bundled me against her chest. I breathed in the lavender scent I'd grown up with and almost allowed myself to relax for the first time since we'd driven out to the museum last night.

Until Mom asked, "How's Trace?"

I cleared my throat. "No change. He'll need IV drips and monitoring and all kinds of other things, but I don't want him in a hospital where Hazel can get to him. I need to figure out how to help him, because I don't know how long he can keep fighting by himself."

I forced myself to take a bite of egg roll and then a bite of rice. I tasted nothing, but the heat, the carbs, and the crunch of vegetable felt amazing after so many hours of nothing but water.

"He strikes me as someone with a strong will," Dad said. "He chose a hard road in life as it is. I'm sure he's faced worse than this."

We both knew that wasn't true, but I appreciated his attempt to be optimistic.

I shoved my rice around my plate. "Where's Gramps?"

"Getting ready for his shift at the pub," Dad said, readying a plate for Mom. "Tory says some weird things have been happening, and she wants him to take a look."

I stiffened and looked up. "Weird how?" What else did I have to deal with?

Dad brushed my hair behind my ear. "Nothing to stress over. A shelf in the kitchen fell yesterday, and one of the paintings in the loft. Old building stuff."

Thank the goddess for that. I did not need any new stresses added to my plate.

The thought of the pub made my heart squeeze with how I would have preferred to be spending my day there than scared out of my mind here, and I pulled my phone out again. Tory had texted a few questions about cleaning supplies, so I answered those, then pulled up Reverie's number.

**Me: Any updates?**

I stared at my phone for a long while waiting for a reply, and finally three little dots danced at the bottom.

**BFF Thief: He's alive. Will keep you posted.**

I wasn't sure if that was supposed to make me feel better, but it didn't make me feel much worse. At least Simon wasn't alone facing whatever he was going through.

Unlike Trace.

A groan escaped the back of my throat, and I pushed my plate away as a lost cause.

"What's wrong, honey?" Mom asked, then closed her eyes and shook her head. "Not what I meant, sorry. Stupid question." She opened her eyes again. "What was that particular groan for?"

"Can we take care of Trace here? Can we avoid taking him to the hospital?"

She pressed her lips together and tilted her head in thought. "We could take care of the basics for a day or so. Certain biological needs might be tricky, but I can take a quick trip for supplies. I have a few things I need to get from the hospital anyway." She levelled me with a sympathetic stare. "But probably not more than a day, Aly. It's like you said, he needs his vitals monitored, he needs to be hydrated. We can only do so much here."

I let out a slow breath. "All right. What do you think the odds are that we could track Hazel down and deal with her in a day?"

I'd done wilder things in twenty-four hours. With Trace's help, but still. I had my family with me this time.

Mom and Dad exchanged a look. "Since we don't know where she is or where to start looking, I don't… I don't really know what to tell you, sweet pea," Mom said.

"Gramps might have a better idea," Dad suggested. "He went downstairs last night, but I heard him moving around, so I don't think he slept much. He probably has a plan or three brewing."

I rose off the stool and gave both of my parents a hug. "Thank you."

Mom took my arm as I made to walk away. "You focus on what you need to do, all right? I want to shower and change, and then I'll head to the hospital to grab what we need and check on Dyl. Then I'll stay with Trace the whole afternoon while you get to work."

I threw my arms around her again and squeezed her tight-tight-tight. "You're amazing."

"You're my daughter."

She kissed my head, then I pulled away before I could break down. I didn't have time to cry yet.

First I needed to drive my fist into Hazel's face, and for that, I needed anger.

I headed downstairs to see Gramps.

# Chapter 25
*Alyssa*

I FOUND GRAMPS lying on the couch in his basement apartment flipping through options on his streaming service. The image of repose and comfort.

Except his laptop sat open on the coffee table in front of him, his phone was in his other hand, and every thirty seconds, he checked one or the other. Waiting for replies to his phone calls and messages.

As soon as he saw me, he sat up. "I'll be heading downtown soon to take over from Tory. Poor thing's run off their feet. I was just hoping I'd hear back from someone before I left."

"I wasn't here to check on you," I said. "I'm here to ask for advice. For direction. I need to know what I can do to help while we're waiting for Trace to wake up." I refused to accept any other alternative. "Who are you waiting to hear from?"

He huffed. "Too many people. Angélique told me she'd get back to me once she had a grasp on what the Quebec council wants to do. I have the rest of our coven mobilizing. The slaughter at the mill raised some eyebrows throughout the city, so I have the more diplomatic members of our family out doing some damage control—and seeing if they can draw in some allies. We need people to redirect the media while we deal with this, among other things. I've been trying to get eyes on Hazel, but the woman seems to be everywhere at once."

"Chip says the same, and if that man can't pin her down, I doubt anyone in this family will be able to." I paced the length of the room, tugged out my ponytail and braided my hair over my shoulder, then released the braid and threw it into a messy bun to keep it out of my face. "I need to stay busy, Gramps. If we can't find Hazel, what about the doorways?"

"Can your computer demon friend help us out with that?"

I squeezed my eyes shut. "Probably. It means calling him, which I hate doing, but he'll want updates anyway."

I was about to ask if there were any other starting points we might pick at when his phone rang. He jumped up, forgetting the device was in his hand, then rushed to answer it before the caller hung up.

"Angel? I'm going to put you on speaker. My granddaughter's here, and she's the one leading this thing."

My heart swelled under his acknowledgement, though considering the amount of shit we were currently shovelling, I didn't know how much credit I really wanted to take.

"Alyssa, bonjour," Angélique greeted. "I won't keep you two long, but I thought you'd want to know the decision the Quebec council's made. Unfortunately, we're not able to help you. We can't risk causing an interprovincial crisis over this, especially with the Ontario Witches' Council currently in disarray. Our recommendation is that you take it higher. SMOAC might be able to step in where we can't."

Gramps and I exchanged a frustrated glance. Given the circumstances, we knew we wouldn't be able to keep the government out of our business, but asking them to come in and take things over was a move neither of us wanted to make. It would say we weren't capable of dealing with our own issues, and the repercussions would be long lasting. The Mooneys could potentially lose their place as the ruling coven of this city.

Gramps's sigh was heavy. "Thanks, Angel."

"That being said," she continued, dropping her voice. "Unofficially, I can tell you the situation in the Ontario council might not be as bad as you think it is. Hazel Blackwood's got her fingers in deep, but there's a network that was aware of her manoeuvres. With Nuñes dead, Pen is raging. She and a trusted unit have cut the spirit witches off, blocked them in."

I thought of the tall blond from outside Hazel's house.

She'd also been there the night we were arrested, silently watching, giving me no opening to get a read on her. I had no idea what we might expect if we tried, but it was better than doing nothing.

The council witch hung up, and I dropped onto the couch beside Gramps. "Do you have Pen's contact information?"

He nodded and pulled his laptop closer to look it up. Within three minutes, he was on the phone again, the call once more on speaker. It rang five times, and I readied myself for it to go to voicemail when a sharp voice said, "What?"

"Penelope Holt, it's Edwyn—"

"I know who this is, Mooney. What do you want?"

She sounded more harassed than aggressive, so I didn't hold it against her. Her partner was dead, her council was corrupt, and she was trying to hold on to whatever she had left.

"We want to help you avenge your partner and bring down Hazel," Gramps said.

"You want to help? Then get your ass into the office and go to work picking up the pieces. Otherwise, I don't have time for you."

"Ms. Holt, please," I said before she could hang up. "We know what Hazel is after, and we know someone in SMOAC has to be working with her to make it happen. Going into the office to have this conversation would be dangerous for all of us."

A beat of silence followed. Another. Another. "Meet me in

two hours where we arrested you."

She hung up, and I sagged back into the seat. "Are all witches into this cloak-and-dagger stuff, and I never knew? I'm feeling really left out."

Gramps patted my leg. "Not all of us, Pip. Some just like to play into the stereotype."

I crossed my arms and twisted on the couch to face him. "You're not exactly one to talk."

He frowned. "What do you mean?"

I took in my grandfather, with his trim white beard, his slightly widened belly on a still fairly muscular frame. The man I'd known most of my life. Which had nothing to do with the version of him I didn't know at all.

"If there's one thing I've learned over the past few months, it's that you have more secrets than a game of *Monkey Island.*"

"Huh?"

"Never mind. Video game reference. Though when this is over, I'll introduce you. You'd enjoy it. My point is you are the most cloak-and-dagger man I've ever met, and you never told any of us. You trained most of my generation in magical know-how. You taught me everything I needed to know about the pub. There was no lack of opportunity to reveal that you were the leader of a witch militia carrying around an amulet that let you persuade people to give you what you wanted. Or that you're some badass magical warrior with tactical knowledge. These details kind of strike me as things a granddaughter should know about her grandfather."

He stared at me for a while, his green eyes piercing. His shoulders slumped. "You're probably right, Pip, and if that's how you feel, then I'm sorry I didn't. But I had my reasons. I liked being your Gramps. The man you turned to when you were on the outs with your parents. Heck, I helped raise you and the others. You're as much mine as you are Mary and Henry's, and I enjoy that. I didn't want to see the brightness in your eyes turn to fear when you looked at me once you learned my history. What I did back then, what me and the guys got up to in those years—it wasn't nice. We always did what was needed and our only aim was to help, but it was war out there for a while. There were riots to quell, uprisings to put down. There is always a power struggle going on, Pip, even when the masses don't see it. We played our part to make sure those masses never saw it. That our families were safe. And yes, I made some decisions I regret, but overall, I'm proud of what we did. But I'm not that man anymore. Or at least, I wasn't. Not from the time I bought the pub. My priorities shifted, and I became a protector of a different kind. A voice for those who needed one and against anyone who got louder than they should be. That's what I wanted my legacy to be. Not everything that came before."

I nodded along, understanding what he was saying but

still not sure how I felt about it. "What about when this stuff started? How surprised are you that we're here? Because, I'll tell you, I'm staggered."

His frown deepened and he held out his arm. I slid under it and shifted so I snuggled in beside him. "Surprised? Not very. The fact that someone like Hazel hasn't popped up more often has been the greater surprise. Disappointed that you're caught in the middle of it? Extremely. I never wanted this for you, Pip. I wanted you to be safe behind the bar like I was. Serving your purpose to our community, keeping everyone safe in a rare and special way. It should have been enough."

My spine sagged under his words, soaking up every ounce of exhaustion over the fact that so much had fallen on me.

He gave me a gentle shake. "But I'll tell you what—if it had to happen, there's no one more ready or prepared or *capable* of handling it. You proved that four years ago when the Firestone Coven tried to push us out of the way, and you're proving it now. You're made of sturdy Mooney stock, and whoever tries to shove past you is going to learn they won't get far. You're what the witches of this city need, Alyssa. I hope you know that."

Tears welled in my eyes, and I wiped them away. "I'm glad I'm there. That I was able to catch things before they got worse, but I hate that I've had to sacrifice so much to do it. I wasn't there for Simon when he needed me—what if I could have helped him? I don't even know what he's going through, but if I'd been at the pub instead of running around after these witches, maybe I could have found out. And Trace. Goddess, Gramps, that's all my fault. He shouldn't have been anywhere near this, and now he's—"

I bit down on my lip so hard I tasted blood, but I refused to let myself cry. When this was over, I would give myself days to cry. Weeks of random sobbing. But if I started now, I wouldn't be able to stop, and Trace needed me. I didn't have room to be afraid that I might have led the man I loved to an early, painful, horrible end. Every drop of his courage and kindness, his humour and tenderness, his intelligence and stubbornness, snuffed out under the pull of a magic he'd sworn never to touch again. He wouldn't have had to if I hadn't made so many mistakes. The regrets were so thick, so heavy, I couldn't breathe.

Fortunately, I had a meeting with Pen to prepare for. I had a next step. I would stay focused on that, and then the next one, and then the next one, until the end was finally in sight.

Gramps kissed the top of my head, then stood up and helped me to my feet. "I'm off to the pub, you're off to the mill. We both have our roles to play in this, and that's what will get us through. Take your dad with you today, though, will you? Might not be the worst idea to have some backup."

"I will. Thanks, Gramps."

"Any time, Pip." He nudged my shoulder. "You're pretty good at this cloak-and-dagger stuff, yourself, you know that?"

I forced a chuckle. "I get it from you."

"You do," he said, all seriousness. "So now it's time for you to go use it."

# Chapter 26
*Alyssa*

I CHECKED IN on Trace before I left, but there was no change. Not a single twitch of his finger. Only the steady rise and fall of his breath. His skin was warm and still held colour, which reassured me we weren't losing him yet, but I only had so many hours left before his body would need more help than Mom or I could give him.

"I have to go out for a bit, all right?" I said. "I'm going to meet with Nuñes's partner. You know, the tall one who doesn't look like she knows how to smile? Probably not likely she will today either, all things considered. But still, maybe I can convince her to stand with us. I might not have an amulet full of persuasive souls, but I can be pretty charming. You're not even able to argue with me on that one."

My attempt at levity fell flat under the squeeze in my throat. I bent down and kissed his forehead. "I'll ask Brody to sit with you until Mom gets back, and then she's going to help make you more comfortable. You let them know what you need."

I waited there, hovering over him, but nothing happened.

With a sigh, I stood up and plodded down the stairs, going in search of my brother before I left for my meeting. I wasn't too surprised to find him shooting hoops in the backyard. He and Dylan had spent most of their teenage years hiding back here, avoiding homework, lectures from our parents, each other—sometimes even as they played together.

"Hey," I said.

He threw the ball and it bounced off the rim, but he caught it before it sailed over his head. "Hey."

"How are you?"

"Good enough." He threw again, this time making the shot. "How about you?"

I shrugged. "Good enough. On my way to talk to a council witch."

Brody froze before his next throw, then dropped the ball to his hip. "Are you sure that's a good idea?"

"She's on our side. I think. Pretty sure. Going to ask Dad if he wants to come with me."

"To hell with that. Let me come with you. You need someone more willing to throw a punch than Dad is."

I smiled. "I'm more than capable of throwing my own punches, Brody. That's exactly why I need Dad. Someone more willing to play mediator if things get tense. Besides, Mom's going to the hospital, so you'll want to hear what she has to say about Dyl when she gets back."

Brody grumbled in his throat and made another shot. I caught the ball as it bounced towards me.

"Can you do me a favour while I'm out?" I asked, shooting and enjoying the satisfying *swoosh* as it sailed through the net.

"What?"

"Can you check in on Trace a few times? Just to… you know. Send me updates if he wakes up?"

*If he doesn't.*

I couldn't bring myself to say that part, so I caught the ball and threw it again.

"Sure."

"Thanks."

One more throw from me, then I passed the ball back to Brody.

"He'll be okay, you know," my brother said. "He made it pretty clear he's willing to fight to the ends of the earth to keep you safe. That means your heart too. He won't break it on you."

I swallowed around the lump in my throat, then gave my sweaty brother a hug before I left him to his avoidance and headed inside to find Dad.

Instead I found Mom waiting for me just inside the door. She'd showered and changed, and now she stood there in her soft pink shirt and flowy white pants looking like the most uncomfortable person in the world. "Have a minute?"

I checked the time on my phone, nodded, and followed her into the living room, more than a little curious about what she wanted to talk to me about—especially if it made her unable to meet my eye. Worry hadn't hit me yet. She didn't look nervous so much as embarrassed, the kind of look parents get before they talk to their kids about menstruation or sex. Mom was a healer, so she didn't bat an eyelash at talking about periods, and that doubled my curiosity.

"It's about Trace's condition," she said as she gingerly sat on the edge of the loveseat.

I couldn't move fast enough to sit down beside her, my heart racing with anticipation. With *hope*. "You've found something? Was it that idea you had? What is it?"

"In my research, I found a ritual that might help. I didn't bring the book home because I wasn't sure if you'd be interested, but if you are, I'll bring it back with the rest of my supplies."

She was hedging. Why was she hedging? I clenched my hands in my lap to avoid shaking her. My patience was not helped when she cleared her throat and shifted in her seat.

"It's... Well, it's not an easy one. Very intensive. Very

permanent. You might not find it suitable."

I sat closer. "Okay. Permanent is good. We want to make sure the souls stay bound." I frowned and pulled back. "Unless you mean that it would keep the souls permanently bound inside Trace. Because I don't know if that's the solution."

Mom shifted again. "No, that part wouldn't be permanent."

"Okay…" I fell silent, doing my best to wait. Obviously whatever this ritual was, it wasn't pleasant, or she wouldn't have such a hard time with the subject, which meant I shouldn't be in such a rush to hear what it was. But my sanity was hanging by a thread. "If you think this is the best bet to save him, then let's get that book to perform the ritual ASAP. What are we waiting for?"

"Well, you'll have to perform it by yourself. It's very… intimate."

I stilled, flushed, swallowed the sudden heat climbing up my throat. "Intimate?"

Mom pressed her lips together and wiped her palms on her thighs. "Trace has done a wonderful job in binding these souls on his own, but it's next to impossible for one person to contain so much power for too long a time. The fact he's managed it this long is a sign of his strength, and I doubt he could have done it with almost any other type of magic. You might have been able to, creating little pulses of atmospheric energy to keep them caged, but it would have taken a lot out

of you. His telekinetic power seems to have created a sort of…
field that's kept them separate. But no one can keep that kind
of passive magic running forever. Especially if we're dealing
with souls from beyond the wall. That's why he keeps losing
control."

She cleared her throat. "Together, however, I think the two
of you could create something stronger. Something that would
hold the souls in place without too much effort from either of
you until you found a way to release them. Everyone here has
seen the way you two manoeuvre around each other. You trust
each other. Your *magics* trust each other, and that's a key ingre-
dient to this particular spell. It's… It's a ritual that's usually only
cast between… between two people who mean a great deal to
each other."

Her meaning sank in, and my mouth fell open. "You
mean…"

"Yes, all right. We're both adults, and there's no need to be
so uncomfortable about it. This isn't the first time we've had a
conversation about birds and bees."

I held up my hands. "You're the one making this awkward."

She rubbed her forehead. "It wouldn't have been, but the
circumstances have changed a little, haven't they? He's not
exactly able to be part of things." Her eyes widened. "And
no, before you look at me like that, this ritual doesn't require
sex. It's just that, from what I've read, sex tends to be a… side

effect. As I mentioned, it's very intimate."

"A side effect."

"Of the binding."

I blinked at her, not sure what to make of any of this. "Can you please start from the beginning and explain it to me slowly? And clearly? It's a binding ritual? I thought you said we should avoid binding rituals."

"We should avoid binding the souls to Trace. This would bind your magics together—in a way you wouldn't be able to undo. If he makes it through, you'll be tied to each other the rest of your lives. If he doesn't…"

My mouth went dry. "I'd halve my magic, with the other half trapped inside him."

Mom dropped her hand onto mine. "It's a big decision, but this is your option. From what I've been able to find, it's the only option. You can ask that Chip friend of yours if he knows of anything else that might do the trick, even on a more short-term basis, but I worry that if Trace doesn't stop those souls soon, they're going to tear him apart." She pressed her palm against my cheek. "I debated telling you at all, but I don't know what you two have talked about in terms of your future. The way you two act together made me think it's not something either of you would dismiss outright, so I couldn't not give you the choice. He's a good man, Aly. I know you two got off to a difficult start with the whole Dara thing, but he's good for you. You've come into your own in a way I've only ever hoped for you since your healing dreams died, and I see the way his entire face brightens whenever you turn your attention on him. I know you won't rush into anything, and maybe we'll find something else, but at least now you can choose."

I swallowed again, not sure what to say. There were so many questions I needed to ask myself. So many questions I wished I could ask Trace, but at least it was *a* solution.

"All right," I said. "I can't—I *won't*—decide this on my own, but yes. Get the book. Please. And then pray to the goddess Trace wakes up in time for us to decide together."

# Chapter 27
*Trace*

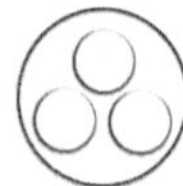

IT WAS LIKE the sun had gone out.

I'd been in darkness, and then the light had come in, a shining beacon of hope and identity. I knew who I was when that light was close by. In its presence, I found myself swimming closer, pressing through the mob of souls trying to haul me back. I gained strength in that light's warmth, and I believed that with some help, I could find my way out of here—safely, without unleashing the spirits swirling inside me.

Then it left. The darkness closed in again and my energy flagged. I forced myself to hold on, knowing the light would be back, knowing I couldn't fail it by disappearing.

But the weight was growing heavier, pulling me down, consuming bits of me that I wasn't sure I could reclaim. All names were gone, and my memories were murky. Everything was being taken over by different memories. Memories of hard labour, of rushing water. Screams, punches thrown.

A sense that these weren't my memories—but were quickly becoming the only self I knew. I didn't even know who the fuck I was, but I knew I had to keep hanging on for *someone*.

*Come back. I'm still here. I'm right fucking here.*

# Chapter 28
*Alyssa*

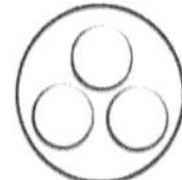

THE DRIVE TO the museum in Almonte was quick and quiet, and I was grateful for one of those things. The million problems I had on my mind had quadrupled after my conversation with Mom, and I would have preferred a bit more time to process what it all meant.

I had a way to help Trace.

That way meant permanently tying myself to a man who'd sworn never to be tied.

I doubted his flirty comments in the cemetery about wooing me and taking the Mooney name could be considered consent for being bound without his knowledge, which meant I couldn't do it. It wasn't an option. Instead, I'd just have to let the souls have him. Let him die and be done with it.

I bonked my head against the window.

"Tough time in there?" Dad asked, shooting me a sympathetic glance from the driver's seat.

"If I say yes, will you ask me a bunch of questions?"

"Not if you don't want me to."

"Then yes. My thoughts are freight trains going at full speed. Lots of crashing into each other, explosions, fires, the works. Not a pretty place."

"Think there will be any survivors?"

"Touch and go at this point, but I'll let you know when the smoke settles."

"Please do. I'll need to know how many sandwiches to order for the funeral."

"All of them. Always all of them. Sandwiches fix everything, don't you know?"

Of course he knew. Dad was always the one making food when shit hit the fan. He was indispensable.

At this time of day, there were plenty of cars in the lot, but since I didn't know which car belonged to the woman we were supposed to meet, Dad found a spot and we started walking towards the mill.

Not far along the path—about the spot where Trace and I had found the first tripwire on the night of our arrest—my phone rang. I pulled it out of my jacket pocket to find *Private Number* written across the screen. Since there was only one unknown number that I could think of that would call me, I drew to a stop.

"I need to get this," I said to my dad. "You keep going, and I'll catch up. Won't be long."

He continued, and I stepped off the path to get out of people's way and answered before Chip could hang up. "Hey."

"Cheers, good," he greeted. "Trace awake?"

I thought of Trace lying in bed, unresponsive, seemingly asleep. "Not yet. No change whatsoever."

He let out a heavy breath. "Shit."

At the particular note of his cursing, I tensed. That was not the tone of a man just checking in on his friend. "Why?"

"Hazel's on the move. Not sure what she's doing yet, and Ameline hasn't been able to figure it out either, but the wicked witch is picking up pieces. Might be to go underground, or maybe to take another stab at those souls, but she's been all across the city, meeting with people. Making phone calls to numbers I can't source. It's like she knows I'm watching and is doing everything she can to keep me out."

It made sense. Everything she'd done from the start of this had been behind the scenes. Just overt enough to lure us in without giving us enough information to make a solid plan. Exactly the kind of control one might expect from a woman with government ties. "Do we know who the SMOAC contact is yet?"

A malicious chuckle sounded down the line and raised goosebumps on my arms. "We do. His name is Tyler Litz. A security officer, been there about twelve years. As soon as I made the connection, I dug through his history, and it turns out he was one of the officers who drove Hazel north to Moongrave nine years ago. I guess they hit it off. They've been in regular communication since then, and I suspect he was involved in the decision to bring her back to Ottawa. The story was that they needed her help on some investigation in a supposed spirit magic ring in the United States."

"He was among the team to go pick her up from Moongrave, I'm guessing?"

"You got it. Then whoops, she slipped the rope somewhere en route."

"Fantastic." I pulled the phone away from my ear and sent a text to Madison with Tyler's name and to ask what his deal was. "I'll see what I can find out about him on my end. What else do we know?"

"Nothing yet, but Am and I are keeping tabs on Hazel. As soon as we have something new, I'll let you know."

"Thanks." I hesitated. "I'm about to meet with a council witch, partner of the one Hazel's people killed. Not sure what she can do to help us, but seems like a good idea to gather allies where we can."

"Want me to poke around?"

"Pen Holt."

"Bah, no need for me to look anything up, she's clean. Boring as fuck—almost as boring as you—but yeah, not one of Hazel's. At least you'll be safe out there today. Trace would kill me otherwise."

At the mention of his friend, my thoughts tripped back to my conversation with Mom, to the confusion and tangled mess in my head. I was on the phone with the only person who knew Trace as well as Trace himself did. I'd never get a better opportunity to ask for input. Even if Chip was more likely to hang up than help me out.

"Hey, Chip?" There was silence on the line, which at least told me he was still there. The question dried on my tongue. What was I going to ask him? Should I bind myself to his BFF without his permission? My stomach twisted into knots. "You know I care for Trace a lot, right?"

"Gag. Yeah, Cheers. You two made that pretty clear the first time you walked into my house. Trace doesn't bring people to my house. He knows better. He broke the rule for you—one of many. But really? Whatever's going on between you? I don't want to know the details."

I chewed on my lip and stared down at my shoe, thinking of Trace's unconscious face. "Why did he do that? Break those rules for me?"

When Chip didn't answer, I was ready for him to end the

call, not wanting to get deeper into this conversation than he already was. But maybe he heard something in my question or got a sense of the reason I was asking, because he let out a heavy sigh.

"Listen, I'm not going to speak for him, all right? If you haven't exchanged your sentiments, it's really not my place. But from an outside perspective and as someone who's known the guy for a good long while, here's what I'll say—he was a wreck after Hazel. He slept his way across the country without a backwards glance at any of those women because, as far as he was concerned, his chest place was a no-go zone. Nine years, Cheers. That's a long time to swear you're done with a good chunk of the population. Then he met you. A few hours in your company, and he's bending over backwards to make sure you live to see the next day. And you didn't even sleep together. So I have no fucking clue what you did to make him do a one-eighty on his entire life philosophy, but the fact that he's sticking with you tells me it isn't a temporary thing. He made a choice. You're that choice. Do not ask me why."

My heart thrummed against my ribs, my pulse shaking in my throat, in my wrists.

"We done?" Chip asked.

"Yeah, we're done."

"Cool."

The line clicked, and he was gone. I slid the phone back

into my bag and leaned against the tree behind me with a heavy exhale. Chip had helped, but I was relieved I didn't have to make the decision here and now. I had time to weigh the consequences of such a huge move—consequences for both of us. But the clock was ticking, and I wouldn't have the option to put things off for much longer.

First, though, I had a council witch to talk to and a SMOAC officer to pin down.

# Chapter 29
### *Alyssa*

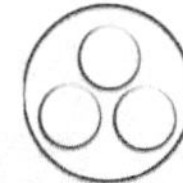

I RUSHED TO catch up with Dad and found him standing with Pen near the damaged pavilion. The area had been roped off for repairs, and I couldn't help my sense of guilt that we'd been the ones to shut down a beloved tourist spot.

But hey, it could have been worse. We could have allowed Hazel to open the door to the supernatural realm and let the mundanes deal with those repercussions. Really, they were coming out ahead.

"Good, you're here," Pen greeted, seemingly unimpressed by my lateness.

"I just got a lead on who's been helping Hazel," I replied, not letting her bully me into apologizing—while also leaving out the personal crisis I was facing. "Looks like the council's not the only organization going through some staffing issues."

A group of people out for a stroll along the walking trail came by. We fell silent until they passed, but the crowd made it clear this spot was too out in the open for such a magical conversation.

"Follow me," Pen said, and she led the way down the wood-framed steps, past the mill, over the bridge, and into the forested area.

Dad walked along with us, looking content to be out for the exercise, and I was more grateful that he was here than I'd realized I would be. Pen did not cut a likeable figure, and I would have to work hard to keep a civil tongue in my head.

Ten minutes later, we stood off the beaten path in the middle of the forest. The trees were widely spaced, the ground padded with a thick layer of leaves, and I was pretty sure no one would be able to sneak up on us.

"All right, talk," Pen said.

I crossed my arms and raised my eyebrow. "We're here because I proposed cooperation. You're not in charge. You're on the back foot because Hazel has you boxed in and you know your hands are tied. So let's cut the attitude, all right?"

Pen clenched her teeth, her blue eyes blazing, but when she didn't argue with me, I understood that her frustration was the only validation I'd get that I was right.

"I'm sorry about your partner," I said. "He was an asshole,

but he was a dedicated asshole."

She dropped her gaze. "He didn't deserve what they did to him. We've been working for months to figure out the source of the corruption. It started so subtly we didn't notice it. Paperwork going missing, decisions getting signed off on that didn't make any sense. Council witches being dispatched to areas with no clear reason why. Eventually, Al believed all these things were to distract us from what was happening here in the capital. So we came to Ottawa to poke around and noticed the signs of increased spirit magic. From there, it wasn't much of a leap to point the finger at Hazel, but by then, it was too late. It has to have been going on for longer than that—since before she left Moongrave—but we can't prove it yet." She met my eye. "But that's an internal problem."

I held up my hands. "I don't want your problem. Hazel's our problem. Whatever's going on in the council, that's up to you." I shoved my hands into my pockets. "Have you heard of Tyler Litz? He's a Smoker, a security officer. But we think he's the person who helped Hazel escape prison."

"Litz." A furrow formed between Pen's brows. "I do know the name. It's been on some paperwork for us in the past. We've worked a few joint"—her eyes flew wide—"son of a bitch, he was in the office the other day, picking up some witches who were due to be handed over to the department. Hours before we found Al. That fucker."

Her nostrils flared, and green elemental magic swept over her hands. She balled her fists at her sides and closed her eyes until her magic settled. "We'll deal with him too. He's mine to take down."

Again, I didn't argue. I understood the need for justice for her friend. It was why I wouldn't let the council be the ones to put Hazel in the ground.

I looked at Dad to see if he had anything to add, but he was staring up into the trees as though we were out here for a nature hike. I knew better than to think he wasn't paying attention. For now he was willing to let me take the lead.

"All right, here's the deal," I said. "We know what Hazel's after. She's trying to find a half-open doorway in the unseen wall so she can open it and move her whole operation into Meril's realm." Pen stiffened, fear trickling into her bright blue eyes. "Obviously, we don't want to see that happen. The Mooney family is going to stop her. What we need from you is assurances from the non-corrupt council that we'll be free to do that however we need to."

She settled her hands on her hips and opened her mouth, and I read refusal in every line around her eyes.

I cut her off before she could say anything. "You can't be sure who's loyal to the council and who's going to screw you over. You might think you know, but you don't really. It makes way more sense for you to focus on that little problem first, don't you think?"

"Listen, Miss Mooney, Al warned me about you. Said you had some really strong opinions and no small sense of entitlement. Trace Wyatt might think he's immune to prosecution because he's Canada's bounty hunter darling, but that's not the case. And you're not protected by either your relationship to him or your connection to a respected witch family."

"Entitled?" I repeated. "Excuse me very much, I do not think I'm *entitled*. I wouldn't be in this situation at all if you'd—"

Dad cleared his throat. "While I'm sure arguments could be made for either side"—I sputtered, but he talked over me—"that's not why we're here. No one in the Mooney family believes they're above the law, Ms. Holt. We're well aware we follow the same rules as everyone else. We also make it a point of family pride to uphold those rules in this city when the council is too busy with the needs of the rest of the province to do so."

Was that a subtle jab? I wanted to give Dad a high five, but he hadn't finished yet.

"We can all agree Hazel is a problem that needs to be dealt with. We have the means, the people, and the knowledge in place to take on that risk. What we're asking of the council is support. Just as you've always done."

Always, sure. After we did all the work, they loved to sweep in and take the credit.

Pen looked between us before settling her attention on my father as the more reasonable of the two. Not an unfair assessment. "You're right that the council is in a difficult position, and we do *appreciate* your willingness to assist us in keeping the peace here in Ottawa."

I sneered at the trouble she seemed to have in expressing her appreciation, but Dad shot me a look, so I pressed my lips together and listened.

"As such, I agree that we can hold back and provide cleanup services after you've dealt with her." She snarled. "That should give me time to crush the problem in our ranks. We're close. My hope is that by end of day tomorrow, I'll have the highest-ranking points of corruption corralled and noosed. If that's the case, perhaps we can provide more support than simply showing up at the end."

She shot me a knowing look, and I shrugged, unwilling to change my opinion until the council proved they deserved it.

"Excellent," Dad said. "Then I thank you for taking the time to meet with us."

Finally, Pen appeared to deflate a little. "Thank you for reaching out. It's not the greatest feeling knowing you've been isolated by someone smarter than you are."

"She's not smarter," I said. "She thinks she is, and she got the leap on us, but we're on to her now. She won't be ahead that much longer."

Pen and I exchanged a look, and I recognized the fire in her eyes as the same one I'd seen in the mirror often enough over the past few weeks. "You're right. Thanks for that. And thanks for the tip on Litz. It'll feel good to tear that fucker down as well."

She held out her hand, and I didn't hesitate to shake it. Dad did the same, and then Pen was gone, taking wide strides with her long legs back the way we'd come.

I stared at Dad. "That's something at least."

"Not a lot of something, but something." He shrugged. "They don't have enough power to act, but they will have enough power to clean up the mess."

I snorted. "Isn't that always the case."

"Seems to be." He rubbed my back. "It all comes back to the root of the problem."

"We need to deal with Hazel."

Which meant I needed to deal with Trace.

# Chapter 30
*Alyssa*

DAD AND I got home to find Mom getting ready to go out. Without saying a word, she pulled a book from her backpack and handed me a large, leather-bound tome, a page in the middle marked with a slip of paper.

My mouth dried, but I accepted the book. "Is he all right?"

Mom set her shoulders, sliding into Healer Mode, which sent a flurry of panic through my heart. "He's still breathing, but the magic is taking hold quickly. I was able to check his vitals—they're strong—and I did what I could to keep his body comfortable, but I don't think we have much more time. I need to go run some errands, but when I get home, if things haven't changed, we should talk about the hospital."

I swallowed and chewed on my lips to keep the lump in my

throat from crushing my windpipe. It took a few attempts to clear it before I could thank her. She gave me a hug, then turned to Dad. "Would you come with me? You can tell me how the meeting went with Pen." She looked back at me. "Brody's at the hospital with Dyl, and Gramps is still at the pub. You know how to reach us if you need anything."

Dad kissed my forehead. "Good luck, kiddo."

I watched them leave, fighting a wave of panic at finding myself alone in the house with an unconscious Trace, with no one to help me if anything went wrong. But nothing would go wrong. Or at least, nothing I couldn't handle. And if I kept telling myself that, maybe I'd believe it. Finally, I got my brain under control and trudged up to my bedroom with the book, once again closing myself inside.

The setting sun cast a golden glow through the curtain, giving a warm, magical radiance to the dust floating through the room. Obviously I needed to open a window and get some air in here.

I settled on the bed and let myself get a good look at Trace. Mom was right: He was fading fast. His colour was worse, an unhealthy pallor soaking into his skin, his pulse quicker, his breaths shallow. A yellow glow followed the blue of his veins up from his chest, his cheeks, into the pale skin around his eyes. I had to believe he was fighting hard, but the souls were winning. Either his heart would give out with the strain, or the next time he opened his eyes, there would be nothing of him left.

"Hey," I said. "How are you doing in there?"

The faintest hitch in his breath, a grimace of pain.

Inhaling deeply, I set the book Mom had brought me on my lap and flipped open the heavy pages. "Mom thinks she's found a way I can help you. A ritual she says is kind of intense. Something we should probably talk about first."

I skimmed through the spell. My cheeks flushed as I read certain passages of it. Intimate, indeed.

"It would weave our powers together at their source," I explained to Trace. "We'd still have access to our individual magic, but working them together would be much easier. On the other hand, it would mean a piece of me would permanently live inside you, and the other way around. So, you know, that's a thing. We still haven't officially gone on a date yet, but that's so passé, right?"

I wished I knew what the extent of the impact would be. Would I be forcing him to want to be with me? To stay with me?

"I can't make this choice by myself, Trace. Not ethically, anyway. You've made it clear the whole *relationship* thing is new to you. This would be going from zero to a hundred and twenty. So I'm going to wait and pray you wake up." I set my hand on his arm and gave him a desperate shake. "Please wake up."

I closed the book and set it aside. There had to be another way to slow things down until Trace and I could talk about long-term solutions. Even if it meant bundling him into the car and taking him to the Peaview so they could keep his body going until we had something to help him. I wouldn't make decisions for him that he might hate me for later.

With my mind made up, I rose from the bed to pace the room and give myself space to think, but a strangled noise caught my ear. I looked over my shoulder at Trace. Was he paler now? There was certainly a layer of sweat on his brow that hadn't been there when I'd come in. I rested my hand on his chest. His heartbeat was rapid and erratic, and as I watched, his muscles flexed and released, as though he were bracing against something. The tendons in his throat went taut, his eyes slid back and forth under his closed lids, and his hands clenched at his sides.

Whatever battle he was fighting, he was losing. I was as sure of it as if he were awake to tell me. I pumped some healing magic into him, wanting him to know I was here, to give him courage and support to stand on his own, but a different magic pushed against me. The veins in his hands glowed yellow, and the light spread up his arms, his neck.

The souls were taking over, and I was out of time.

"Fuck, fuck, fuck, fuck."

I hurled myself off the bed and reached for my phone to

call Mom, or Gramps, or anyone who might help. But what could they do? None of us could climb into Trace's head and drag him out. Even if we raced him to the hospital, the best doctors couldn't keep these souls at bay. If he even lasted long enough to get to the hospital. The only option in front of us— the only option I had—was this ritual.

Cursing, I slammed my phone down, locked my bedroom door, and rushed back to where I'd left the book.

"I hate this, Trace. I fucking hate this. Please wake up so I don't need to make this choice for both of us."

Tears blurred my vision as I flipped the pages back to the start of the ritual. I set the book beside us and climbed onto Trace's lap, straddling his hips.

I couldn't rush this. For so many reasons, I had to set my panic aside and come into this as calm and assured as he needed me to be.

"Okay," I breathed. "The ritual calls for both parties to work together, but I guess we can skip over all the suggested ways for the partners to get comfortable in the ritual state of mind because, unfortunately, that's not an option." I groaned. "Goddess, Trace, I pray there's enough of you left in there to work with me on this, but I'm only taking it so far. You have to wake up."

I glanced at the page again, grimacing at the insistence of skin on skin. It was apparently a key factor to make the spell work. But I had my limits. This man was unconscious, unable to give consent, which meant I was walking on very thin ice.

I settled for removing my shirt and lifting his to bare his stomach, then stretched out across him so our chests pressed together. His skin was warm, feverish, and there was no mistaking the way the yellow magic had centred on his middle, spreading its power out from where he'd kept it bound and where that binding was fading. The veins that had made their way up his face and wrapped around his eyes were glowing brighter, and more were spreading down his stomach to his legs.

Breathing through my fear, I shifted the book so I could spread my weight and prop my elbow beside him while I continued to read each step.

"Both parties need to allow the other one in to complete the binding. That's something at least," I said around a grimace. It meant I could only take this ritual so far without Trace's cooperation. But it also meant that if he wasn't aware enough to work with me, to make his informed decision to agree to the binding, then the ritual would fail and he would die.

As I read, I rubbed Trace's arm, desperate for him to show some sign that he knew I was here.

My stomach was tied up in knots, and I had to suck in breath after breath to ensure I didn't vomit all over the bed. I didn't know what to do. I didn't know what the right choice was, but what I did know was that the idea of the rest of my life without Trace left me hollow. The way he looked at me as though I were a fresh-baked cinnamon bun, the way he ran his fingers through my hair. The way he called me princess. To lose that—to never experience any of those things again when there was something I could do to save him…

And what about the rest of the world? Trace had been so much more than a vehicle for two-century-old souls. He'd captured dangerous criminals across the country for almost a decade. He was a national hero, brought to this point because he'd sacrificed himself for my sake.

All these reasons to force the issue and save him, but I could only be so selfish. I would throw him the rope, but that was as far as I'd go. If he was too far gone to grab hold of it, I'd stop. For my sake, for his. Either he woke up and agreed to this, or I'd have to let him go.

A sob caught in my throat, and I forced myself to read through the next steps, then closed the book, closed my eyes, and laid my head on Trace's chest, needing the contact. Not only for the magic but for my sanity. Trace had become such a source of comfort and reassurance, and even in his current state, there was no one I wanted to lean on more.

Focused on his racing heartbeat and the flush of heat under his skin, I sank into my magic, searching through the waves of faint, shimmering lilac until I located the source of the power coursing through me. It was bound to everything I was. To my genetic makeup, to my personality, my past. It was as much a part of me as the blood that ran through my veins—and I was ready to share it.

I released a slow breath. "I'm going to draw on my magic and nudge it towards you. When you feel it, I want you to take it, okay? I'll try to talk you through what I'm doing, but once I focus on my magic, I might not be able to. So just… if you're still there, please watch for me. Please, please, *please* still be there."

With my thoughts on Trace, it was easy to coax my magic out. I focused on where that swirl of yellow power was centred and pressed mine towards him, offering it to him. I felt the moment it soaked into his skin and mingled with the silver and yellow magics currently fighting beneath me. I sensed the moment those powers stilled, confused by the new addition, and then how they curled around mine, testing it, exploring it.

My eyes flew open with a gasp, but I wasn't looking at the room around me. I couldn't. I was too caught up in the wild sensations of someone else's power stroking mine, surrounding it, enveloping it. I was no longer in my body but inside Trace's, stretching within him, nudging his power, urging him to acknowledge me.

And the closeness—it was like nothing I'd ever experienced before. It was beyond intimate.

Enough so that I retreated. The sensation was too much,

too intense. Too invasive.

Trace's body lurched again, and again that yellow power spread. With my power still inside him, I felt the souls pulse and grow, getting stronger, doing everything they could to absorb Trace's beautiful silver magic.

Gritting my teeth, I pressed in a bit further, focusing on the silver and ignoring the yellow. The souls weren't what needed to accept me—Trace was. He had to notice me. I needed him to *notice me*.

He pushed me away, a brutal shove, an instinctive rejection to protect himself.

A moan of frustration escaped me, but I refused to back off.

"Come on, Trace. I need you. Please accept me. Please let me in. Please let me save your life."

But when he rejected me again, I couldn't help but wonder if I'd already lost him.

# Chapter 31
## *Trace*

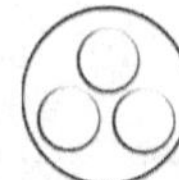

I DIDN'T UNDERSTAND what was happening. The souls were overpowering me, crushing me under their growing weight. I'd fought them off as long as I could, but I was so tired, and the light was gone, and I was lost in the dark clawing for a way out.

And then the light was back, and for a brief, blessed moment, I felt my strength and motivation returning. I wasn't alone anymore, and if I wasn't alone, maybe I stood a chance.

But then it wasn't only me and the souls in here. A third presence had slid between us, asking to be let in, and the only thing I could think to do was eject it. I didn't need more forces confusing the problem. I needed to focus.

I tried to remember the face I was fighting for, but it had

left me along with every other thought. All that existed was my magic and the souls. The entire universe could disappear, and it wouldn't matter to me as long as I came out on top. Or at least kept the souls from consuming me.

The third power returned, wedging itself between me and the souls, and I shoved it away again. What was happening? Had the souls found a way to divide and conquer? Was I now fighting two enemies?

My flagging strength couldn't handle it. I was exhausted. If there was another foe in here with us, I might as well give up right now. Eat my regrets, swallow my remorse, and retreat into the darkness.

Except this new force wasn't dark.

The reminder of that light drew me back, and when the third power stretched inside me again—a strangely pleasurable sensation—I paid attention to it. Its signature was… It was familiar.

*I didn't know you witches could recognize each other like that.*

A woman with star-filled eyes had said that to me once.

Reverie.

Fae. Succubus. Helping me to save…

*Alyssa.*

Her name came to me at the same time I recognized the magical signature that slid through my veins as though the woman herself had slipped her fingers through my pores to take up residence under my skin.

It felt incredible. I'd never experienced anything like this in my life, and I wanted more of it.

I reached for her with my magic, running it alongside hers, and with every contact, the sensations grew more delicate, more intense. Like dark chocolate syrup dripping over a chilled strawberry. Like champagne trickling down the side of a crystal flute.

Her magic coiled around me, embracing me, and I returned the favour, trailing magical fingers down her magical spine, until it was like I could *see* her in the weave of power. The souls were still there, still straining to overpower me, but it was no longer only me in here, and Alyssa's power was stronger for being well rested. She spread herself inside me, taking up more space, pushing the souls to the fringes of my being. It wasn't a solution, but it was such a sweet reprieve that I felt my body shudder.

My body. There it was. For too long, I'd lost awareness of it, but now I sensed warmth on my skin, felt the weight of something on my chest. My senses remained dulled, my thoughts too scattered and pulled in too many directions, but it was a start compared to where I'd been since the souls had dragged me under.

Alyssa. My light. Proving yet again that she was the only beacon that mattered.

Her magic shifted, this time weaving through mine, inter-twining with it as though forming a knot and pulling my magic into her as much as hers had settled in me. I didn't know what she was doing, but I trusted her. I trusted that she'd found a way to guide me home—to bring me back without letting these souls loose. Whatever it took, I would do it.

Together we strung our power together, creating a net that nothing would be able to unravel. It was so similar to the way we'd worked our spells in the waking world that the effort came naturally, even if it felt so much deeper, more erotic. As we went, the souls were guided back into my centre. Their power waned and ours grew until, for the first time in what might have been forever, I felt in control of myself.

My body shuddered again, this time with a growing need. I became aware of a cotton bed cover under my back, a pillow under my head. Of soft hands coiling through my fingers where my hands lay on the bed.

The scent of sweet aloe vera. The soft tickle of long hair on my chest.

All these little details combined with the sensation of Alyssa's magic wending its way through mine hurled me out of my head. I opened my eyes, blinked against the too-bright golden light shining into the room, and searched for her.

I found her draped across me. Her bare shoulders were rounded where her forehead rested on my chest, her ponytail trailing over one side of her neck to tickle my ribs. I pulled one hand free of hers to stroke my fingers down her cheek, and she sat up with a gasp, staring down at me in wonder.

"You're here," she whispered. "You're back." Her eyes widened. "We can stop. I don't think it's permanent yet. I can pull my magic back. We can—"

I bumped my hips and sat up, wrapping my arms around her so she stayed straddled across my lap. When she opened her mouth to keep going on about whatever she was going on about, I silenced her with a kiss. I needed to kiss her. I needed it as much as I needed air.

Her bare chest brushed against my T-shirt, and I ran my hands down her spine, just as I'd done with her magic. She shivered against me, and her hips tensed, as though she longed to grind against me but was stopping herself. She didn't need to stop. Goddess, I did not want her to stop.

Even as we kissed, I sensed her magic pulsing inside me and nearly hit my peak right there.

She pulled away from me, her gaze serious, wary, but as heated as my blood—just on the point of boiling. "How do you feel?"

"Incredible," I said, catching her mouth again. "High as the fucking sky. Whatever you're doing, keep doing it."

Once more she pulled away, earning herself a low growl of frustration from me. I needed more. I needed all of her.

"By the sounds of it, you're capable of dubious consent at best." She caught her bottom lip between her teeth. "I'm going to pull back. We can stop the ritual until you're clearheaded enough to talk about it."

Ritual?

I blinked, trying to catch up.

Only now did I realize what she was doing. I'd heard of rituals like this. Rituals between lovers to merge and amp up their power. I'd been right that she was working to support the binding I'd created for the souls, but that binding would be permanent. This feeling I had of her existing within me, of me existing within her, of her being as much a part of me as the souls currently were, would stay that way forever. No undoing it without severing her power. Halving her strength and mine.

*We can stop*, she'd said.

We could. I was awake, and she'd bolstered my power, at least for the moment. We could end this ritual, I could attempt to reinforce the bindings on my own, and we'd be no worse off than we were before.

Maybe it would be the responsible decision. I'd only known Alyssa for a total of a few weeks. After years of being on my own and swearing off all other emotional, romantic attachments, I'd thrown myself into circumstances with this woman that tested that rule on a regular basis.

The practical part of me knew the smart thing would be to

disengage. To continue on my own as I'd done, and if I wanted to see where things went with Alyssa, then fine. We could take our time getting to know each other. Maybe I could take her out to dinner on an actual date.

But I hadn't gotten where I was in life by being practical. And although my history would suggest the results were fifty-fifty about that being a huge fucking mistake, I couldn't look at my life right now and see it that way. Yes, we were facing a potential supernatural civil war if Hazel got that doorway open, but if Corrick hadn't tracked down that amulet and kicked things off to begin with, I never would have met Alyssa.

Everything came back to her, and I'd already accepted there was nowhere else in the world I would rather be.

But this wasn't only about me. She'd given me the choice, but what did she want? Was she offering to do this only to save me, knowing what she would be agreeing to? What she might be sacrificing?

The expression in her eyes was inscrutable. Pain and desire, confusion and concern. I opened my mouth to ask her, but the words caught in my throat. Fear of rejection? An inability to crunch all my feelings and opinions and decisions into a few comprehensible words? Whatever the reason, they wouldn't move. I looped my fingers through hers and slid my magic between us, continuing the weave we'd started. When I reached the end of my loop, I paused and left it open to her whether she wanted to join me.

She stared into my eyes, uncertainty lurking in the green. Her kiss-swollen lips were parted, and it took everything in me not to pick up where we'd left off. I wouldn't. Not until I knew where we were headed.

Questions filled her expression, and to assure her of my answer, I gave a slight tug on her magic, securing the portion of the knot I'd tied. This was what I wanted. To keep going. With her.

Tears spilled over her cheeks as she, just as slowly, finished the knot, tying off that section of the binding so we could move on to the next. With every pass of our magic, every tightening of the bond, my skin grew warmer and my lower stomach grew tighter, more blood rushing south than remained in my head. I wrapped my arms around Alyssa, needing the contact, needing the friction, though I hated that it was such a tease.

A tiny sound escaped the back of her throat, and she squeezed her eyes shut. I watched her skin flush, the red tint creeping up her chest, over her neck, across her face to spill into her cheeks. Her fingers curled into my shirt at the shoulders, and I held her more tightly against me, the bare skin of her stomach squeezed against mine. It wasn't enough.

Keeping one arm around her, I pulled off my T-shirt and threw it on the floor. At the increased contact, our magics seemed to grow even closer, the weave that much tighter, that much easier to bind.

I kissed her shoulder, gliding my lips over her soft skin. The scent of her was overwhelming. I would never get enough of it. Of her. Of her magic.

Her nails dug into my back, creating a flash of pain that felt so amazing my thoughts blacked out. I gripped her waist, ran my fingers up her sides, skirted around the edge of her breast. She arched her back, inviting me, and goddess help me, I accepted. With a flick of my fingers, I released the hooks of her bra and slid the straps down her shoulders before tossing the whole thing away. The weight of her breast filled my palm, and her nipple hardened under my thumb.

A whimper escaped her as she lost the battle and rolled her hips against mine, creating such delicious friction I released a groan of frustration when she stopped.

"We—we don't need to—" she rasped. "It's not officially part of the ritual."

Was this woman mad? Did she not know the depth of what I felt for her?

"Fuck the ritual. This feeling has nothing to do with whatever spell we're working. It's the feeling of your magic winding inside me. From the first time my power played with yours, I've been addicted to it. It's otherworldly how good you feel inside me." I stilled my hold on her. "But if you want to stop, we don't have to—"

Her mouth was on mine, her tongue invading my lips, her hunger melding so perfectly with my starvation that we devoured each other as I rolled her onto her back. With little effort, I tossed my sweatpants onto the floor, then set to work unbuttoning her jeans, pulling down the zipper. She butted in when I took too long, tearing her pants and underwear off her and throwing them off the bed to join mine. I trailed my fingers over the cat paw prints tattooed down her hip, nudged her legs apart, and sank between her thighs, her beautiful skin so smooth and soft and so fucking perfect that I had to take a moment to savour the view.

"Goddess you're beautiful."

I bent to kiss the inside of her wrist where she cupped my face, her forearm, her shoulder. Then I ducked my head and sucked one of those perfect nipples between my lips, glorying in the way Alyssa's body responded. The sounds she made, the way her body moved—everything was perfect.

And all the while, our magics played. They continued the binding without our input, as naturally as if they'd been created to work together, and I found myself wondering about fate and destiny. Inevitability. As our magics tightened, the binding around the souls tightened as well, the cage thickening, growing more stable and ensuring all that dangerous power remained contained.

When the final knot was tied, I slid inside Alyssa. She

clawed at my back, releasing a muffled moan into my shoulder. I hooked my hand under her thigh, drawing her knee up around my hip. She was everything I'd ever dreamed about. Everything I'd ever longed for. My magic had been incomplete until I'd met her, and only now did I appreciate how much I'd been missing.

With gentle thrusts, I worked myself deeper, and she met every roll of my hips, her breaths growing more ragged, her noises desperate, as though I still wasn't close enough. I captured her mouth with mine and gave her what she was silently pleading for, driving myself home as my vision burst with stars and our magic surged around us.

# Chapter 32
*Alyssa*

I'D BEEN RAISED embracing my magic. Learning it. Controlling it. Coming to know it as well as I knew the swell of my moods and the shape of my body.

In this moment, I realized I'd known nothing at all.

With Trace wrapped around me, inside and out, I felt new. Exactly the same and completely unfamiliar all at once.

His body moved with mine, his skin as slick with sweat as mine was with desire, and I clasped him to me as though the smallest gap of space were a crime. He braced himself on his forearm beside my head, and I watched the flex of his biceps, the lines of his muscles across his chest. My gaze travelled up his neck, where the veins of yellow light had disappeared, and up to his beautiful violet eyes, once again streaked with silver.

Beautiful. Perfect. Mine.

I kissed him, keeping my eyes on his, never wanting to look away again. He was mine, and I was his, and there would never be any separating us.

The thought should have sent me into a panic. I'd bound myself to a man I hardly knew. We were permanently linked in our efforts to save him. What if I hated the way he ate soup? What if he grumbled every time I threw on the same sitcom for the fifteenth time in a row?

But the fear never came. There was only a deep certainty that I'd made the only decision I could, and I would savour the good and accept the bad, and we would make the most of whatever future we had together.

At least now we had a future. Even if only for a few days.

Trace thrust into me again, and my breath caught as my pleasure climbed higher. I wrapped my legs around his waist and kept him against me, needing him deep, needing more of him. Always more. I pulsed out with my magic, and his responded, tying together around us in swirls of silver and purple, and the brush of the two sent shivers rolling through me, adding another sensation to our lovemaking that was wholly new to me.

His eyes rolled back as he felt it too, and I did it again, driving us both higher. A growl escaped his throat, and he kissed me, just as hungry now as he'd been before, and the roll of his hips, the crashing wave of his body, moved faster, more erratically. I gave into it, revelling in every shift. I ran my fingers down his back, grabbed his firm ass, pulled him deeper into me. I nipped on his ear as he trailed his mouth down my neck.

In all the weeks we'd danced around each other, wondering what our first time would be like, I'd never imagined this level of desperation. I'd thought we might take it slow, exploring each other, discovering the secrets the other had to offer, but I had no time for that sentimentality today. The eroticism of that ritual, the heightened sensations of our magic, made my very bones scream now, *now*, *NOW!*

I crested the peak and tumbled over the edge with a scream that Trace caught between his lips. My entire body shuddered, falling again and again and again, and I held on as Trace rode towards his own end with a madness that gave away the depth of his need. His muscles tensed as he buried his face in the crook of my neck, and we both sagged into the bed covers.

His breaths were heavy, his body was heavy, but I didn't urge him to move. I wrapped my arms around his neck and kissed the top of his head. Then again on his forehead, then on his nose when he looked up at me, and finally on his mouth.

He kissed me back, this time slower, tender. The heat in his gaze was gone—though the desire was still there—and I stared into the hues of his eyes that I'd come to know almost as well as my own.

"I love you." I hadn't realized I was going to say it until the words were out, but there was no panic, no wish to draw them back in.

It'd be too late now anyway.

His smile was warm and filled his eyes with such intensity that I knew what was coming before his lips formed the shapes. "I love you too."

"Phew. That could have gone badly."

His smile widened into a grin as he kissed me again. "Normally, I would have preferred to tell you *before* we tied our magics together." His gaze softened. "But I'm glad you took the initiative. Thank you for saving me."

I brushed his hair out of his face. He needed a haircut; it was getting a bit long. "Thank you for trusting me." The worry I'd felt when I'd started the ritual returned, and I looked away from him, staring deeply into the spreading shadows of my room. "I'm also sorry. You weren't conscious, and your body was giving out, and I feel so bad for assuming that you—"

He shifted his weight fully onto his arm so he could use his other hand to guide my face back to his. The slight movement caused him to shift inside me as well, and I sucked in a breath at the wave of pleasure and slowly rising return of my earlier need.

"No apologies, princess. You were the only thing keeping me going in here." He tapped the side of his head. "Everything else was gone. There was only you. Only your light guiding me home. I told you that, remember? I meant it, and now I know it for certain. You are everything I need."

My throat tightened, and I held on to him as he rolled onto his side. He pulled out of me as he did, and a whimper of disappointment slipped from between my lips. I felt empty without him, like a void had been formed. Yet my eyes widened as his magic surged within me, replacing that void with something else—a different kind of pleasure. Deeper, visceral.

Trace chuckled, his violet eyes darkening. "Well, this will be fun."

I narrowed my eyes at him and returned the attack, sliding my magic over his, tickling it, teasing it. His breath caught, his lips parted, and his length stirred. "Holy shit."

I didn't stop, curious to see how far this new connection might take us. He exhaled heavily and rolled onto his back, one hand fisted against his forehead, the other curling into my covers. I swirled the magic around us, sent it burrowing deeper into his, then lightly trailed against it. The sensations were intense. Like the softest, coolest breeze against bare skin. A feathery touch. A soft breath.

My body responded along with Trace's, all the satisfaction of a moment ago drifting away under this fresh surge of arousal.

We had things to do, people to end, worlds to save, but

right now, I didn't care about any of it. There was only this newly formed bond, only us. I rolled on top of Trace, settled my weight over his hips, and stroked myself along his length. He grabbed my hips and dug his fingers in as he arched his back, pressing himself more firmly against me. His eyes slitted open, giving me a glimpse of the violet lurking beneath, and I bent down to kiss him as I angled myself to take him inside me again.

This time, I rolled my hips to take him all the way on the first go, and he groaned as he thrust into me, driving deeper. I watched the flex of his stomach, relieved to find no yellow seeping through his skin. Curious, I homed in on the magic inside him and was awed by the magical net I discovered there. It was flawless. Tightly woven with no gaps for the yellow to seep through. Yet when I pressed myself into the net to see what existed beyond, there they were. All those souls, waiting, sleeping. If they were frustrated at being yet again bound, I got no sense of it.

"Come back," Trace said, luring me out of our power into my bedroom. I smiled down at him, happy to be exactly where I was, then gasped as he stroked my magic with his, raising goosebumps all over my body. He eyed my breasts hungrily. "Oh yeah, that's going to be really fun."

He sat up and gripped me to him, and I held on tight as we took each other to another, higher peak.

# Chapter 33
*Trace*

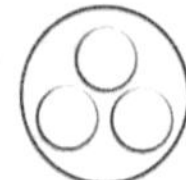

THE SUN HAD set and our bodies were beyond sated by the time Alyssa and I finally curled up against each other under her bright purple comforter. Her frame moulded perfectly against mine, the first time we'd done this flesh against flesh, and I held her tightly, not wanting to give up this moment even as my thoughts turned down darker streets.

Especially as they did. Because they had no pleasant directions to head in until we solved the problem of Hazel.

"We need to lure her in somewhere," I said as I nuzzled Alyssa's ear.

She hugged my arms. "I know. I've been thinking about how we can best do that, and the only idea I've come up with is that we find another badly sealed doorway. According to Chip, she's been checking out other locations, probably to see which one would be easiest to open." Her shoulders tensed against me. "I was also thinking we could use this to our advantage to help you."

"How do you mean?"

Her fingertips followed the wrinkles in her sheets. "Well, what if we lure her in by opening the doorway ourselves… and using it to release your souls?"

My mouth went dry and my hold on her tightened. "That's a thought. A brilliant one." I kissed her neck below her ear to reassure her I wasn't being patronizing.

"But?" she asked, hearing it anyway.

"But also terrifying. I want these souls gone as much as you do, and if what Earl said is true, then we have to look at getting them across the wall, but until the souls are fully through the doorway, they're vulnerable. If Hazel interrupts the ritual—or if someone on Meril's side realizes what we're doing—it could bring a whole lot of hell down on our heads."

"It's risky," Alyssa agreed. "But it could be our best chance to deal with both problems in one go."

"I'm open to giving it a shot as long as we have the support of the coven. We'll need a lot of power to hold the doorway steady."

"You'll have it."

Not wanting to let her go, I kept one arm vice-gripped

around her while I reached for my phone with the other. One-handed, I unlocked it and scrolled through my messages. Nothing from anyone important. It made sense. Chip would have known I was out and been messaging Alyssa instead.

I sent him a quick text to let him know I was awake and to put Alyssa's idea into action. She watched my message emerge and turned her head to kiss my neck. As if I would ignore her suggestion. She'd more than proved she was as capable of forming these strategies as I or anyone else in her family was. She needed to have more confidence in herself.

Message sent, I set my phone down and leaned over to kiss her. "You are amazing, and the sooner you realize that, the happier we'll both be."

"I *feel* amazing," she said, "and right now that's counting for a lot. After the last couple days, I didn't think I'd ever feel like this again. Hell, I didn't know I *could* feel like this."

"I am pretty good in bed," I replied in my cockiest tone, then flashed her a grin to tell her I understood exactly what she meant. I'd been with enough women over the past ten years, but nothing like this.

Not even with Hazel, who I'd believed—in my teenage naivety—to be the love of my life.

But no, that title belonged to Alyssa.

My soul darkened with the thought of what awaited us, and Alyssa brushed her fingers over my cheek. "It's going to be okay," she said. "We're going to get through this."

"I know." I kissed her again. "How can I have any doubts now? It's always been you and me, princess, but now it's you and me in a way no one will see coming. Hazel thought she'd seen the best of us in our last fight? She has no idea."

The gleam in Alyssa's green eyes—the satisfaction and anticipation of showing the world what we were now—reached deep into my chest and filled me up.

"I love you." We'd said it enough times over the past few hours, but the need for her to hear it, to know it, to know she wasn't in this alone, consumed me.

Her eyes widened as if she'd seen something in my face that surprised her, and the meaning behind her returned "I love you" set a fire burning in my chest.

If Hazel stormed the house right now, I would take her on without hesitation. I would burn the world to keep Alyssa safe.

My phone vibrated. I expected a return text, but the incoming phone call made me reach again for the phone to answer it.

"You're awake," Chip said in greeting. "About fucking time. I hope you're rested, because we've got trouble."

Alyssa groaned and closed her eyes. "What now?"

"Hazel's getting desperate. She's calling in all her forces, and they're heading back to the house in Rockland. What's left of it, anyway. Not sure why they think that's the best spot for them, but whatever. It's not like the council's going to stop them, and the fucking Smokers seem to have something bigger going on to distract them. Fine. We don't need them. But there's a lot of them, Tracey-boy. Hazel pulled all her people out of the council and a few of the feds. Whatever she's planning next, it's going to be aggressive."

More fighting. Of course when her plan failed, she would go for more fighting. The woman was nothing if not a hammer.

"Any luck finding a doorway?" I asked.

"A few potentials. I'll text you the list as soon as I have them narrowed down. But even if we choose the one she's most likely to go for, I hope you have a good battle plan."

"We'll be ready for her. Is Am—"

"I'm here," Ameline cut in, "and I'll be ready. Whatever you need me to do."

"Which I fucking hate, for the record," Chip said. "I would very much prefer she stay here with me." She murmured something, and he grumbled under his breath. "Since that's not going to happen, fine. But you'd better keep your promise to watch her back, or you and me, Trace? We're done."

He hung up, and Alyssa stared at me in wide-eyed wonder. "Did Chip fall in love?"

"You know… I think he might have."

"Goddess help us."

We dragged ourselves out of bed late the next morning, got dressed, and headed downstairs hand in hand.

Despite how hard I'd fought against those souls, I felt as though I'd slept for a week. Alyssa looked a little more worse for wear, and I worried something had gone awry with the ritual and she'd accidentally given more of herself than she'd taken. But when I tugged on my magic and found it just as securely tied within her as hers was within me, I breathed a little easier.

No, she just hadn't slept well in days. Instead of having sex with her the third—or at least the fourth—time, I should have encouraged her to get some rest.

We found her family in the living room hunched over what looked like a diagram. Gramps looked up when we came in, stared at each of us, and grunted once before returning his attention to whatever he was working on. Henry glanced our way, blushed, and refreshed his water glass with the pitcher on the table, but Mary's expression was downright smug. The others in the room seemed confused, but they shrugged it off and joined Gramps in focusing on the gameplan.

"What is that?" Alyssa asked, pulling me over to an empty spot on the couch where she could see the large sheet of paper. Since there was only one spot, I sat first and pulled her onto my lap, unable to let her go. That she didn't fight me for space and instead rested my hand on her stomach to keep me rooted against her told me she felt the same.

"It's our battle plan," Gramps explained. "We're pulling in the rest of the Mooneys, and I need to know where everyone's going to go before we head in. We can't decide this in the moment."

I nodded. "That's a smart move. You know Hazel's people will be doing the same." I filled him in on Chip's warning call, and his brow furrowed as he stared at the figures scribbled across various sections of the map.

"Do we know numbers?"

"She came with fewer than twenty and we took down more than half," Alyssa said. "If she pulled everyone else, we should prepare for at least twice that many."

Mary groaned and rubbed her hand over her face. "We'll need healers as well as fighters, and this family only has so many."

"Can you ask any of your friends from the hospital?" Henry asked.

She nodded. "There are two or three who might be willing to step into this with us. Tiff's in the know about most of it, and she's frothing at the mouth that the council didn't step in when it could. And Noelle is furious with this coven for the number of souls they've harvested. They'll both be happy to see these people go down."

"That's a start," Gramps said. "They won't need to get anywhere near the fighting, but having them on hand will be a good safety net. Fortunately, what this family does have are fighters." Grief cut through his features. "Too bad Dyl's not with us. That boy can strike a punch or ten."

"Who says I'm not?"

The voice came from the doorway, and Alyssa was on her feet, flying towards her brother. She threw her arms around his neck and hugged him so tightly he winced.

"Oh, sorry," she said as she pulled away. "Are you still hurt? Of course you're still hurt, you were almost dead." She smacked his arm. "So what do you mean 'who says I'm not?' You're not getting anywhere near this."

Dylan grinned, that roguish smile that had always told me he was a guy who liked to find trouble—though today it lacked its easy confidence—and dropped his arm around Alyssa's shoulders. "You think you can boss me around, little sister? I'm in good shape." With his other hand, he tugged up his shirt to expose his abdomen, where a deep white scar now crossed from shoulder to stomach. "See? Fit as a fiddle."

Gramps shook his head. "The doctor gave you permission to leave, but you're not in fighting form."

Dylan scowled. "Like hell I'm not."

Brody came into the room behind him and punched him in the other shoulder. "Listen to the old man, bro. You're going to have to sit this one out and watch me get all the glory."

"There is no glory in this," Mary said, her voice firm and angry. "Both of you sit down and stop talking like this is some play fight you're signing up for in the Underground."

My eyebrows shot up as I took another look at Dylan. Maybe it shouldn't have surprised me that Alyssa's brother fought in the illegal supernatural fights, but it did. Probably because Alyssa herself was such a rule-follower. But a lot about him now made sense.

Dylan's shoulders slumped, and Brody shoved him into the living room. Val stood up and made space in the armchair for her brother, but he pulled her back into his lap when they sat down. She rolled her eyes when he tried to tickle her and elbowed him in the ribs. His face paled at the impact to his healed wound, and his sister turned her nose up at him.

"If you can't take an elbow from me, you're not going into a fight with a spirit witch. And that's final."

Apparently his youngest sister giving him orders hit harder than anyone else, because he dropped his gaze and nodded. "Yeah, all right. I'm out." But his eyes hardened when he looked at the map. "But I can see about five ways you're guaranteeing we lose, Gramps. Let me at that plan."

He shifted Val out of the way, unceremoniously dumping her to the floor—earning yet another eyeroll—as he dragged the chair closer and set to work.

"Kyle, Grayson, and Brody are strong, but they also don't have the same experience as some of the older witches. Aunt Courtney is a decent warder, so she should be over here with

Kyle, but Jennifer, she's a powerhouse. She could be on her own over here and stand up well."

He took us through the rest of the family, organizing them into categories and teams that would best use their abilities. Gramps watched on with pride shining in his eyes, and when Dylan caught that look, his face flushed. It made me wonder if his Underground fights had been to prove himself in his family's eyes, which clearly wasn't necessary. Alyssa returned to my lap and leaned into me, watching her brother with the same respect in her expression, and when Dylan wrapped up, she gave him a nod of approval that made his shoulders straighten.

"Good job, m'boy," Gramps said. "I forget sometimes I'm not the only leader in this family. All right, so we have a start. We're bringing a lot of atmospheric magic to this party, along with some elemental, and Trace's telekinetic power. As for the spirit magic…"

He raised an eyebrow, and I shook my head. "If all goes well, they won't be coming out to play this time." My grip around Alyssa's hand tightened. "But we won't need it."

Henry frowned, then looked at us again and his eyes widened as the change between us finally clicked. Mary was already nodding. "You two will be the strongest players here, but if I could make one adjustment to Dylan's plan, I would say you shouldn't go in together."

"Oh?" Alyssa asked, sounding like she was ready to argue

that point.

"Hazel watched Trace fall. When he shows up at this next fight, she'll suspect he's weak. I think it would benefit everyone to have her believe it."

"Let her underestimate me," I said.

"Exactly. She believes she knows you, and to be fair, considering how close she got to opening that doorway last time, she does. So we let her guide the play while we herd her into position."

It made sense. If we were going up against that many strong, trained witches—even without the demonic witch—we needed to make sure we controlled the field. If Hazel believed I was coming with my power drained, struggling to hold on to the souls, she would focus all her efforts on me, and in doing so, she would open herself up to be overwhelmed by the power I now shared with Alyssa. The sooner we took Hazel down, the faster the rest of her people would scatter.

"I don't think we'll be enough," Alyssa said. "To bind her, absolutely, but not if we're fighting her off at the same time. Everyone else will be focused on the rest of her coven."

I gave her waist a squeeze. "You're forgetting the other type of magic we'll have at our disposal."

She turned to face me, the question in her eyes.

"We have a time witch."

IT TOOK CHIP another few hours to send Trace the list of best doorways, and another hour for us to plot them on the map to figure out which one would benefit us most for location as well as magic.

"One thing Hazel was right about was keeping away from people," Trace said. "If we're looking at an outright battle, then being in the city centre isn't an option."

I thought of the fight with Clyde Corrick and had to agree with his assessment. We'd been lucky that the club had been large enough to accommodate the sheer number of us, and that it had been winter, when everything was nice and isolated, but in the middle of spring, when everyone wanted to be outside enjoying the change in weather, we couldn't take the chance that mundanes might get drawn into the crossfire.

"That crosses off the gateway in Mer Bleu and Princess Louise Falls," Gramps said, scratching those off the list.

"Pine Grove could work," Mom suggested.

Dad shook his head. "If anything happened to those trees, or at Pinhey Dunes, we'd get slammed by conservationists." He shrugged. "Also, it would be heartbreaking."

That was my father, ever the scientist with the heart of gold.

"That cuts out most of Orleans, as well as the locations close to downtown." Mom frowned and looked down the list. "Not the worst thing to lead her back out this way."

The country had its benefits for so many reasons, but it also meant we'd be farther from any supernatural hospitals to deal with the injured. Dylan had been lucky Mom was with us when he was hit. The Almonte Hospital was wonderful, but they didn't have a large enough supernatural unit to deal with any witches that fell in the line of magic.

I brought up a map of the city on my phone and pinned each location on it, trying to figure out the one that would best suit our needs. The ones in Quebec crossed into Quebec Witches' Council territory, and they'd made it clear they didn't want to get involved, so that was another three off the list.

Our options were narrowing, and my insides twisted with uncertainty. Hazel would know all these doorways existed as well, so we were racing against her to choose the best one.

Finally, my eye fell on the winner, right in the middle of Ottawa's Experimental Farm. According to Chip, the doorway was small, almost sealed, but the power leaking through it suggested it was located in a prime spot in the mirror realm. As long as we went out at night, we could be confident that mundanes wouldn't be walking around, and if we gave Pen the heads up, the council could ensure the perimeter was clear. It would be even better if word reached one of Hazel's people within the council. They would pass the information along to her, raising the odds Hazel would come out to meet us.

I laid out my idea to the others, and when it was met with nothing but approval, I experienced the same sense of pride I'd caught in Dylan's eyes earlier. A pride that was reflected in Trace's gaze when I turned to look at him. He kissed my temple, and I leaned into him, drawing on his support and what I now recognized as love, something that had been growing between us so slowly I hadn't put a name to it.

"All that's left is to get Hazel's attention and bring Ameline into the plan," Trace said.

I clenched my teeth at the thought of the time witch taking the brunt of this encounter on her shoulders. If she agreed, she'd be holding Hazel in a two-second time loop while Trace and I bound her. It would be strenuous, finicky work that would take all her concentration and would require more Mooneys than we could spare to protect her while she did it, but if it worked, we would be set.

So many ifs, but from the outside looking in, there was no denying it was a strong idea. Our best chance of success.

Trace was already texting Chip the details so he and Ameline could meet us near the farm, and I turned my thoughts to Hazel. We had the number she'd texted Trace from, but I doubted it would still be in service the way she'd been jumping through phones. No, if we wanted to flag her down, we'd have to go big. Sparkly.

I thought of my conversation with Trace this morning and knew it was time to drop that particular bomb on the family. They wouldn't like the idea, but the logic was sound.

I cleared my throat to get everyone's attention, then let the bomb fall. "We need to open the doorway."

"Excuse me?" Val asked. "Isn't that what we're trying to prevent?"

"Ultimately, yes, but if we stake out a doorway and get Hazel's attention, she'll assume it's too well guarded and go target one of the other doorways. We need to control this battlefield, which means making her believe it's worth the risk to confront us. If we crack the doorway open, she'll see it as half her work being done for her and will likely come finish the job."

Trace nodded. "That does track with what I know about her."

He shot me a look, a silent question in his eyes about whether I would mention the rest of it. I understood his concerns about rushing the job. Those souls were embedded in him. We couldn't just grab them and toss them into the ether. It would be a delicate process and risk so much if it failed. But if the doorway was open, how could we ignore the opportunity to save Trace's life?

"If it's possible, we should also look at learning the ritual to pull the souls out of Trace. Before Hazel reaches us."

Gramps rubbed his upper lip and stared at the map. "We'll need a lot of magic to do it. Those doorways may not have been sealed perfectly, but the wards are strong. Look how many corpses Hazel needed to get the last doorway even halfway open. And we won't be dealing in spirit magic. As for getting the spirits out of Trace, the ritual's not overly complicated, but it is time consuming. And diplomatically challenging. Meril won't be best pleased if we're caught dumping souls without permission."

I thought of Madison. A great-something granddaughter of the queen beyond the wall. If anyone knew how to get that doorway open and deliver the souls safely, she could figure it out. But I set the thought aside before it had fully formed. She'd worked hard to separate herself from that side of her family. To ask her to get so close and draw the queen's eye would be the act of a horrible friend.

Still, maybe there was something there to work with.

"Do we know anyone from the mirror realm who could help us open the way?" I asked.

Gramps pressed his lips together and looked to Mom, who heaved a sigh. "No, but I have another ritual we might be able to use."

I raised an eyebrow. "You've been pulling a lot of rare and powerful rituals out of your bookcase these days, Mom. There something you want to tell us?"

With all four of her children staring at her, Mom's cheeks flushed with indignation and she sat up straight. "No, there is not. If you kids had taken an interest in the more academic nature of your magic, you'd have the same knowledge, but two of you decided to focus on fighting, and the other two have been more focused on your mundane careers and left your magic more or less ignored. So don't look at me like I'm the strange one."

While I gave her an amused smirk at her snarky answer, I couldn't help but feel put in my place. She made a good point. I'd trained with my magic my entire childhood, but it had always been to learn how to use what I had and that was all. I'd dug more deeply into it on my path to become a healer, but when that had been interrupted and I'd taken over the pub, I'd stuck to the basics. Having Simon's chaos magic to consider at work had been a good excuse to keep my hands off my power, but now that I was faced with yet another major crisis, I felt like a child who hadn't applied herself in school and was now staring at an exam worth half my grade.

"What's this ritual, then?" I asked without any attitude.

Mom met my eye and seemed to recognize the earnestness behind my question, because her shoulders relaxed. "It's a way to work spirit magic without harvesting souls."

My heart jumped into my throat, and Trace tensed beneath me. "Excuse me?" I asked.

"Voluntary soul-workings," Mom said. "And it would have to be voluntary, because we'd be using our own."

"I didn't know that was possible," Val said. "The only thing I've ever heard was spirit magic equals bad."

"That's because this ritual is incredibly dangerous and complex. It'll require a lot of concentration, and not all of us will be able to cast it." Mom sent Trace a pointed look. "I recommend you not even try."

"I think that would be wise," Trace agreed.

"But I could?" I asked.

Mom hesitated and looked between us. "It might not be smart for you either, Aly. Not with your magics tied. You just bound those souls. You don't want to risk snapping the binding."

My stomach curled with anxiety. "Then who? If this ritual is so dangerous, I don't want anyone taking it on if I can't. We already lost Uncle Tony. We almost lost Dyl."

"If Hazel wins, we'll lose a lot more than that," Gramps said, his shoulders slumping. "Your mother is right. It's the best way to open that doorway, which is the best way to lure Hazel into our plans and stop her. We have to take the chance."

I suddenly regretted voicing my idea. If it meant the cost of another family member, I didn't know if my heart could take it. But I also couldn't argue with Gramps's logic. Hazel could not win.

"I'll put in a request for volunteers," Mom said. "We'll need at least six people. Eight would be better, but I'm not going to force anyone's hand."

"I'll do it," Gramps said.

I gritted my teeth to stop myself from protesting. Of course he would volunteer. He was the head of our coven and he felt responsible for the souls being unleashed and setting us on this road in the first place. But he was also older. His magic was strong, but his body wasn't as sturdy as it used to be. I worried he wouldn't have the strength to keep his end stable.

By the worry in Mom's eyes, she felt the same, but she nodded. "With your power behind it, we should have no trouble nudging this door open a crack."

"I volunteer as well," Brody said, and at that, Mom's eye twitched.

"We should look to the older members of the coven first," Dad said. "That way if anything goes wrong... well, we've had our time."

My brother shook his head. "You have the power behind your magic, but you need at least a few of us who can hold steady if your strength falters. I'll be one of those people."

"Me too," Val said, and the shock that spread through my body was greater than my horror at what my family was agreeing to. My sister, the drama queen kindergarten teacher, was offering to put her life on the line for this battle? I'd never known her to be so self-sacrificing.

Her stare was hard as she looked at Dylan, then Brody, then me. "The three of you have been putting yourselves into the line of fire for weeks now. Do you think because I'm the youngest that I'm not capable of doing the same?"

"Of course not," I said. "I think you have just as much power as any of us."

I knew she did. I'd seen it in the fight for Mooney's Pub four years ago and in her determination to show up every time our family dealt with a problem. But that didn't stop me from worrying about my little sister.

"Consider it a done deal, then. That's three of us. We'll get the rest once we gather everyone together," Val said firmly, her teacher voice in place.

No one else had anything to say.

We had a plan, we had a location—now we just needed our enemy.

# Chapter 35
*Trace*

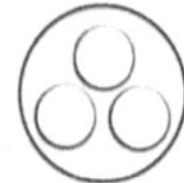

I DROVE ME and Alyssa to Nepean early so we could double-check that our location would be a good one and have enough time to make changes if we needed to.

Alyssa's family wouldn't be far behind, and Chip and Ameline would meet us there. It felt so similar to our trip to the museum in Almonte that my stomach did somersaults with every passing metre, but I did my best not to be overwhelmed by the uncertainty. We'd known what we were getting into the last time as well, but on Wednesday, Hazel had called every shot. Here, we'd be in charge, and I prayed to the goddess that slight shift of advantages would be everything we needed to come out victorious. And maybe that I'd be walking away without this burden in my centre.

Alyssa rested her hand on mine, and I turned my palm up to loop my fingers through hers. Her face had a slightly green cast to it, and I knew she felt just as nervous about how tonight would go as I did. Her family would be putting themselves on the line for our success, and even if we won, it was possible we would be grieving by tomorrow.

I didn't know what to say. Some part of me wanted to apologize, as though Hazel were my responsibility. The rest of me wanted to reassure her that everything would work out, but those words turned to ash in my mouth. This wasn't the time for guarantees, and Alyssa would rightfully disregard any I tried to offer.

So we sat in silence as I parked in the lot behind the strip mall, then we got out and crossed the street towards the farm.

The Experimental Farm was a fascinating feature of Ottawa's landscape. Acres and acres of field right in the middle of the city, split with walking paths that opened the way for the more energetic members of the community to take an active commute to work on bicycle or foot. Alyssa and I joined the after-work wanderers as we made our way to the tree in the centre of the field. The paved path gave way to a dirt trail when we rounded the crop of wheat and came to stop at the base of the large trunk.

Here and there were small copses of gathered cedars, giving shade and hiding the outbuildings from casual view, but this tree stood on its own. A twisted ash with its branches stretched high as though communing with the sky. Faint magic pulsed from its bark even from a few metres away, and I stared up into the full branches.

"I've walked by this tree so many times," Alyssa said, "and I never would have known a doorway to the mirror realm existed here." She squinted at the tree. "I can't even see the magic from here, it's so subtle."

"Meril's people hid them well," I agreed, and with her hand in mine, we approached the tree.

The magic grew stronger as we got closer, and deep in my centre, the souls stirred. A whisper of their power flowed through me—so gentle I might not have noticed it if I wasn't paying attention. The magical weave containing them was serving its purpose, and for the first time since I took those souls into me, I didn't worry they would break free and take me over.

I heaved a breath of relief, almost of peace. Despite the trials we faced tonight, in this moment my outlook on the future had never been brighter. I felt more at home, more complete, than I'd ever imagined I would feel.

"What?" Alyssa asked, watching me, her green gaze running over my face before landing on my eyes.

I thought about shrugging off her question, not wanting to get into all the sentimental nonsense out here on a busy Friday afternoon, but as I looked at her, as I remembered what we faced tonight, I chose not to hide. Who knew how many more opportunities I would have to bare my soul to her.

I took her hand. "Because of Hazel, I ran for my life for three years, and it was awful. But I've had a lot of reason to look back on my past, and I realized that those three years were just part of it. I ran to Hazel because there was a lot of stuff going on at home I wanted to avoid. After SMOAC sent her to Moongrave, I worked hard to become the best bounty hunter I could be, but I was still running. Running from the mistakes I'd made, from the versions of myself I'd left behind." I swallowed the lump forming in my throat and clung to the connected magic tying us together. "Then I met you, and I think—I think for the first time in my life, I've found a reason to stop running. Maybe even…" I shrugged. "Maybe even put down a root or two."

Alyssa's eyes were glassy as she rose on tiptoe to wrap her arms around my neck. Her dark purple sweater was soft under my hands, her curves so tantalizingly close beneath the fabric. "I would like to put down a root or two with you, Trace."

I cast a side-eye at the tree. "Is it really corny that I made that metaphor while we're standing next to a magical tree?"

She grinned. "Yes."

I kissed her, slow and deep, as I pulled her against me, in awe once again at how perfectly she fit. From the road, someone cheered and clapped, no doubt thinking I'd proposed and she'd accepted, and I did nothing to dispel their assumption. We'd already bonded together in a way far beyond paperwork and government approval, and if Alyssa ever wanted the white dress to go along with the commitment, I wouldn't shy away from it.

Our magic surged between us, a gentle lap of the tide, and I groaned as Alyssa pulled away, knowing we had more important things to do here. Also knowing this would not be an appropriate place to let our magic play… for so many reasons.

Alyssa kept her hand in mine as we did a circle around the trunk, searching for any sign of where the doorway might be strongest. We found it against the side of the tree facing the centre of the farm. Just a trickle of extra magic, but enough to reveal where the seal had been left unfinished. Exactly the opening we'd need to draw Hazel in.

Now all we needed to do was wait for sundown.

I WAS A bundle of nervous energy as we waited by the tree, but I also felt solid in our decision to be here. Instinct told me we were in the right place. This was the best location we could have chosen, with the best team, and the best strategy.

Believing that did nothing to remove my terror that we might lose as much as we gained, but no one here showed any hesitation in the roles they'd taken on.

Spread out across the empty field were thirty Mooney witches, who were hard at work warding the lanes around the field to prevent any mundanes from inadvertently walking into our fight. While the council was supposed to arrive to help with that, none of us were prepared to trust them completely.

While they worked on protection, another six of us stood

in a ring around the tree. Gramps led the ritual to open the doorway, chanting the words that had pulled his spirit towards the surface, blending his familiar purple magic with the yellow I'd come to fear. All the power it offered, all it threatened to steal.

Val and Brody stood on either side of him, their positions and the flow of their magic mirroring his. Jennifer and Sonya stood opposite each other beside my siblings, both of them focused, their magic strong and steady. Across from Gramps stood Aunt Hilary, and her magic glowed with an intensity I worried might be noticeable from beyond the ward. She was pouring everything she had into this spell, and I hoped she remembered we weren't actually trying to throw the door open, only nudging the gap a bit wider.

More Mooneys stood on the edges of the ward, some standing within the copse behind the outbuilding where they might go unseen by Hazel's people until they were close enough for our family to close in. The dark coven would undoubtedly know they were there, but that wasn't the point. Everything we'd set up was a matter of clawing for advantages wherever we could grab them.

Trace stood with Ameline, close enough to the tree that they would be on the front lines to face Hazel when she arrived, but far enough not to disrupt the ritual in progress. Once the doorway was open enough, Trace would get into position to start releasing the souls, but only if the coast was still clear. Otherwise, we'd need to keep the doorway stable until we'd dealt with Hazel. Such a critical balance, and one that threatened to topple if we missed our mark.

I stood with my family, pretending to add my magic to theirs. We hoped that if Hazel believed I was distracted by the ritual, she'd be unprepared for me to attack. It was worth a try, but I missed Trace's steadying presence by my side. Yet when I tugged on his magic, he responded immediately, letting me know he wasn't too far. Together, we could stop her.

I didn't let myself think of anything beyond that. I couldn't. Not unless I wanted my anxiety to run off the rails.

Stars glittered overhead, and I swore I caught a hint of the green and purple of the northern lights swirling in the sky, a shimmering reflection amid the stars, like water over dry land.

It was only because I was so focused on those lights that I caught the faint flash of something in my periphery. If I'd been staring into the darkness, I might have missed it.

I summoned my magic as vibrations ran along the ward, letting us know someone had crossed the barrier. Three witches ran forward, green-and-yellow magic flying through the air towards the Mooneys standing guard around the ritual casters. It seemed we'd been right about what would attract Hazel's attention. Too bad it meant Trace's souls were still a target.

Hazel was smart to not attack the casters themselves. They

were doing the work for her as far as she believed. But it also meant Gramps and the others would have to work harder to keep the spell stable, fighting against any other power that attempted to lend their magic to ours to force the door open.

Trace's magic surged with mine as the attacking witches moved in. We both grabbed our power and launched it towards them in a counterspell that was both bulkier than I was expecting and so much more powerful. It hit two of the three witches square in the chest, and I watched how it not only devoured the spells the witches had been about to cast but wrapped around them and snuffed out their power altogether.

A strangled gasp rumbled in my chest at the sight, but I had no time to stand in awe over what we'd done. The third witch was still coming, and by Ameline's stifled scream, there were more coming up behind me. Trace focused on witch number three while I spun around to face the new arrivals.

Six more witches bore down on me, and my heart slammed against my ribs as I threw a ward up to fend off the sudden onslaught. As soon as the first hits landed, I dropped the ward to retaliate. Ameline beat me, summoning her time magic and reversing events by two seconds, forcing the witches back before they could draw on more power. I grabbed the opportunity to sling my atmospheric magic at the nearest two. The pulse sent them flying, and Mooneys spilled out of the shadows to stand around them, throwing out a magical net that bound the two witches together, leaving them unable to access their power.

The other four pushed through Ameline's spell, but Ameline was ready for them. Instead of reversing time, she sped it up, and they lurched forward, moving in closer, faster than expected, with no time to defend themselves. Thrown off balance, they scrambled to catch up to the lost moments, and the attempt gave my family a chance to bind another two witches while I released a flow of atmospheric power that wrapped around the final two, creating a vacuum of air around them. They clawed at their throats as their faces turned red, then purple, and they collapsed into the grass.

I barely had time to catch my breath before I turned around to find yet more witches coming for Trace. Four of them, elemental magic swirling between them mixed with the telltale hint of yellow spirit magic.

Blasts of light and magic, shouts and screams, sounded from all around me, and I knew the other Mooneys had been pulled into the fight. How many had Hazel brought with her? How had she rallied all of them?

I didn't know why I was surprised. The world had taught me time and again that some people were always willing to be swayed towards the groups that promised them the most power, regardless of the cost to anyone else. All she'd had to do was vow to change their lives, and they'd fallen into line.

And she was right. Many of them would face their final change tonight. I hoped they believed it was worth it.

A pained cry burst out behind me, and I whirled around to find Gramps on his knees. The yellow magic around him was so bright I had to squint to see him through it, and horror churned in my gut as I realized what was happening. Someone had boosted his power so he would channel it into the doorway, and it was taking all his effort to hold that power back without taking it into himself. He didn't have Trace's telekinetic magic that would allow him to create a cage around it. If it broke through his defenses, it would absorb into his blood and kill him. Unless he found a way to shut it down.

I ran to his side and threw my magic around Gramps, doing what I could to help take some of the weight off him. But there was so much magic. As soon as I got close, I gagged on the feeling of that yellow power sliding down my throat, choking me.

Brody and Val were struggling to hold their spell steady; Val's mouth was open in a silent scream, while Brody's face was slick with sweat. Jennifer and Sonya were also wavering, their control fading. The only one still standing strong was Hilary, but she was working against the others, still channelling all her magic into the doorway. What was she doing? If she didn't stop, the door would open.

I lurched towards her and slammed into her side, breaking

the ritual and taking her to the ground. Yellow magic sprayed like sparks throughout the darkness, and the tree lit up as though the leaves were filled with fireflies.

Jennifer staggered on her feet, and Sonya collapsed to the earth, but Gramps fought on. The yellow power around him hadn't dissipated, still trying to consume him, and I didn't know how to help. His face was grey, and he clutched his hand to his chest. He met my eye, and in his gaze, I read all kinds of apologies I didn't want to acknowledge. I opened my mouth to cry out, but Gramps closed his eyes, held out his arms, and let go. Purple magic surrounded him and wrapped around the yellow. They battled each other, each one vying for dominance, and all the while, Gramp's jaw, eyes, mouth twitched with discomfort and determination. Finally, purple swallowed yellow and both drew into his centre before disappearing. His eyes flew open on a gasp, and he toppled onto his back, making no move to catch himself. He lay unmoving, and I screamed and dropped by his side, desperately scanning him.

He had a pulse, but he wasn't snapping out of his stupor. His magic was there, I detected no injuries. There was only what I'd seen—that yellow power contained in the purple. What had he done?

Flashes came to me of Trace lying exactly the same way, but his souls had been caged. What was happening inside Gramps that I couldn't see?

"Come on, Gramps. The fight's not over yet."

My concentration was torn away from him by the approaching sounds of battle.

Brody shoved me away. "I've got this, go!"

I was ready to shove him in return when a growing sense of magic tickled the back of my neck. I jumped to my feet and whirled around to find Hazel approaching. She wore that smile, the smug one that said she'd gotten exactly what she wanted, and I scowled at her.

"I should have known the temptation to look across the wall would be too great for you," she said. "You all say you want to stop me, but I know the truth. You want what I'm after. You never would have thought of going after it yourself, but the idea of someone else taking it first… it's just too much, isn't it?"

"You're wrong," I said, panting through my grief, my rage. "You're not a trailblazer, Hazel. We're not looking at you as a visionary or an evil mastermind. You're just a bitch. A bitch who's so focused on ruining the world for her own ambitions that it never occurred to you others might not want the same things."

Her grin widened. "Indulge me, then. What do you want, Miss Mooney?"

I wanted so much. For Trace not to have those souls inside him. For Gramps to come to. For this night to be over. And maybe all of that might be possible if we overcame one major hurdle. "To see you back in your cell in Moongrave Prison. Maybe this time in a nice little home in the Frostmines."

At the mention of her previous home—at the idea of the added horror of maximum-security confinement in the Frostmines—Hazel's eyes narrowed and her grin turned feral, more of a snarl than a smile. Magic floated over her hands, so much yellow that her natural ability was washed out under that of the souls she'd harvested. The hair on the back of my neck danced and goosebumps rose on my arms at the force of it. She was so damn strong.

But so were we.

A trickle of orange power hovered in my peripheral vision, and Hazel was so focused on me that she didn't notice as it wrapped around her. Caught her. Bound her to that two-second moment in time. Her eyes widened, then the snarl returned as she was pulled backwards, one-two.

"Trace!" I shouted, but he was already by my side. His magic—*our* magic—worked together, surging between us in stunning swaths of silver-purple ribbon that flared out and wrapped around Hazel. She fought against Ameline's binding, but her daughter kept hauling her back in two-second stints. Our net tightened around her legs, and she toppled to the ground, cursing us both as she continued to fight off her daughter.

Sweat dripped down my brow, and through the blur of it, I made out Ameline's twisted expression. The effort she was using to pin her mother down was too much. We had to work faster or she would slip.

I pushed more magic out, working with Trace to create a magical net similar to what we'd created around the souls, but Hazel was too strong.

She shoved us away and our work was shredded as we both flew backwards into the grass. Ameline cried out, and for a moment I was terrified Hazel would turn on her own daughter. But when she climbed to her feet, she only had eyes for Trace.

"You, you, you. It's always you," she growled. "Always getting in my way. Always making life harder, harder, *harder*. I won't let you ruin things for me again, Drew. You can either help me today, or you can watch your little witch as I finish what I started the last time we met."

I didn't have time to brace myself before Hazel's magic surged into me and wrapped around my soul.

"Your souls or hers?" she asked. "Tick tock."

# Chapter 37
## *Trace*

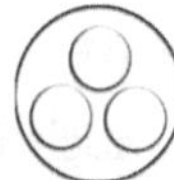

ILURCHED TOWARDS Alyssa with a yell as her eyes widened and Hazel's spirit magic wound under her skin.

Was it my imagination, or did there seem to be a yellow glow around Alyssa as she fought against the power that held her? The sickly hue sank into her, creeping through her, highlighting the veins along her neck and soaking into her eyes.

"One more step and I pull," Hazel warned. "There will be no saving her, no putting her back together."

I stumbled to a halt, nearly losing my footing, and stared in horror at the scene playing out in front of me. My magic mixed with Alyssa's should have been capable of binding Hazel, but we hadn't had enough time to practise together to work as quickly as we needed to. Hazel was stronger, and she was more experienced. With Ameline, we'd been three against one, and she'd managed to get the better of us.

Ameline was still on the ground behind her mother, chest heaving with panting breaths.

On the other side of the tree, Brody and Val knelt next to a motionless Gramps, while Jennifer and Sonya had gone to get hold of Hilary. The ritual had ended, but I *saw* the magic emanating from the crook of the tree where the doorway had been hidden. Not hidden anymore. More open than it had been. Hazel wouldn't need much more effort to remove the remaining barrier.

Or for me to do it. Which was my only guarantee of giving Alyssa a chance to survive.

Not that I was fooled for a moment into thinking Hazel would let her go. She would yank Alyssa's soul out in front of me as punishment for acting against her nine years ago regardless of what I did. But if I refused, it would happen *right now.*

I held up my hands. "All right, Hazel. I'll help you. Please don't hurt her."

Alyssa's lips parted on a silent plea, and I wrapped my magic around hers, giving it a gentle tug in a way that I hoped she interpreted as a need for her to trust me. We had to buy ourselves time. I would steal any seconds I had to come up with a plan.

"You have five minutes," Hazel barked. "I want that doorway open and the souls of all these other people harvested before I let her go. You do that and maybe I'll let you both live."

Yeah, right.

I turned my back on her and walked towards the tree, using the opportunity to take stock of the field around us. Along the edges, Mooneys fought Hazel's coven, and the fight appeared evenly matched. Bodies littered the grass and lanes, and I caught the spots where the ward around the battle had grown patchy. We were running out of time in more ways than one. If the ward fell, we risked any passing mundanes witnessing the results of our magic. We risked upheaval in the balance of the world. If that happened, Hazel wouldn't need to worry about this doorway opening. Queen Meril would tear open every single one and drag all supernaturals back into her realm. Then she would close the gateways for good.

A shudder ran through me, and I turned to stop in front of the tree. The doorway called for power, and said power hung thick in the air.

Lessons from all those years ago came back to me. A younger Hazel spouting visions of the future. Of the two of us sharing unlimited power, of the necessary sacrifices we needed to make to achieve that power. Not sacrifices of our own, of course, but of the victims we'd gathered to fuel her rituals. I pictured Emile, Kurt, and Nathalie as we'd been, the four of us eating up every word this bitch spoke and believing the promises she made.

But she'd never been prepared to share. She'd wanted to use us for everything we could do for her, and then she would have crushed us under her heel and kept us there. I'd been her lover, yes, but I'd been nothing more than a tool for her to use. Just as I was now.

What she didn't appreciate was that I wasn't the same naive kid I'd been back then. I saw through her lies, through her games, through all the bullshit she heaped around herself in the hopes that it would hide what she was really after: relevance.

I looked from the tree to her, caught the murderous glint in her eyes and the tightening in her jaw as she strengthened her grip on Alyssa's soul. Alyssa hissed through her teeth, remaining statue still, as though afraid that any small movement might be enough to tear her apart.

My heart was in my throat. My nerves were strained to the point of snapping. Fury burned along my veins, waking up the souls deep within me, but I refused to use them. Alyssa and I had worked together to contain them, and there they would stay until I found a way to release them. They were safe from me—and from Hazel.

The power lingering around Gramps, though…

I reached for it, allowed Hazel to see me working the spell she'd taught me when I was eighteen, and pulled it out of him. Hazel watched me, not the magic, and I had to work on the assumption that she couldn't see what I was doing the way Alyssa could. Alyssa's eyes were round with horror, her mouth open, on the edge of a scream, and I worked quickly to put her at ease. The yellow magic that poured out of Gramps was tied up in the purple he'd bound it with, and I set to work unravelling them, leaving his atmospheric power untouched. Once it was free, I distinguished another subtle difference between two separate magics—a purple-tinted yellow and a darker, green-tinted yellow. Gramps's soul tangled in the souls someone had pushed into him to amplify his power. This knot was more delicate, and I had to stay aware of the ticking clock as I worked. I didn't want to hurt Gramps, but I wouldn't put Alyssa in more danger by taking my time.

Bit by bit, I peeled away the magics, leaving Gramps's intact and letting it settle back inside him while drawing the other to myself. It was unwieldy. Heavy with the burden of having been stolen and used against the will of whoever it had been stolen from. But I controlled it using the knowledge and memory of a life I'd sworn never to look back on.

Hazel's eyes narrowed in distrust, and I went through the motions of directing the spirit magic into the doorway. It shifted, widened further, and Hazel's shoulders sagged as she leaned forward in eagerness, ready to witness her dream coming true. I nudged the door open a little wider than any of us had intended when we began this ritual.

Alyssa thrashed against Hazel's hold again, but I didn't turn to look at her, not wanting to give myself away too soon. Shouts sounded around me, gasps of horror as the other Mooneys registered what I was doing, and I prayed to the goddess they kept their distance. I prayed they realized one move towards me or Hazel would risk Alyssa's life. I would have bound them all in place to prevent that from happening if I could have afforded the energy. Instead, I stayed focused on what I was doing, concentrating hard on the power now surging from the opening doorway. It was strong. Untainted by the mundane energies that wove through our magics regardless of how far back our bloodlines went. I handled it carefully, keeping my movements subtle. Let Hazel believe I was only trying to open the doorway. Let her believe I was obeying her as I'd always done. I suspected she was ready to believe it. That her time away—that my past betrayal—weren't enough to make her conceive of the depth of my hatred for her.

The temptation was there to try to release my souls at the same time, but there was too much going on, too much risk that my hold on them would slip and they would reveal my intentions. I begged them to be patient, promising release as soon as we could.

Winding the yellow magic around the doorway to keep the stolen souls in place, I reached for the power drifting out from beyond the unseen wall. I stifled my awe at the way the pure white magic danced through the air and brushed against my skin. It stung like a sunburn. A red-hot knife that would slice me to pieces if I weren't careful. I wrapped it in the yellow magic, then strengthened it with my and Alyssa's combined power.

Playing my role, I widened my arms, letting Hazel think I was about to release the final burst of magic that would throw the door open.

"That's it, my pet," she crooned. "Open the door and let a new age begin. We'll step through together, just as we were always supposed to. You'll be my consort as we soak up whatever power Meril's been hoarding over there, and when we return, the world will be ours. I can see it now, Drew. The future is beau—"

I launched the combined magic directly at her chest and sent her tumbling head over heels across the grass with a piercing shriek. With the force of the blow, the doorway slammed shut, blocking off all access to the mirror realm.

Smoke rose from the burns in her shirt and a nasty red welt across her chest, but not nearly the damage I'd been hoping for. Unfortunately, her time in Moongrave hadn't dulled her reflexes, and in no time, she was back on her feet, her teeth bared as she reached for the magic binding her to Alyssa. My stomach dropped out from under me, terror gripping every cell in my body. I launched a desperate attack at the yellow magic threatening my partner's beautiful soul. Our joined magics struck the spell, sending vibrations in both directions along the binding, and Hazel and Alyssa let out screams that rattled my eardrums. Hazel shook her head to clear the effect of the assault, and I wrapped my magic more securely around the binding, carefully drawing Hazel's magic out without taking Alyssa's along with it.

The process was finicky, and I was too focused, only saved from having my own soul torn out by Alyssa's scream of warning as Hazel launched her magic at me. I threw up a ward just in time, but Hazel's spell rattled through it, whittling away at the protections until it was little more than a shredded shield.

"*Enough!*" she shouted. "Enough games, enough play. Everything you know about your magic is because I taught you. You were nothing. Your family wanted nothing to do with you, you had no friends, no *future* until I came along. And this is how you repay me?"

Every word was a slap, but the palm across my cheek no longer carried any weight. What did it matter what the past looked like when my future was right in front of me? I had family. I had friends. And I would fight to the death to protect them.

I summoned the rest of my magic, pulling on my deepest reserves, borrowing from Alyssa until I sensed her stores running low. With all that power pooled, I prepared myself to throw it. Hazel anticipated my move and launched another spell my way, this one binding my arms to my sides, caging me, stifling all the power I'd summoned.

"I had hoped to keep you alive." Her full lips drooped in a feigned pout, one she'd always believed made her look seductive and powerful. But the blow I'd struck must have hurt more than I'd realized because the downward pull of her lips was more of a grimace, and the combined expressions made her look like a child throwing a tantrum. "It's too bad you're so desperate to meet your end."

She pulled back her hand, her fingers crackled with power, and I turned my gaze to Alyssa, wanting my last sight to be of her face. Tears streamed down her cheeks as she struggled to summon her magic, desperate to save me. I silently begged her to take advantage of Hazel's distraction to take her down the moment I was gone.

Hazel's spell lit the air, and I braced for pain.

# Chapter 38
*Alyssa*

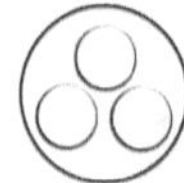

A SCREAM ESCAPED me as Hazel launched her spell aimed straight for Trace. It was too late to redirect the magic, and I was too far to shove him out of the way, so in a panic-filled haze, I grabbed hold of my magic and launched an atmospheric pulse in his direction.

By sheer luck, my spell hit a microsecond before Hazel's landed, and Trace flew out of range, the air ripped from his lungs as he crashed to the ground, rolled, and sagged down. I worried I'd cracked a rib or two, but ribs could heal—something he wouldn't have been able to do if Hazel's spell had hit him. Not if the ground where he'd stood, now a rotted patch of compost, was anything to go by.

Hazel whipped towards me, her expression feral, and I

stepped back as if that would save me. I was too exhausted to summon a ward. My magic begged me for a break, for a chance to recharge.

"Always getting in the way," she said as she stalked forward. Power crackled at her fingertips. "I thought Corrick must have been weak to have been brought down by the likes of you, but now I see you really are that much of a pain in the ass."

"I'll take that as a compliment," I shot back. "How did you hear about Corrick, anyway? How did you know about the amulet? How did you plan any of this?"

If I could keep her talking, maybe I could scrounge up enough power to defend myself if not stop her. It was a small hope, barely worth having, but it refused to go away. Plus I was curious. How could I not be? After the events in The Scorpio Lounge, Dara's people had swept in and cleaned up everything that had happened. Corrick himself was gone, likely dead. Who else had he told about his plan?

Hazel sneered, condescension oozing off her like mould creeping down a shower drain. "Do you believe you were being subtle? You can't wipe out a dozen of the city's strongest magic users, get dragged in front of a fae duchess, and transfer that many souls into a person without attracting notice."

Pity replaced the scorn. "You really thought you hid it all, didn't you?" She tutted at me. "Silly girl. You have so much to learn about the darker side of this world. Too bad for you,

you're learning too late."

I barely had time to throw myself out of the way before her spell zinged past my ear. Smoke puffed into the air where the magic hit the ground, and bile churned in my gut with how close that had been.

Not wanting to waste the power now leaching back into my blood, I summoned just enough to throw a similar pulse to the one I'd launched at Trace. Hazel went airborne before she landed on her back, and I was ready with a follow-up by the time she shook off the blow.

A glance at Trace showed him slowly getting to his feet, one arm wrapped around his middle. I'd definitely done some damage. But he was breathing, which was what mattered.

I turned back to Hazel in time to watch her stand up, another yellow-tinged spell already between her palms. I rushed to summon a ward, but Trace stepped in with a silver-purple spell that caught Hazel around her wrists and thrust her hands upwards. She had no choice but to release her spell if she didn't want to send it into her own face.

She snarled, tore her hands apart to rip through the binding and readied another attack, this one filled with so much power goosebumps bubbled over my skin. Trace paled and stepped in front of me, and I scrambled to find the magic to create a shield strong enough to fend that behemoth off.

Yet the more power I tried to channel, the more it slipped

through my fingers. Nothing I had would defend us against that thing. I reached for Trace's hand, and he gripped my fingers tightly enough that my bones screamed. I didn't care. That pain I could handle. At least it would give me something to focus on during whatever agony was coming.

Hazel froze.

My first thought was that she'd had a change of heart, figured out some new, better way to destroy us. But the flare of her nostrils, the widening of her eyes, told me that whatever had halted her attack hadn't been within her control.

I looked to Trace to see if he was responsible, but his attention was fixed somewhere behind Hazel. I followed his gaze to where Ameline stood on shaking legs. Blood dripped down her nose, but as Hazel's hand retracted, the tingle of magic in the air let up. I sucked in a breath, the tension around my lungs easing, but the relief was short lived as Trace drew on our power and created a spell almost as massive as the one Hazel had wielded.

Murder flashed in his eyes. A rage so deep and so mixed with old hurt and fresh pain that I suspected every wound this woman had ever inflicted on him was included in it.

He was going to kill her with that spell.

I didn't blame him. To a point, I hoped he did. Hazel had caused so many people so much pain, and the council and SMOAC had both proved they couldn't be trusted to contain her. Why not let her die here and now and let the nightmare die with her?

If anyone else had stepped in to bring her down, I wouldn't have shed a tear.

But this was Trace.

He'd told me earlier that he'd spent his entire life running away from his past. From the things Hazel had made him do. I knew him. He wasn't a cruel man, and he wasn't one to take a life unless it was necessary. Ameline had her bound. Maybe only for a second or two, but in this freeze-frame moment, we had all the power. Killing her would be an act of vengeance, not justice. And as soon as Trace snapped out of his fury, he would realize that, and it would eat at him.

After everything Hazel had put him through, I refused to allow her to get her claws into him in a way he'd never be able to recover from.

So before he could launch his beast of a spell, I gathered every scrap of magic I was able to muster and threw it at Hazel, binding her magic, her limbs, her mouth. I wrapped the magical net so tightly she fell to the ground, board-straight.

Trace lurched forward, shoulders heaving as he sucked in air, and slowly—so slowly—his spell dissipated. I watched the war take place within him as he glowered at Hazel, the way his shoulders sagged and his hands balled into fists.

I saw the moment he made his choice.

His hands came up, magic flowing between them… and he added his spell to mine.

Together, we pulled the net closer, securing the rough edges. Our silver-purple magic, beautiful and unbreakable, covered Hazel from her head to her toes, with no possibility that she could break through it. We'd created around her what we'd crafted around the souls within Trace, and I would recommend to whoever escorted her to Moongrave that they keep those bindings tight until she was safely in the Frostmines.

When she was completely bound, with no freedom for her magic to move, Trace broke the spell and stalked towards her. On shaking legs, he dropped to one knee.

"Today, I'll show you mercy, but you get no third chance. If I see you again, I won't settle for binding you. I'll make sure I watch you breathe your last breath."

He shoved himself to his feet and strode away from her, finally putting her behind him.

# Chapter 39
*Trace*

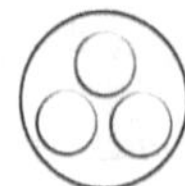

Ameline stumbled on her feet, and I ran to catch her before she could fall, not wanting Chip to cast me out because the woman scraped her knees. As soon as I moved, Alyssa did the same, rushing to Gramps's side and skidding so hard, I caught the flinch of pain from her torn skin.

"Is he…" she asked her brother, unable to finish the question.

Brody shook his head, but his eyes were bright with unshed tears. "He's not waking up, but he's breathing." He looked towards me. "It's like what happened with you, except I don't get any sense of magic. I don't get a sense of anything."

I wrapped my arm around Ameline and helped her walk towards the others, needing to see the man for myself. Again, I fought a wave of guilt that I knew wasn't rational. I hadn't had anything to do with Hazel escaping Moongrave. Yet she'd been the ghost of *my* past, of *my* mistakes, and here she was drawing the people I loved into her chaos. I also worried I'd made things worse by pulling the tainted souls out of him somehow. I couldn't see how——the burden of holding them would have been more strain on his system than my efforts to remove them, but the fear remained.

I rested my hand on Alyssa's shoulder as she ran her fingers over Gramps's chest, applying every bit of her healing knowledge to assess what was wrong with him.

"There was magic," she said, a note of panic creeping into her voice, though the tightness gave away how hard she was working to hide it. "I saw it when Trace pulled the souls out. It has to be in here somewhere." She squeezed her eyes shut, drew in a breath, and when she opened them again, her expression was calm. "Where's Mom?"

Brody stood, scrubbed his pale face, and looked over his shoulder to where we'd parked the cars in an apartment parking lot nearby. "I'll go get her."

Val shook her head and pulled him back down. "You sit, I'll go. You nearly drained yourself in that ritual."

His lack of arguing was telling of how right she was.

Val took off at a halting sprint while the family gathered closer.

Belatedly, I remembered we hadn't been the only ones fighting, and I looked around at where the rest of the Mooneys had battled Hazel's people. All the fighting had stopped. What survivors there were of Hazel's coven must have scattered or submitted and agreed to be bound because, of the people remaining around the field, three-quarters of them were standing while the others were on their knees, their hands behind their backs. I wouldn't have been able to make out those details in the darkness if it weren't for the glow of the magic binding them, and now that the initial shock was over, I shook my head in awe that I could actually *see* it. Finally I understood Alyssa's expression of wonder when she watched our powers play. Magic was beautiful.

While we waited for Mary to return to check on Gramps, I helped Ameline sit down, then made my way around the field to get an idea of where things stood. Over a dozen of Hazel's people lay dead, and nearly half as many Mooneys. No one I recognized, but that didn't make the pain any less. These were Alyssa's family members, and while we'd all known the risks before coming here tonight, that didn't mean their losses didn't hit hard.

Tears stained the faces of the survivors. Many were wounded, accepting minor healing from those with the ability to help. I hoped the other healers Mary had brought with her from the hospital would join her now that the threat was over.

The sooner we got people off the farm and cleaned up the scene, the better for everyone.

I hated how many funerals we'd be attending in the weeks to come, and I prayed to the goddess that Gramps's wouldn't be one of them.

Once I was sure no other danger remained, I returned to Alyssa's side. Mary had arrived. Her brow was furrowed as she sat with her fingertips against Gramps's temples and her other hand on his chest. We stood around her, barely breathing, waiting for her diagnosis.

Finally, she sat back with a sigh. "We'll have to get him to the hospital for a full assessment, but I—I don't know what to make of it. He's alive. That's all I can say right now."

She delivered the news with perfect professional detachment, but as soon as the words were out, she crumpled in on herself and began to sob. Henry limped in, sank to the ground beside her, and bundled her against him, tears welling in his own eyes. I wasn't sure where he'd been fighting, but I was relieved he'd made it through. Gramps's condition would be a hard enough change for the entire Mooney clan. He was the head of their coven, the head of their family, and it wouldn't be a fast matter to sort themselves out.

Small blessing, but at least now they'd have the time. Hazel had been dealt with. Everything else could wait.

Courtney strode towards us, the set of her jaw hard. A

bruise was blossoming across her cheek, and blood stained her shirt from what looked like a nasty burn on her shoulder, but she stood strong as she surveyed the family.

"With Dad out of commission, it falls to me to keep things organized," she said, her voice raspy with fatigue and restrained emotion. "Mary, you and the healers see to triaging the injured. Patch up those who can go home and organize transportation to the hospital for those who need it. Jennifer, reach out to the council. They'll need to send the cleanup crew. Tell them to be prepared to identify their own. Mooneys will remain a part of the security detail until such time as the council arraigns them. We're not taking chances that any last moles in the organization will let these bastards run or silence them for good."

She didn't receive much more of a response from the dazed Mooneys than a few absent nods, but that didn't stop her from turning to the next huddled group. "Hilary, get up."

Her sister didn't even raise her head, and Sonya looked down at her, nudging her with her shoulder.

"Get. Up," Courtney repeated, her voice laced with a hint of exhausted magic as her frustration flared.

Hilary's shoulders tensed, magic swirled around her— barely wisps of it left—then practically climbed up Sonya to get to her feet. When she looked up, I was struck by how empty her eyes looked, as though she'd given everything to that door- way. More than she was supposed to.

Courtney met her stare, and her jaw tightened as she glared at her sister. "I understand that you're grieving right now, so we're going to set this conversation aside for the time being, but once we've all had a chance to process what went on here tonight, I'll be asking what the *fuck* you thought you were doing. You nearly upended the entire plan by unleashing the realm's magic into this world."

Hilary didn't flinch, didn't show any sign of guilt. Gramps might have been the one unconscious on the ground, but Hilary was just as lost, her soul just as drained. Just as buried. Missing?

I couldn't help but worry what repercussions she would face in the fallout.

"Mom?" Kyle called as he and Grayson—bleeding, exhausted, but on their feet—rushed towards Hilary. "What's going on?"

Grayson frowned, glancing between the sisters, but Courtney didn't bother to explain. "Take her home," she snapped. "And keep an eye on her. Her head's not on straight."

Kyle's eyes narrowed, and I braced for him to lash out at Courtney for her lack of empathy, but he must have realized the change in dynamic—that he wasn't currently looking at his aunt but at the acting head of their coven—because he bowed his head, turned on his heel and gathered his mother up without saying a word.

Finally, Courtney turned to Alyssa and me. Alyssa rose to

stand at my side, leaning her weight into me to keep herself from falling. I wrapped my arm around her shoulders and did the same. I needed to sit down. I needed to *sleep*. But first we needed to deal with the consequences of what we'd done.

Courtney's throat flexed with a swallow, and she took a moment to scan the field, grief and fatigue flickering through her eyes. "You two did well here tonight," she said, and glanced over at Ameline. "You as well. You fought a tough fight, made some difficult decisions, and your gambles paid off." Her eyes hardened. "You were lucky. I don't know what game you were trying to pull there, Trace, but it could have gone incredibly badly. You might have dragged the entire country into a war no one would win."

I worked my jaw but didn't answer. She wasn't wrong. I'd known I was taking a risk, but in the face of Hazel's almost-win, my options had been limited.

Her shoulders sagged. "But I'm not about to give you shit for something that didn't happen. We all learned a lot tonight about our limitations. Our family has worked so hard to keep the peace in this city for so many years, but now I have to wonder if the only reason we've been successful is because we haven't been tested hard enough. This—this opened my eyes to a lot of things. Dad taught us how to use and control our magic, but he always guided us as a family. Now I have to wonder if we need to start training as an army."

She shuddered. "A thought for another day. For tonight, let it be enough that we survived. The sun will rise in a few hours, and no one outside this farm will know how close they came to that not happening. Let's keep it that way." She looked between us again. "I know you're tired, but would you mind staying here until the council arrives? You're both in the best position to give the report about what went down here."

"Of course," Alyssa said, and I squeezed her shoulder.

Courtney sighed and trudged away, weighed down under her new mantle. But she'd shown she had what it took to wear it, so I had no concerns that the Mooneys would be in good hands until Gramps woke up.

My phone buzzed in my pocket, and I pulled it out, amazed that it had survived me throwing myself around this field all night. I read the *Private Number* on the screen and knew exactly what I would get when I answered.

"She'd better be fucking all right," Chip said. "She's not answering her phone."

Ameline must have heard him, because she reached into her pocket and hauled out a phone that hadn't fared nearly as well as mine had.

"Do you care about the rest of it or just her?" The silence on the line told me enough so I handed the phone to Ameline. "Here. Put him out of his misery, if you don't mind. The world will thank you."

She twisted her lips in a wry smile and headed off to talk to Chip.

"I still can't wrap my head around that," Alyssa murmured. "I've never seen that man show an emotion for anyone."

"That's demons for you. Heartless, soulless bastards until something shakes them out of their routine and sends them into a passionate rage. There is no in between."

At Alyssa's pained expression, I kicked myself for my lack of empathy. Considering she was currently missing her best friend at her side, she was no stranger to demonic unpredictability. I pressed a kiss against her temple.

"If I don't sit, I'm going to throw up," she said, and I walked us towards the tree.

I dropped against the trunk, and Alyssa settled between my legs, leaning into my chest.

She tilted her head to look up at me. "I'm sorry we didn't get your souls out."

"It's all right. We knew there was only a small chance that part would work. Probably for the best that it didn't. The last thing we need is for Meril to stomp over here and put us in our place. We'll find another way." I bent to kiss her forehead, needing to reassure her that I wasn't disappointed by the outcome. We'd done what we'd come here to do.

"How are you feeling?" she asked.

"Me? What about you? You're the one who nearly had her

soul ripped from her chest." I tightened my arms around her, sliding back into that moment, reliving my terror that she was about to be stolen from me.

She shrugged. "That's been more or less the norm for the past few weeks. I'm fine. I'll lose myself in tea and sitcoms until the nightmares fade." She leaned her head to the side so she could meet my eye. "And maybe some other enjoyable pastimes."

I smiled and kissed her. "We've only just gotten started, princess. If you think I'll be able to keep my hands off you for ten minutes together over the next six months, you're sadly mistaken."

Alyssa's eyes widened. "Six months? That's it? I would have thought your stamina was better than that."

I laughed and hugged her against me. Her fingers stroked the back of my hand, and she turned her face so she nuzzled my neck. We were both covered in dirt and blood, but neither of us cared. We were alive.

"I didn't mean are you okay physically," she said, pressing her point. "We made it through. It's over. We won. We have so many reasons to celebrate."

"But?" I knew where she was going with this and wanted to let her know it was okay to ask.

"But this will hit you differently. All those things Hazel said. Facing her again. It's okay if you're not okay."

I kissed the top of her head. "I'm okay." She looked up at me again, her gaze searching, skeptical, and I chuckled as I kissed the tip of her nose. I couldn't keep my lips off her. "I'm not just saying that. I thought it would be hard. I thought I would have all these memories come up that dragged me back to those days, how I felt then, what I've carried with me. But all it showed me was how far I've come. She hurled those verbal attacks like she expected them to destroy me, but they didn't touch me."

"Were they true?" she asked.

I nodded. "Pretty much. My parents weren't around all that much, and when they were, they were more interested in each other than me. And we moved. A lot. By the time my dad retired and my folks settled in Alberta, I was past the age where making friends was easy, so I was by myself. The perfect mark for Hazel's ambitions. She saw my potential, and she reeled me in. I was so desperate to belong that I followed without question. Classic story."

"Where are your parents now?"

I expected the question to hurt, but again, I felt nothing. Not even numbness. Not hiding, not running, not ignoring. Just… behind me. "I don't know. They stopped talking to me after I was accused of practising soul magic. I went to them before I went on the run, and they told me to get out. They were ashamed of the accusations, and I don't even know if they cared if I was guilty. So I left and never went back. They might be blood related, but they're not my family. That's what I realized when Hazel was hurling those words at me. She was wrong. You're my family. That's all I need."

Alyssa's magic stroked along mine, and I shivered. "All you need?"

"To start," I said, nuzzling my lips against her ear. "Keep doing that, princess, and we'll be giving your family a show."

She gave my magic a squeeze, then released it, and I kissed her temple again. I couldn't stop. I couldn't believe we were here. That we'd made it this far.

"I'm scared, Trace," she murmured, and I hugged her tighter.

"I know, princess, but he'll pull through. You know he will."

"And you?" she asked, even more softly.

At first I didn't know what she meant until I felt the light pressure on the bindings around the souls in my chest.

"Yeah." I kissed her once more. "We'll figure it out. Working together, there's nothing we can't do."

# Chapter 40
*Alyssa*

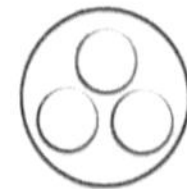

I APPRECIATED TRACE'S optimism, but he was quickly proved incorrect about what we, even as a team, were capable of.

First the council swept in, and although we did our best to keep some control over the cleanup operation at the farm, we were quickly cast out, stuck behind wards that refused to budge no matter how much magic we shoved into them. By the time the ward came down, the council had stowed all of Hazel's fallen as well as the Mooneys in body bags for transportation to the supernatural coroner's office. I thought Aunt Courtney was about to wrap Pen in an atmospheric spell and pop her head from her shoulders, but she managed to rein in her temper.

She did, however, demand that she receive copies of all the paperwork of what happened to the surviving members of

Hazel's coven, and given her position on the council, Pen didn't argue with her. Especially when Courtney made it clear that any sign of laxness in how these witches were treated would be taken up the ranks to SMOAC.

By the time Trace and I made it home, it was five o'clock in the morning and the sun was rising. We showered together, and despite all my hopes of what our second shower together might be, we were both too tired to do anything more than wash each other down and get rid of the blood and gore of the day.

Considering the brutality of the battle we'd fought tonight, the two of us were in relatively good shape. Bruises and a few minor wounds, but nothing that wouldn't heal with a few days' sleep and some gentle TLC. Most of our injuries were internal. Emotional and magical. When we crawled into bed and wrapped around each other, I barely had the energy to tell him I loved him before we fell asleep.

We woke up late the next afternoon, and the scoreboard of Team Tryssa versus The Rest of the World reflected even worse for us. Madison had texted to let us know word had reached Meril about Hazel's goals and extra guards were being placed on those semi-open doorways, which meant our plan of sending Trace's souls through one of them was gone. An hour afterwards, Pen called to give me the heads up that Tyler Litz had gone missing, along with a few other people in his inner circle. Part of me hoped he'd been among the corpses at the farm, but I guessed our luck wasn't nearly that good. No, he'd probably smelled trouble on the horizon as soon as the council had taken steps to close in on Hazel, and he'd wisely taken his leave. If he was smart, he'd disappear and never raise his head again. If he did, he'd be SMOAC's issue.

"Do you get the feeling our problems aren't over?" I groaned as I stared at my ceiling.

Trace nudged my cheek with his nose, his warm body pressed against mine. "I'd say they're over for a little while, princess. We wouldn't want things to get boring. But let's see if we can't fill that time with something just as heart racing."

The next morning, sated and happy, I managed to haul myself out of bed, get dressed, and drive to Mooney's Pub. It was five o'clock and Somerset Street was quiet. Trace was at home in bed, enjoying the sleep of a man who'd spent the last few months fighting and suddenly found himself at peace. I wanted him to take advantage of it. I also wanted a bit of time to myself. Some space to think. Since the fight at the farm, I hadn't wanted to be alone for a moment. Trace's company had been all that kept me from breaking down in belated panic attacks. Or right-on-schedule panic attacks. I'd been grateful for his steadying presence, the calmness of his voice, the gentleness of his touch.

This morning, I felt a bit steadier on my feet. More able to sit in this quiet car and consider what the future looked like. What other problems I faced.

The largest one was right in front of me. With Gramps unconscious and Simon gone, I was left to manage the pub alone, which meant I wouldn't have as much time to run the floor. I hoped Tory was willing to stick around a while longer to fill the gap because I would need the help.

I exhaled slowly and scanned the back door. The full dumpsters, the shimmer of wards on the door and windows. Just as I'd left it, yet also not. I had no idea what I would walk into when I stepped inside. Had Tory moved anything in the office? Had any other shelves collapsed? Would there be new marks on the floor I wouldn't know the story behind? Would some of my regulars have moved on? Would there be new faces?

As my anxiety started to rise, I rubbed my palms against my legs and breathed until my heart rate slowed. It was fine. I'd been away from the pub for a few days before. Tory knew what they were doing. Nothing would have changed that couldn't be changed back.

Not giving my thoughts time to build into a full spin, I grabbed my purse, unlocked the door, and marched into the pub.

As soon as I breathed in the familiar air of beer and cherrywood and food, my blood pressure dropped and my shoulders sagged. Whatever changes, this was still my pub. This was still as close to home as my apartment or my parents' place. That I'd ever doubted it would be otherwise was laughable now that I stood on the familiar creaky floorboards in the familiar nook at the back of the pub.

A sudden noise from inside the office made me reach for my magic and the keys in the front pocket of my purse. No one else was supposed to be here. I'd confirmed Tory wouldn't be in this morning, and the first of the servers wouldn't show up for at least another half hour.

I didn't call out to see who was creeping around in the staff-only room. Instead, I slid my keys between the knuckles of one hand and wrapped my magic around the other, ready for any kind of fight. After what I'd gone through with Hazel, if someone thought it was a good idea to rob me, they were in for a very bad day.

Keeping my steps light and my approach quiet, I crept towards the office, then slammed the door open, hoping to take whoever was inside by surprise.

My eye fell on the intruder, and my heart stopped at the familiar stretch of muscular back, the shock of auburn hair.

"Simon?"

He spun around, his hands up, his amber gaze fixed on my magic-wrapped hand. "Lys," he breathed. His throat bobbed with a swallow. "Hi."

Rage rose up to stamp out my fear. "'*Hi?* That's all you

have for me?"

"You're right. I'm an asshole. I should apologize."

"For starters."

I pulled my magic back and crossed my arms, leaving my keys where they were to make a point.

"It's been… a long couple of weeks." He looked around the office. "Can I pour you a coffee and fill you in?"

"Make it a whiskey. Generous with the pour." I didn't care about the hour. If I was finally going to hear what had been going on with my friend, I needed something bracing.

He gestured for me to lead the way, and I pulled a stool off the bar to take a seat. He set to work prepping the drinks, leaving the performance for after opening hours. For me, he simply poured—far more than a tipple—and added a moderate one for himself.

Then he started talking, and I sat, riveted, as he told me about the hit to his head that had triggered his demonic nature, which had drowned out everything. Something about vying for the infernal throne? Mating with Reverie? By the time he finished, I understood more about his attitude the past few months than I ever thought I would, and I went around the bar and threw my arms around him without a second thought.

"I'm glad you're alive," I said against his broad chest, so happy to have his familiar arms around me. There was nothing like a Simon squeeze, especially when I had worried I'd never experience it again.

"Likewise," he said. "You look…" He pulled away to scan me over, and his brow furrowed. "Well, like shit, if I'm being honest."

I took one last sip of whiskey before setting the rest of it under the counter for my coffee later. "Gramps is in a coma. The healers think his soul got… dislodged when he was using its power to try to open a doorway to the mirror realm. They're trying to set things right, but they don't know if they'll be able to."

Simon's eyes flew wide. "What? Lys, infernals, fuck. What the fuck did I miss?"

I filled him in on all of it, and the relief of pouring my heart out to my best friend meant so much that my cheeks were soaked with tears before I'd finished, and I was tempted to pull the whiskey back out for another sip. It felt like another piece of my life had fallen into place. Between Trace, Simon, and my family, I would be ready to face the hurdles remaining.

Like what was going on with Jet, and why Madison hadn't replied to any of my texts. Like how the family dynamics would change now that Aunt Courtney was at the helm—especially if Gramps never recovered.

But for today, my anchors were here, and when Mooney's Pub opened for the day, I was able to greet Davis with a bright smile as he took up his usual place on his usual stool, even when he waved away my enthusiastic greeting with his regular order of a pint.

Being back at work was a much-needed break, and the longer I was here, the more I appreciated that nothing had changed while I was gone. My regulars were still my regulars, and the new people were happy to come in and check out our simple menu and fantastic lineup of drinks. The old patter came back to me as though I hadn't been screaming battle cries for the past week.

Only a few witches gave me curious looks, the rumours about me having grown more outlandish in the community after my run-in with Clyde Corrick and now against Hazel. How many of them knew my connection to the council or to the woman who'd escaped Moongrave Prison? Did they know how close Hazel had come to opening a doorway between our world and the realm beyond the unseen wall?

I didn't know, and I didn't care. Because it didn't matter. None of it mattered anymore. We'd saved the day, and I felt like a superhero. I channelled the feeling as I saw my way through the rest of the day and into the evening. My feet hurt after my few days away, and my arms shook with all the weight I carried. I was sweaty, I was exhausted, my face hurt from all the smiling, and I felt fantastic.

By the time Simon and I passed the reins to Becca and our closing staff, my soul felt fulfilled.

As we headed to our cars, Simon stopped me. "You'll message me if you need me?"

"I will," I said, meaning it. Because I could. Because this was normal. "You too?"

"You know it."

"Say hi to Reverie for me," I said, and his bright smile—over a *half-succubus*—made me roll my eyes with a smile of my own.

I drove home and, just as I'd done outside Mooney's, for a while I simply sat and stared up at my house. I spotted my tenant, Ann, through the window of her apartment on the main floor. She appeared to be arguing with her cat, which was a normal day for her. And upstairs…

Trace stood in the kitchen window, staring down at me with a smile. Goosebumps bubbled across my skin as he stroked my magic, and fireworks went off in my lower stomach at the hint. Interesting that the effect worked from so many metres away. We'd have to play with distance. Could be an interesting experiment.

Then he raised a pizza box in offering, and my heart exploded a tiny bit.

Okay, so I'd fallen in love with a man who was housing hundreds of other souls inside him, our magical oversight was corrupt, our government was a bit shaky, and my grandfather seemed to have misplaced his soul for the time being.

I was strong, and I was resourceful.

y dream of becoming a world-

had been crushed, I'd believed myself

w I knew I'd been more than capable—I just hadn't

found my team yet. With that void finally filled, I would enjoy this reprieve while it lasted, and then I'd go out and kick some ass.

Feeling alive, buzzing with energy, and more than a little turned on, I got out of the car and headed upstairs to enjoy some pizza.

# Thank You for Reading

Thank you so much for taking a chance on an independent author. We're living in a wonderful age where it's easy to upload a book to the internet, but that doesn't reflect the blood, sweat, and tears that go into making a book the best version it can be. It takes time, patience, perseverance, and to have the final result end up in a new reader's hands is the best reward. You are the reason we keep writing, so thank you.

If you enjoyed the read, please help support the author by leaving a review at the retailer where you purchased the book. Reviews make a world of difference for an author, helping us reach new audiences and bringing more people into the worlds you've spent time in.

For exclusive character content, announcements, promotions, and special offers, sign up for Krista's mailing list at https://www.kristawalshauthor.com/pages/about-the-author

# Acknowledgements

My heart is filled with so much love and gratitude for everyone who's read Alyssa's story so far and found as many reasons to root for her as I have.

To everyone who wants to join the Mooney clan? Consider yourself one of them. As we've seen, they embrace all like-minded people.

Special thank you to Kate Sparkes for being my constant support.

To Emily Stewart, my fantastic editor

To Noelle, Traci, Rachel, Beba, Angie, and Tiffany, my wonderful beta readers, who not only helped me catch some pesky timeline issues but also highlighted all the reasons I fell in love with this series.

To my writers groups for your suggestions and advice, both in the writing and in all the business decisions that come after the writing. You know, the ones I often don't think about until I have to.

To my ravens, my wyverns, and my Patrons—you guys are support rockstars, and I couldn't be luckier to have you in my corner.

To Chris and Bit, thank you with all my heart and soul for understanding when my brain goes into "idea" mode and I leave chores half unfinished or start talking in tangents about people you've never heard about. Thank you for the hugs and snuggles, the laughs, the constant questions. You give me reason to keep going.

# About the Author

Known for witty, vivid characters, Krista Walsh never has more fun than getting them into trouble and taking her time getting them out.

When not writing, she can be found reading, gaming, or watching a film – anything to get lost in a good story.

She currently lives in Ottawa, Ontario with her husband, toddler, and epileptic blue heeler.

You can find her at www.kristawalshauthor.com or at the local Second Cup coffee shop... but only if you come bearing a Vanilla Bean Latte, half-sweet.

# Other Works by Krista Walsh

## Epic Fantasy

*The Meratis Trilogy*

*The Cadis Trilogy*

*The Nayis Trilogy*

## Urban Fantasy

*The Dark Descendants Series*

*The Ghostmaker Trilogy*

*The Immortal Sorceress Series*

*The Hour of Witches Series*

## Romantasy

*The Rogues of Golthwaine*